I0638660

JASON C. MYERS

CRIMINAL
ENTERPRISE

A
SOUTHERN
CRIME
DRAMA

VOLUME 1

Palmetto Publishing Group, LLC
Charleston, SC

Copyright © 2016 by Jason C. Myers.
All rights reserved. No portion of this book may be reproduced, stored in a retrieval system, or transmitted in any form by any means–electronic, mechanical, photocopy, recording, or other–except for brief quotations in printed reviews, without prior permission of the publisher.

For more information regarding special discounts for bulk purchases, please contact Palmetto Publishing Group at Info@PalmettoPublishingGroup.com.

ISBN-13: 978-1-944313-32-6
ISBN-10: 1-944313-32-X

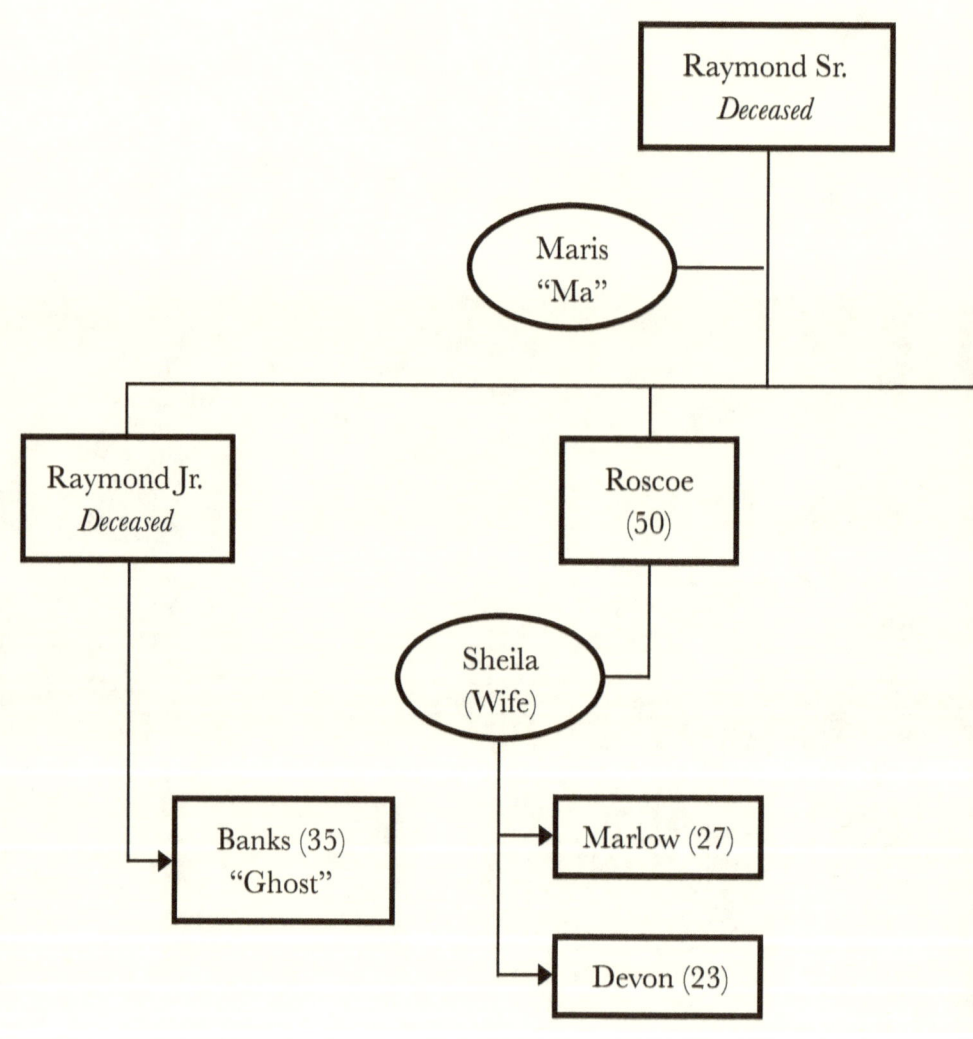

JOHNSON FAMILY TREE

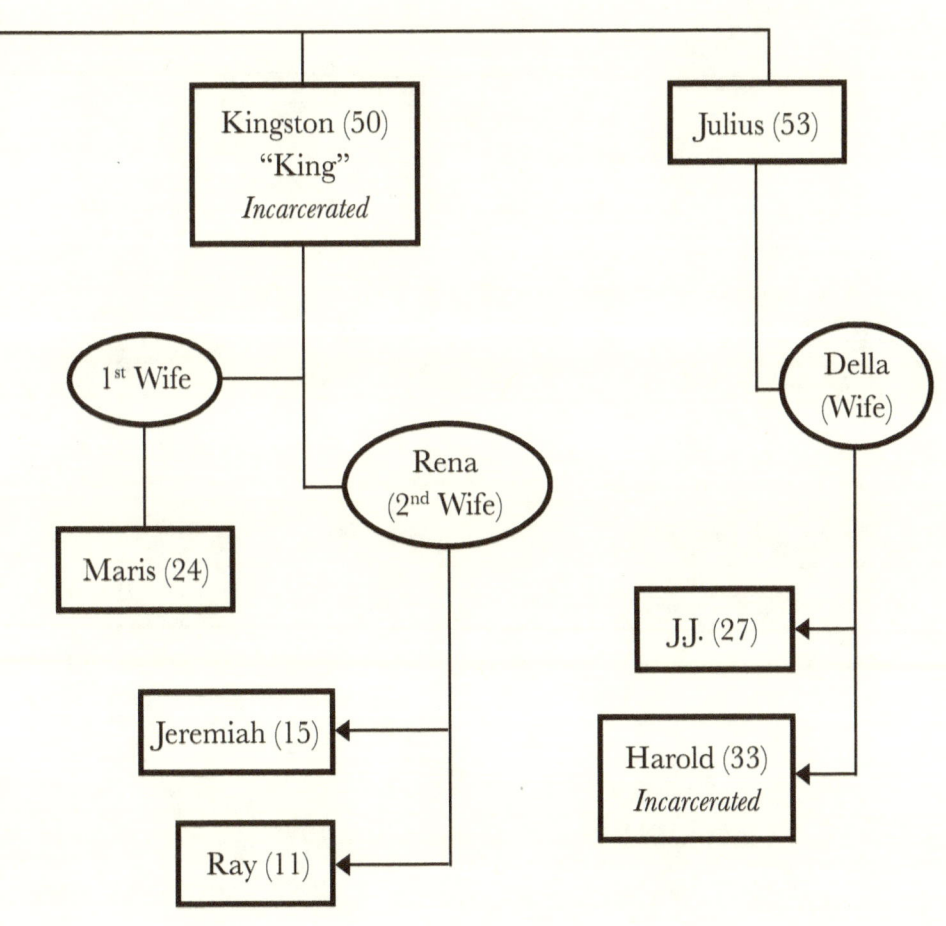

CHARLESTON GROUP

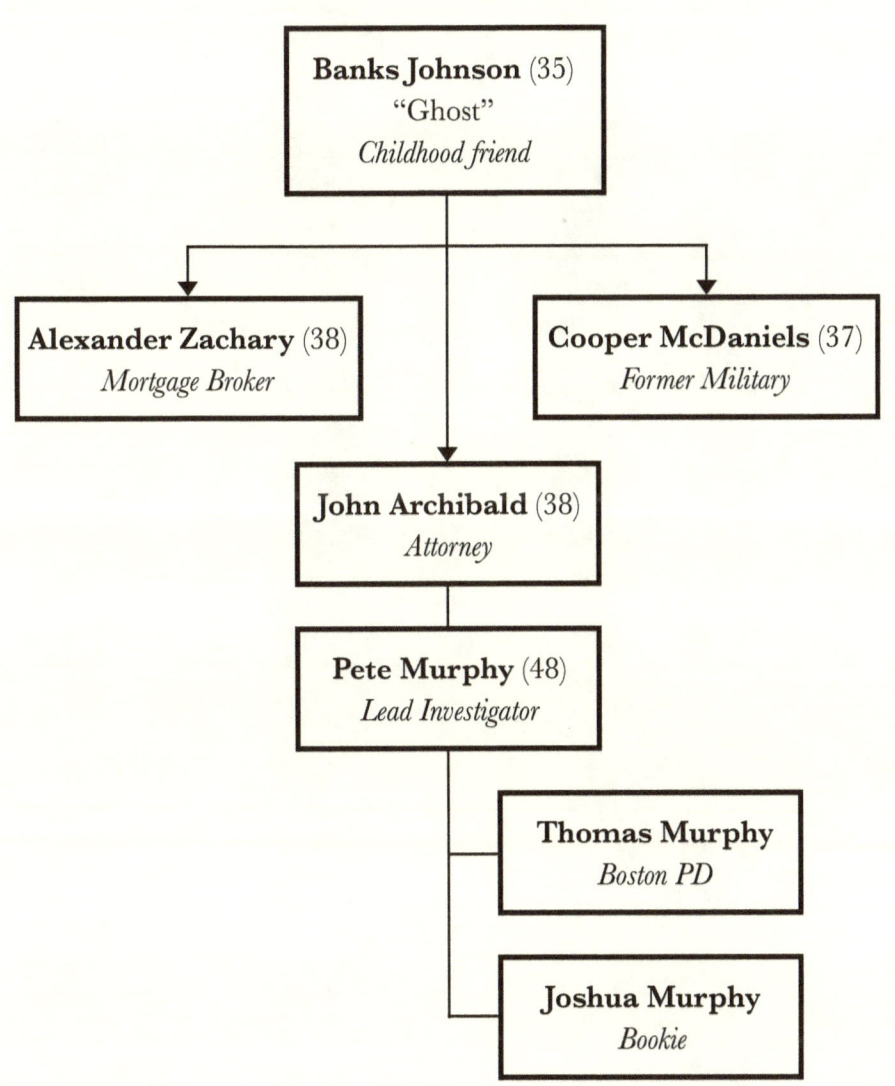

Banks Johnson (35)
"Ghost"
Childhood friend

Alexander Zachary (38)
Mortgage Broker

Cooper McDaniels (37)
Former Military

John Archibald (38)
Attorney

Pete Murphy (48)
Lead Investigator

Thomas Murphy
Boston PD

Joshua Murphy
Bookie

ALEXANDER ZACHARY

"Coop, slow up; we're losing the truck behind that minivan," I said to my driver and co-conspirator, as they would call him. Cooper got in the right lane and waited while the gray former U-Haul carrying roughly $5 million in small bills came back into sight beside us. The truck in route from Palm Beach, Florida, carried that special cargo, along with the worldly belongings of the Alford family, who was moving from South Florida up to downtown Charleston, South Carolina.

The term "continuing criminal enterprise" refers to the federal status for major drug trafficking, also known as "The Kingpin Statute"; and apparently this is what you would call myself and the people I now work with, but it sure feels a long way from how this all began. Our interest in the truck was obviously to safeguard the money held within the bowels of a compartment in its underside, which on the way down had been filled with various narcotics from their source in the Atlanta area. Our trip had begun on the return voyage, and that was as close to the action as either one of us got; but nonetheless, under the terms of the CCE Statute, we were a part of this entire empire.

"We're going to need to stop outside of Gainesville for some gas," chirped the radio sitting in the dash's cupholder.

"Copy," said Cooper in a monotone, military kind of way even though that was in his past.

As I sat in the passenger seat preparing mentally for the next steps in the process, I couldn't help but think of a man I had never met and hoped I would never meet in my life, who was the reason I was spending quality time in traffic safeguarding his money. I found it ironic that our kingpin was really named King.

While there was a guy name Kingston Johnson who started this whole mess, he was already in jail, so I wasn't really sure how the statute would apply, seeing as the Feds had already gotten him once and it had only made things worse in terms of his overall operation. Being put in jail made him rely on others and a level of cunning that frankly I didn't think he even knew existed until he was forced into a six-by-nine cell and had no other choices. Now it did help that he had a nephew named Reginald "Banks Johnson," who happened to be a computer genius at MIT; but involving him, while a minor miracle for the drug distribution side of the family, was far from a slam dunk. Turned out Banks was a wunderkind at logistics, and the applications of computer science did wonders for the overall safety of their deliveries. With Banks at the helm, the distribution network had been booming for the last three years, with a perfect record in terms of delivery and with no busts since King had gone inside.

My involvement in this entire criminal conspiracy came at the hands of my lawyer and one of my best friends, no less. Just remember, if someone asks you: "Hey, do you know how to launder $500,000 in cash?" even if you do know how, the answer to the question is always a resounding "No, John, and don't ever mention that again!"

"Zack, you know it's times like this I can't decide if I hate Kingston or John more because of this entire operation," said Cooper. Cooper was another friend now tangled up in our business of choice. Cooper was an ex-special forces operator who now acted as our chief of security. For what, I wasn't really sure; we never really named ourselves anything . . . it's not like we had business cards or a website.

"I go with hating John," I replied as the rain pelted the windshield of the Ford F-150 as we drove north up I-95, passing Jacksonville and heading home to Charleston.

"I mean, he is the one who got us involved."

"Well, I guess you really could say that Banks is the reason we're all criminals," I said while thinking even that was a stretch—we all had our own reasons for taking the money and becoming responsible for others' actions. But really, where does one sign up to join a criminal enterprise, you may ask? It really didn't start like you would think it would; ultimately, it all started with a chance encounter and the fallout went from there.

Where do we start? I guess the beginning is as good a place as any, but first you need to understand a little bit of history because it is the history of all of us that binds us together and creates our present.

The Black Mafia Family or BMF was based out of Atlanta and was responsible for a distribution network covering most of the Southern states. Now I know what you're saying: How does a thirty-eight-year-old white guy in Charleston, South Carolina, get tied in with the Black Mafia Family? It's simple: I didn't. But you need to understand the backstory of the rise of one Kingston Alfred Johnson, better known as King to his friends. I personally had never even met King and at the same time never desired to visit him since he was sitting in a medium-security federal penitentiary in Atlanta, Georgia, for crimes unrelated to the drug trafficking that was now occurring. Well, maybe the money he had on him had something to do with it, but that was a different story. He was actually busted with weed and money, but now the entire organization was involved in the distribution of cocaine for the Sinaloa Cartel. Back to the BMF and its fall from grace or, more importantly, its members' incarceration, which created a job opportunity for King Johnson.

Demetrius "Big Meech" and Terry "Southwest T" Flenery were originally from Detroit, Michigan; but during the 1990s and into early

2003, they established a network for cocaine distribution that stretched from California up to Michigan and back down to Florida with numerous points in between. They established the BMF in the late 1980s; and at the time of their arrest, it was estimated that they moved more than $270 million worth of coke and 2,500 keys a month. The reality is, it was far more than those numbers; but in the grand scheme of things, for them to get arrested, it was plenty. In 2005, members of the BMF were indicted and subsequently arrested, with the brothers being placed in the federal system around 2007, each serving thirty years. Both were scheduled to be released in 2032, when they would both be over the age of sixty. Both they and their group were sentenced under the CCE Statute, or the Continuing Criminal Enterprise Statute, which is used for major drug traffickers.

How does this play into our little band of professionals?

Enter one Kingston Alfred Johnson.

King, at this time, was strictly a "weed guy" in the College Park and Midtown areas of Atlanta. What the federal government did not understand was that one of the most basic economic principles in our country was free enterprise and one of the most basic principle of our economy was supply and demand. Just because you got rid of one set of drug dealers, if you didn't do anything about the demand of the general public, then it was just a matter of time before the supply stepped right back into the fold to meet the demand. I think this was the biggest epic fail of the so-called war on drugs. For every BMF they arrested, there was another group that would get promoted and step into the shoes of the group that had just departed. There was no win when there was a need that was as great as the demand for drugs in the United States of America. People wanted to and would get high. It was just simple economics: As long as people wanted it, someone would get the supply to them.

Kingston was unique in the fact that he was already doing business with some of the same people, namely the Sinaloa Cartel, and let's just say that when the BMF went out of business, they decided Kingston was no longer just a "weed man"; instead, he was offered a promotion. The cartel had product to move, whether King wanted to move it or not; he was going to work with them or face the consequences. Think of the scene from *The Godfather*: they made him an offer he could not refuse. This was not the kind of promotion that could be turned down, mind you, and not the kind of job that really minded if you ran it from a federal lockup in your home state. And the best part of the story was the federal government had no knowledge that they had one of America's fastest rising drug dealers already in jail.

KINGSTON JOHNSON

"Open cell A-5," called out the jailer. "Johnson, you have a visitor."

A wiry six-foot-two former athlete rose from his bunk and walked to the gate of his cage. His gait showed the fluid movement that had made him a minor division one basketball prospect, but whom had been held back by grades that did not meet par. Undiagnosed dyslexia and a lack of interest in education did not tell the story of a streetwise individual determined to succeed at all costs—even from a minimum-security work camp in Atlanta, Georgia.

The federal pen in Atlanta is broken into two sections, with the medium-security level of inmates held in one part and a work camp set up for inmates considered to be minimum-security risk. USP Atlanta had been the home to such notables as Al Capone, Mickey Cohen, and one of its most recent residents, James "Whitey" Bulger, Jr.

Kingston Johnson, while not nearly as notorious as the aforementioned inmates, nonetheless was currently one of the most powerful and wealthy detainees. He also happened to be one of the most unknown gangsters to inhabit the halls of USP Atlanta, and that's just the way he preferred it. The facility that housed him smelled of cleanser and the unique body odor of men living in close quarters with one another. The beige floors and similarly colored walls held roughly five hundred bodies in the smaller work camp.

"Hey, King, how you doing this week?" chirped the pleasant voice at the other end of the telephone as he picked up the receiver.

"Just fine, Della; how's Mama this week?" replied King.

"Well, she's doing a little better, and the doctors think the new medicine is helping with the MS," said Della. "It's a blessing she's getting along as well as she is."

One of the main reasons King got placed in USP Atlanta was to be close to his mother so she could visit, given her condition. A minor win in his plea bargain that landed him in Atlanta, even though with Mama Maris now confined to her own type of prison in the form of a wheelchair, the visits had become far less frequent, with Della or his wife, Rena, taking her place the majority of the time. Rena was not really his wife; but for all purposes she was, as she was the mother to Jeremiah and Ray, his two sons.

"Tell her to listen to the doctors and make sure she's taking the meds they be giving her."

Della looked at him with glassy eyes. "I sure hope she makes it till you get out; you know, that pneumonia last October scared us all."

"Don't you talk like that; you know she'll be just fine till I get outta here to see her. Maybe these new meds and doctors will make it so she can get on up here to see me again.

"How is Jeremiah getting along in school?" Kingston sat up straight and looked at his sister-in-law through the glass separating them.

"He got two Bs and received his first letter for basketball from Georgia Southern!" exclaimed Della. "That's what I wanted to come and tell you. Already getting noticed and he's just a freshmen!" she said with a proud smile on her face.

King smiled for a brief second, then replied, "That's great, but tell him not to let that go to his head. He better keep them grades up or the basketball don't matter none. Get Roscoe to remind him what happens with no grades . . . nothing without no grades." King saw the look on Della's face change slightly at the mention of her brother-in-law.

"I'm staying on him, King, don't you worry. Your son is in good hands. Now your daughter, that's another story."

Kingston looked away and avoided her gaze at the mention of Maris. He stood up from the visitation table and walked to the window. Kingston looked out, thinking about his first born child.

"What's she doing now?" he asked his brother's wife.

"She's got hooked up with a boy that's no good, if you know what I mean. Out at all times of night at those clubs," Della replied. "All she does is sleep all day, missing her shifts at the store. Her and Rena can't even be in the same room with each other."

"Time's up, inmate!" the speaker buzzed, ending the meeting and reminding King just where his place in life was at the moment.

No time for weakness, no time for feelings about his daughter from a failed first marriage—if you could call it that. Never anything formal, just a daughter and loads of regret.

"Tell Julius to get Archie up here to see me,." King told Della. "Ain't nothing I can do for Maris today from here!"

Della stood up and hugged him goodbye. "You know, King, it just ain't right that you in here for something that's legal now," Della said.

"Life isn't always about fair, Della. You watch over my kids and tell Rena I love her," King replied as he walked away from his sister-in-law, back to his world as he knew it now.

His world, away from his family and back into the cage, where he was as unassuming a prisoner as he could possibly be, with no outward signs of what was going on outside the prison's walls. He thought to himself, Can't think about them now, back to the grind. Back to what I am and what I do.

Both the women named Maris in his life were in different kinds of trouble, and there was nothing he could do for either one of them. The reality was that King was doing time for something that was now legal in other parts of the country. Marijuana was now legal in many states for recreational use, but King was behind bars for transporting weed along with roughly $2 million in cash. Facing certain prison time, he was left with few options to provide for his family; his only choice was to adapt and to change.

JOHN ARCHIBALD

"Law Offices of Archibald, Howle, and Regan," spoke the blonde with slightly showing roots in a Southern drawl into the phone as she worked the lines directing traffic. The firm of thirty-plus lawyers with hundreds of clients in midtown Atlanta never seemed to let her get back to her daily Facebook regimen and Instagram photo hunt.

"I will connect you, hold one second. . . ." as she connected the call to Mr. Archibald's secretary, Janice.

"Mr. Archibald's office. . . . Oh, hello, Mr. Johnson, I will see if he's available," said Janice with a sweet tone of recognition and seriousness that underlined the importance of his call.

"John? You alive in there yet?" Her tone had changed to a nurturing if not concerned melody.

"Depends on who it is?" muttered the other end of the intercom.

"Julius Johnson," she spat out the words ringing him to life.

"Yep, give me one minute, then connect him," John said as he rose to rubber-like legs and a slight headache that registered as he moved his head off the plush $8,000 couch in his office, which overlooked the city from One Atlantic Center in the heart of Midtown. Last night's dinner still rang in his ear, and the slight hangover of a wine and four-course meal at Smith & Wollensky made him still slightly foggy. What was that girl's name again? Not his impromptu date with Mary Ellen, but the one at the bar . . . he would have to ask Patrick, the bartender, if he knew her name. That amazing brunette in the blue dress.

Rising to his feet, he quickly did an inventory of his faculties as he grabbed his headset and clicked on his Bluetooth, ready for the day and the inevitable task that was managing the Johnson family and their burgeoning criminal empire.

"Julius, what's up?" The light went solid as he answered the bell once again. John closed his eyes so the room would stop spinning, but little helped the four-alarm hangover he was currently experiencing, and talking to Julius would most likely not help his mood improve either.

"Not too much. Jeremiah got his first letter from Georgia Southern."

"The first of many, I'm sure. Can I assume his father is proud? John spoke into his Jawbone headset. He briefly leaned up to steady himself only to collapse back down on the couch. His only salvation now was that he had closed all the blinds, blocking out the midmorning daylight trying to enter his foggy reality.

"Yes, we just spoke to him and he wanted to make sure you could still be around to see him in the next rotation," bleated the voice on the phone.

"Of course I'll be there this coming Friday as scheduled; is there anything he needs to discuss in reference to his case that he specifically mentioned we need to review?" asked John while resting his head on his cushions and praying for the call to come to an end.

"No, nothing major, but I do have his monthly magazines and some books for him; I'll have R. J. drop them by your office tomorrow if that's fine with you?"

"Sure, no problem; ask Roscoe to hand them to Janice, and I'll make sure King gets them," replied John, all the while regretting the relationship that regulated him to monthly meetings with his client and current partner: one Kingston Johnson.

"Give Ma Maris my best, and let me know if the doctors are doing a good job for her."

"Thank you for getting them to come see her, Mr. Archibald. She sure do appreciate the extra attention, being in her condition and all."

And with that, the call ended and the messages contained in the delivery would reach the man in charge. The predetermined sequence and information really didn't matter to John because his role was simple at this point yet so complex that he could barely remember how it all started. But as soon as he did, he would require another round of bourbon and the attention of something that looked beautiful both dressed and naked to help him forget. And with that, he lay back down on his couch and pretended to be working on all those billable hours he created from his corner office overlooking the landscape of the jungle below. He tried to forget how he got here and all at once remembered why he'd done what he had to begin with and the lives he had altered as a result.

He rang his intercom. "Janice?"

"Yes, Mr. Archibald?"

"Can you confirm my reservation for this evening and my flight for Friday evening to Charleston?"

"Your flight is with Delta, flight 2223, and takes off at 4:00; you should be on the ground by 5:00 p.m. I have the car service scheduled to pick you up and take you to your condo downtown."

"Thanks, Janice, you're the best. I'm heading out to lunch for an appointment. We'll be getting a care package for Mr. Johnson delivered tomorrow; please put it in my office for my visit on Friday. Thank you."

And with that, John sprang up off the couch and began lumbering to his private executive shower, which he shared with his partner just one office over. At least being one of the most prestigious criminal defense lawyers in the Southeast had some privileges like a private shower and your own executive assistant to schedule your lunches and flights—even if he was at the beck and call of a guy that just a few short years ago had threatened to kill him and now required his presence one Friday a month for the foreseeable future to deliver his mail. Interesting, sometimes, how life dealt out its own little ironies.

"No problem. Enjoy your lunch," replied his faithful assistant.

If she knew the care package was essentially the monthly reporting to the CEO of the largest drug distribution network in the South, she might have handled it a little differently.

The system itself was not unique, not something that hadn't been thought of by criminals before him, and would probably be the same years after his stay as a guest of the federal government ended. It was both simple and at the same time complex because unless you knew the code, it made no sense. In the case of King Johnson, it was unexpected because he wasn't technically in jail for intent to distribute marijuana across state lines, which was essentially a gift negotiated by his criminal defense attorney—one John G. Archibald—but nonetheless still meant jail time, which did not sit well with the King. None of the guards in the minimum-security unit that held King looked at him as a drug kingpin, and this anonymity was part of the plan.

While John had been able to get the gun they found thrown out, re-ducing the sentence, he had not been able to keep the King out of jail altogether, even after charging him a half million in cash to do so. The rub in the entire situation was that King was caught with roughly $2 mil-lion in cash as well as the gun and several hundred pounds of pot driving from Alabama back to Georgia, thus creating the situation in the first place seemed to be lost on deaf ears, in King's opinion. So while facing the next decade in prison, he gave John one of two options: John could help King with a new business opportunity or he could end up dead and buried somewhere in the state of Georgia at the hands of the more, let's say, "violent" part of the organization. John picked option A, and his journey into the underworld began.

COOPER McDANIELS

The sweat drenched his shirt even in the mild winter Charleston temperatures as he ran down near the end of Folly Beach just south of Charleston. The 8-mile run was the end of his own personal regimen, which had begun at 4:00 a.m. that morning for the former Delta operator who was now a full 4 years past his official retirement from Uncle Sam's service.

"Morning, Coop. You want some coffee and the usual?" asked the girl behind Lost Dog Café's counter as he entered at the conclusion of his run.

"Sure, thank you, Sam," the long-haired and bearded runner said as he sat at his usual spot in the back of the restaurant, where he could see everything and everyone coming and going. Even at this hour in this location, he was wired and ready to go at a moment's notice. The odds of any such activity were nonexistent, but nevertheless, Cooper was ready for action and treated each day like it could be his last. His outlook on life had forever changed after his removal from the work he loved, and his respect for those in charge of our country was lost at the same time. Cooper was still as fit as any man in service and was wired the same way.

He sported a tan even at this time of year, as he had just returned from a surfing trip to the Pacific side of Costa Rica. He had spent several weeks beating around the beaches down there and returned after the holiday to pick back up his current post working with John and Alex.

"You going surfing later?" asked Sam, who looked like a cross between a bikini model and a pot-smoking hippie with her braided hair and nose ring. She was rail thin with just enough curves to catch the eyes of the café patrons. She had several noticeable tattoos peeking out from various locations on her body.

"Thinking about it, that storm has the water kicked up; should be some action out there today."

Truth be told, the waves and their action did very little for Coop after years of combat and the war in Iraq, then Afghanistan. The previous night's mission had been nothing more to him than a babysitting trip that had gone off without a hitch; it offered nothing in the way of excitement. Had something gone wrong, like the truck getting pulled over, the cover family of Jack and Mallory Alford would have swooped in to attempt to head off any potential issues with interested police or state troopers. The real Alford family was none the wiser that the exceptional deal they got on movers had absolutely nothing to do with a great referral from the real estate agent and more to do with the fact that they were relocating from South Florida and the Johnson South Florida branch just happened to need to move $5,243,000 to Charleston to be laundered. The drivers were members of the Johnson organization working undercover as movers. They drove the truck filled with blow south from Atlanta and after the Alford's worldly possessions were lured into a different truck, complete with cash, they headed north to Charleston. The entire operation was coordinated and overseen by two complete strangers and by the faux Alford on-site. The real Alfords were actually staying at a hotel in South Beach, compliments of their realtor team from Charleston, while their move was being handled for them. But, hey, those were the kinds of services and perks you got from Jack Mercer and the Mercer Realty Group when you bought a

$2 million-dollar home in the downtown area of your new city.

A small vibration let Cooper know that his iPhone was receiving an incoming request for a FaceTime chat. He looked down to realize it was his daughter, and his demeanor changed as he took the call.

"Hey, baby girl, you getting ready for school?" Coop said with a smile and tenderness that had not been there only seconds before.

"Yes, sir. Did you do your run this morning?" asked the blonde with braids from the screen in front of him.

"I sure did, and now I'm grabbing breakfast. Did you finish reading that Berenstain Bears book I sent over last week?"

"I sure did, and I did it all by myself," responded the smiling face.

"Well, that makes me proud, baby doll. Is your mother there?"

The screen moved in and out of focus, and a stern voice came on the line: "We need to get her tuition money to the school by Friday, and I need you to pick her up from school by 2:00 p.m. this week—I'm heading out of town." The now clear face of a less-than-pleasant former Mrs. Cooper McDaniels could be seen.

"Good morning to you too, Lauren," Cooper said while holding the phone back a little farther. "Shouldn't be a problem. I'll transfer funds to you today, and I'll pick her up."

"Sorry—not trying to be short, but these early mornings kill me; and I'm still getting used to the new hours at the hospital. Night shifts are not all they're cracked up to be."

"I'm sure they are. The offer is still on the table if you need a little more money. Contracting work has been good here the last few months, and I have some extra if you or Rebecca need anything. I can do more, and I'm happy to do it."

"I know, Coop, but it's just . . . this is something I need to do on my own. All those years while you were gone overseas, I depended on you and the money too much. I really want to get this job started and cover myself on my own. I hope you can understand. I mean, we are divorced."

"Understood, Mrs. McDaniels, but the offer is still on the table.

"Tell Becca I'll pick her up on Friday, and we have plans to hunt some shells near The Washout on Saturday."

The Washout was a stretch of beach toward the north end of the island where surfers congregated. The land mass tightened, and there were only rocks between the paved road and the beach. No massive mini hotel homes down this far on the island. The stretch of beach offered the best surf in the Charleston area. The old Morris Island Lighthouse lay farther to the north—a lone statue in the water, as the inlet had long eroded away, leaving the faded red-and-white-striped lighthouse as a beacon out in the sea. It was out of use but still a landmark that could be seen as far away as Sullivan's Island and the Isle of Palms, which were on the other side of the Charleston Harbor.

"Affirmative, Sergeant Major McDaniels," replied Lauren. "Becca, tell your Daddy to have a good day," she said as she passed the phone back to her eager seven-year-old.

"Bye, Daddy, I love you and I'll see you Friday!"

"I love you too, and I'll see you soon," replied Coop, silently thinking to himself that he had been outside her window just hours earlier, checking in on the two ladies in his life. Checking in on Becca as well as the new night sitter Lauren had hired to stay at their home while she worked at her new job as head ER nurse at Trident Medical Center, which was a little north of Charleston in the Summerville area. Cooper had strongly opposed the idea, but at the same time, with limited visitation and an otherwise decent relationship with his ex-wife, he eventually gave in. Secretly he thought this new job could lead to more opportunities for him to spend time with his daughter if the need arose—something he had failed miserably at during his time as a solider and a husband. His new career path did pay well, and it did give him time to be at home, so he could make time for Becca—and if Lauren would have him back, then her, too. Sure, this line of work was not necessarily aboveboard, but at the same time, he was out of options.

Going back overseas was no longer something he could do without losing his daughter altogether. He had been able to repair his relationship with Lauren over the past few years, but the absence that cost him his marriage was not going to cost him the time he had left to spend with his daughter. Thankfully, John had been able to get an attorney in town to work out a reasonable divorce and custody arrangement. After his discharge from the military, Cooper had found out the hard way that there were just no decent jobs for ex-military guys whose basic best skill was killing the enemy.

After a few miserable months as a security guard on a Brink's armored car, his phone rang and it was Alex—or, as he called him, Zack—with a job offer. Growing up in rural South Carolina, Cooper was used to guns; they had been his business card in the military. The only differences with this job were: he was working with some of his best friends from growing up and it gave him the money he needed to help raise his daughter. As John and Alex put it, he was their guardian angel; and given the circumstances of how this had all begun, Cooper sure hoped he was never needed for anything more than driving and watching.

But just in case, he was going to be ready and would be there for his friends, just like he had been overseas.

"Sam, let me get that coffee to go; I think I'm going to hit those waves while I can this morning."

ALEX

After getting back from South Florida, I had to get to work on my part of the equation. I normally didn't go within a hundred miles of the deliveries, but anytime the amounts got over several million and I knew I was accountable, I would ride shotgun with Cooper to keep a set of eyes on the money. I had absolutely no contact with the drugs, and I took some peace of mind from that disconnection, but ultimately we were all guilty. Getting us all out of this without going to jail was the only plan I really had in mind.

John, Cooper, and I grew up outside of Charleston in a small town called Moncks Corner; and we all went to school together from roughly middle school through high school. We had played sports together, including baseball and football, and in general had been together all the time. Moncks Corner was like many small towns in the South, where football was king on Friday nights and church dominated Wednesday nights as well as Sundays. Hunting, fishing, and boating on the lake were as much a part of life as anything else in our town.

We had gone to elementary school in a building that was nearly a hundred years old with old heart pine floors and at least ten layers of paint that had built up over the years. The old brick schoolhouse was directly across from the local Baptist church on the main street of town. We had local small businesses like a neighborhood pharmacy that served milkshakes as well as a locally owned grocery store. When we were growing up, there had been no such thing as Walmart, Walgreens, or Target in our town.

We had all played together, we had learned together, and we had primarily eaten together courtesy of Ma Maris, the Archibald family's housekeeper. Ma Maris had helped do the laundry, cook the meals, and clean the Archibald home. John's mother had died when he was young, and his father had been heavily involved in local politics; his hours as an attorney had kept him away from the family home. Ma Maris would have dinner ready for us each night, and her Southern cooking was a way of life for all of us after some sporting event or after church. For all intents and purposes, Ma Maris had been the closest thing to a mother John had growing up.

When we were in middle school, Ma Maris's grandson Banks came to live with her, moving down from Atlanta after the death of his father. Banks had no mother and was raised by Maris Johnson. Maris had worked for John's family, and part of compensation included living in the guest house behind the property. Banks and John had become best friends partly because of their common connection of not knowing their mothers and barely knowing their fathers. Banks just became part of the group, and it had been that way ever since.

While not an athlete, Banks was tremendously smart and the term "computer geek" fit him like a glove. It was his work with computers and math that got him a full ride to MIT, one of the first students from our high school to make it to that institution. Banks was a few years behind us, but already taking some of the same classes and as many advanced honors courses as they could throw at him. Reginald "Banks" Johnson was one of the smartest guys I had ever met with a computer and a genius at games like chess, playing at almost a master's level.

Like a lot of kids in small towns in South Carolina, we had our share of fun and our share of scraps with the law growing up. It was one of these scraps that may have been the tie that bound us all together. One night in our junior year, we had all been out running the roads in Cooper's beat-up old truck. We had a spot on a friend's land with an old, run-down hunting cabin. All of us kids would meet up there and do the types of things that high school kids did—namely drink beer, play music, smoke cigarettes and the occasional joint around a bonfire. In general, a good weekend night for any high schooler in any Southern town in America. That particular night had been unlike many others. It had been a crisp night in the fall after a home football game win.

We had been together with roughly ten to fifteen other kids, hanging out doing nothing much. The house was down a dirt road that was shaped like a "U" with two entrances off the same road. The cabin was on roughly two hundred acres with no electricity, but it had a working fireplace and plenty of firewood in the surrounding forest. The house's ownership was of question, but a friend of a friend swore we had permission to be on the premises. At least that was the way we always took it, and for the most part the property was always open unless someone was out hunting on a Saturday in the dove fields, which were adjacent to the property.

From what I remembered, that night had been nothing special until we saw two sets of headlights come down the road, and all of a sudden one set went blue. At that point, everyone had decided it was a better idea to scatter into the woods instead of staying close to the house. Beer cans and small dime bags of weed flew in various directions, away from their owners. Kids scattered and went everywhere. The only problem with this plan was that the kids with cars parked by the house had nowhere to go; and with full coolers of beer in the backs of most of the trucks, it wouldn't take a police officer very long to put one and one together and issue some underage drinking and possession tickets to anyone they found.

John and I had been inside the house by the fire when the cops came, which left us no opportunity to run; but we were able to hide the beer cans and attempt to sober up as quickly as possible.

"All right, you boys, come on out here," said the deputy. They had followed another group of kids down the road and watched them throw a beer bottle out the window at a sign; their interest in the car had turned into them following the vehicle to our sanctuary of high school youth. John, a few girls who'd been inside, two football players, and I walked outside the little cabin.

"Who do we have here?" asked the light that was concealing the officer's face.

"John Archibald and Alex Zachary," said John with no hesitation in his voice. This wasn't the first time he'd been caught drinking a beer—and probably wasn't the last.

We walked out of the cabin and into the light of a half moon. I could faintly see my breath as I got out into the November night air. The lights from the cop cars splashed blues and reds off the pines surrounding the property. Two spotlights whipped out on the sides of both cruisers, shining their search beams into the woods separating the property from the dove fields. The five of us walked out of the house to join the rest of the group in front of the first police car. The headlights formed off the rear of the silver Tahoe they had followed down the dirt road. The area between the two, about twenty to twenty-five feet, was illuminated. The officers placed everyone in the group between the two cars in a kind of impromptu holding pen without walls. The house was to the right of the cruiser and Tahoe; and our cars, including Cooper's SUV, were parked to the right of the house in some underbrush. Our group had been behind the cabin by a fire pit that had still been burning and was surrounded by coolers and chairs. One officer walked over, opened the coolers, and saw the cans scattered behind the light in the thick underbrush. The silver of the cans shimmered as his Maglite shone over them.

"Well, well—I don't think your daddy will be too proud to have his son get a ticket for underage drinking," said the officer.

"Officer, we don't have any beer on us. We were just meeting some friends out here by the fire. At best, we're just in the wrong place; but this is Timothy Gregorie's land, and we have permission to be here," John spouted, his inner lawyer already taking form at the age of seventeen. It also helped that his father had been a lawyer and had happened to be on county council at the time.

"You guys and girls line up over here by the patrol car in the light so we can see you all," said a second, sterner voice. By this time, a second deputy sheriff's car had arrived at the scene. Obviously it was a big night in the old county. They had most of our group by the patrol car, the exceptions being a few of the football players who had run into the fields as well as Cooper and Banks, who were also still missing. The deputies were looking at the license plates and figuring out who was whom when Cooper and Banks came out of the woods to join the crowd after a few more calls from the cops over their car's PA speaker.

"We know who you all are. Cooper McDaniels, come on out," the amplified voice pierced the night. The license plate on Coop's old GMC, registered to his father, had given him away. Cooper was also a defensive back on the team that had won the state a few years earlier when he still got playing time as a freshman—a rarity at that time in our school.

Without notice, the deputies had begun looking through a few of the cars and had opened up Cooper's SUV.

Cooper and Banks came out together and stood by the truck while the deputy searched it.

"Bingo! Officer Sheppard, come over here, sir. We have some weed," shouted one of the deputies searching Cooper's car. The amount was insignificant, but there were multiple dime bags, and this created an issue. "Looks like we have five or six bags of marijuana in here; that's intent to distribute."

The two officers called over Cooper and Banks and began questioning them.

"Who does this belong to?" one deputy said as he shone the light on Coop and Banks.

The reality was it belonged to all of us. Being high school kids, the only areas we could get drugs from were the rural black areas; and at that time, that was their method of delivery: small bags of weed sold individually. High school kids being high school kids, we had each bought a bag along with two for two girls we were friends with at the time, who just happened to not have gotten them from us the day before. In fact, the only person who hadn't bought a bag was Banks, who didn't smoke weed very much, which probably had more to do with economics at the time than anything else. Banks just didn't waste his money on buying weed; and honestly, we were all friends, so he could just smoke any of ours when we could get some. I was the son of a dentist, and Cooper's parents were both employed by the local power company. John's family was very wealthy for our area; his dad had political power and was one of the favorites to eventually run the county when the current regime changed hands.

It had been at that point that everything changed—and not for the better.

"I bet the black kid is the responsible party. Hook him up, Tom!" And with that, Banks had been singled out as the only black kid in a group of affluent whites. To say that Banks was scared would be an understatement. I could see the fear and confusion in his face as he was handcuffed and placed in the back of a cruiser.

"The rest of you kids, we're calling your parents; and each of you will receive a citation for underage drinking—unless someone claims this beer!" chimed in one of the other officers.

Without thinking it through, I took a step forward and said, "The weed and the beer belong to me. Banks didn't have anything to do with it!" I stood alone in front of one of the officers, who stared at me with a dumbfounded look of disbelief that someone would actually take responsibility for both.

John looked at me with an anger in his eyes that I had very rarely seen. "Officer, I think you need to let everyone go at this very moment!" he called out.

A silence fell over the group until one of the officers replied, "Well now, why should we do that, Mr. Archibald? Because you think your daddy is some hot shit?" The officer approached John, his leather boots crunching on the underbrush as he strode over to John's position behind me. He got directly in John's face and shone his light, blinding my friend, but John stood tall.

"You should let us all go because it's the right thing to do, given the situation," John said with his eyes closed, not flinching.

The officer pulled the light back and replied, "The right thing to do?" He chuckled. "You think the laws of our land don't apply to you, Mr. Archibald! You boys and girls have beer and weed, and it looks like you have your very own drug dealer out here with you. That black kid in the car is going to jail!" said Officer Sheppard with no feeling in his voice.

"I mean it's the right thing to do since you illegally searched my friend's truck in front of all these witnesses," said John, his eyes now open and staring into the officer's face. "And I don't need my father to get out of this one; any old attorney will do since we also have the eyewitness accounts of fifteen people gathered at a private residence. "You only have cause to search the vehicle you followed onto the property. You have no right to search a parked car without a proper warrant!" John said, now almost slightly yelling.

"Randall, come here for a minute!" sounded the PA from the sheriff's car, which had arrived and now held Banks in its backseat. With that, the officer broke off his engagement with John and walked to the third cruiser. A window on the passenger's side rolled down and a discussion commenced. By the deputy's body language, I could tell that it was not going his way.

The door opened and a fourth officer stepped out into the fray. The new officer was a black deputy I recognized from football games; his name was L. P. Shelton. Officer Shelton came over to the group. "All right, all of you shut it down," he said to the other officers. "Boys and girls, you know you should not have booze or weed at your age. It's a road to disaster for you all. I scrape kids like you off the roads after parties like this. . . ." He paused for a second. "We are going to confiscate all the alcohol and weed, and consider this a warning to you all." Officer Shelton walked back to the other two officers.

At this point, a hush fell over us as the two officers grabbed up some coolers; then Officer Sheppard opened the back door and uncuffed Banks, sending him back to the crowd.

"I want you kids to stay out here and sober up by that fire; don't go get no more alcohol tonight!" said Officer Shelton. "You kids stay away from that Green Hill area. I know that's where that weed came from, and we'll be down there watching it over the next few weeks."

With that, he turned and walked back to the car. Both cruisers cut off their lights, turned, and headed straight down the dirt road, back out into the night.

A stunned silence was the best way to describe the tone.

The two players finally came back from the field, and one exclaimed, "Shit, they didn't take my handle of Jim Beam from the cabin. Let's get on it!" Each of the boys were thinking of the sticky sweat-burn of the bourbon.

Cooper, John, Banks, and I looked at one another and with a quiet recognition of friendship went back to the SUV and got inside to head home. Our night was over, but our friendship was just beginning.

"Man, I thought I was gone," Banks had said as we loaded into the GMC to head back to town. He still had a look of shock on his face, even thought it had been thirty minutes since he'd been in cuffs.

"Not as long as I'm around," said John. "We take care of our own. What they were doing wasn't right."

Cooper got behind the wheel and didn't say anything as he drove us back into town and over to John's house in Pinopolis, a little peninsula a mile outside of town that led into the largest manmade lake in the state of South Carolina. The area had large, older homes with access to the water. John's house was almost a hundred years old and beautifully restored on about four acres, complete with a guest cottage that housed Banks and his grandmother. There was a dock with a pontoon boat we all used in the summer. It was the kind of home where you knew your neighbors and they knew you. A tight community of people who still went to church on Wednesday nights and football games on Fridays. A sleepy alcove about forty-five minutes away from Charleston.

"Man, you know, Maris was cooking shrimp and grits tonight with some cornbread. I bet there's some leftover," John said with a smile on his face. There were always leftovers when Maris cooked; she knew she was cooking for four growing boys as well as the Archibald family. Maybe our night wasn't over after all; it was going to be spent in the Archibald kitchen eating good food and telling this story again among ourselves all night long, as long as John's dad was asleep or at least upstairs.

"Man, Alex, you were about to take that bust for everyone?" Banks asked me.

"Yeah, I guess I was. Wasn't right to let you go it alone," I said. "You didn't have nothing to do with that weed. Good thing I think I left a joint at John's house too."

Cooper finally spoke up. "Now you talking my language!" He gave me a high five as I sat in the passenger seat. We pulled up the driveway; and the lights shone on the large, white columns of the Archibald property, a two-story home with a kitchen off the back.

It had been a night to remember and a night with meaning for all of its participants. A night that would bind us together for years to come as we would remember we had one another's backs at all times.

For better or worse, that night of innocence was one of the last times we would be innocent. But one thing I could never forget was that had it not been for John's quick thinking, Banks's path in life could have been altered forever—and not necessarily because he was guilty of anything. The cops had been more than willing to single him out just for being black, and I thought that was a lesson Banks would always remember.

REGINALD "BANKS" JOHNSON

The ping of the computer called and read the email. It was a high-end computer setup similar to what you would expect any high-level computer geek or hacker to have.

"What the fuck are we doing about Agora!" from the gamer known as Rogue.

"Nothing you can do; they're recoding and it will pop back up. I'll let you know. For now, go to the designated chat room on Alphabay," replied the avatar for Ghost, also known as Banks Johnson. The other players were all contacts within the Johnson family network up and down the East Coast of the United States. These contacts were the younger generation or relatives of connections the Johnson family had known for decades, since the times that the original four brothers ran weed all over the eastern seaboard. Banks had taken them and their communications online, and business had grown ever since.

"Oh, and kill those damn orcs on your left for me!"

"Got them," pinged the user known as Death Angel.

"Agora is dead, just like Silk Road and Silk Road 2.0; business will keep moving as usual. Let your team know the new room and access codes. Send me a message via Telegraph, and I'll get back to you with new passcodes and usernames for Alphabay. Make sure all of your contacts have the new website, and then send the passwords via Telegraph only. Have the messages set to auto-destruct after one read, so tell them to be sure to remember their passwords."

Telegraph was a newer phone app that allowed the user to encrypt a text message with a self-destruct feature that would permanently delete the message after a certain amount of time. At the time, not even the NSA had the ability to break the encryption in time to view the message before it would be gone forever.

The new usernames and passwords were to the Dark Web or Deep Web, which could only be accessed with specific Web addresses, servers, usernames, and passwords. In short, it was an invitation-only party whose location changed often. The dark Web allowed them to conduct business in secret and avoid using phones and other trackable methods to communicate. It also made it easier for drug suppliers and buyers to connect and made things like selling on street corners obsolete. This level of sophistication protected the dealers and their suppliers and kept necessary barriers between them. Couriers would have no idea whom they were selling for and, thus, could not snitch on people if they were taken down. All anyone knew was the coke came from Mexico, and that in itself kept everyone in check because of the fear instilled in them by the cartels. The lower-level guys had no way to rat out those higher up the food chain, and the thought of ending up beheaded or in a barrel in the desert kept most in line—because they could never be sure whose coke they were handling.

The fear and the resulting discipline were things the Johnson family took full advantage of, as only the top connections in the major cities had access to Banks; and none of them even knew where he was located.

"Send the message to the new phone number I just posted. That number will be good for the next twenty-four hours. I'm out. Good luck, guys."

With that, the user known as Ghost logged out of World of Warcraft and turned his attention to one of his other five computer monitors, all burning with life that was the Darknet, already moving his orders and notifying his buyers to move from Agora to the new locations on Alphabay and Nucleus. Staying not just one step ahead of the game, but basically running a completely different race that ended before the Feds even started. Banks was also several thousand miles away from US borders, so tracking him down would prove to be nearly impossible.

Silk Road had been the first online black market of sorts started by a guy named Ross William Ulbricht, who was currently under indictment for creating the website, which allowed its users to buy anything from magic mushrooms to cocaine—users could even order up a hit man. The ordering-up-a-hit-man part is apparently where the federal government drew the line in the sand, since they charged him with conspiracy to commit murder. The concept of a black market on the Web wasn't new; it had been, ironically enough, started by some students at Stanford and MIT in the late 1970s and was called ARPANET. Its purpose was to make connections to score cannabis. Marijuana was actually the Johnson family trade. Banks had hoped he would never have to participate in that side of the family business; but with his uncle Kingston in jail, he had to help out.

Maris Johnson, his grandmother, had multiple sclerosis and was confined to a wheelchair. Multiple sclerosis was a bitch of a disease that included wonderful symptoms like loss of vision, loss of the use of one's limbs (in her case, her legs), pain, fatigue, and numerous other life-threatening things that in general destroy one's quality of life. Currently there was no cure for MS; but if treated properly, it could be managed better than it could have been as recently as a decade ago. At this point, managing Ma Maris's disease was the best Banks could hope to offer her. She had been the rock in his life, raising him after the death of his father, Raymond Jr., and the disappearance of his mother.

An incoming ping from Dr. Hashan Patel of the Mellen Center for Multiple Sclerosis in Cleveland: "How is Maris responding to the new regimen of drugs?"

"Seems to be doing well," responded Banks. "Thank you for taking on her case with your current workload and research schedule."

"No problem, and thank you for the donation from the Johnson Foundation. I'll make sure the tickets to our gala get to you if you'll shoot me a good mailing address."

"That won't be necessary, Dr. Patel; I won't be able to make it."

Not that Banks Johnson, a thirty-five-year-old computer science graduate of MIT would be able to attend since he wasn't even in the country and didn't have plans to be anywhere near the US for some time. Running an Internet drug empire was not easy, and not something you wanted to do while sitting at a computer within reach of the FBI and DEA—not that either of them knew he or the organization even existed. But that was the way it was supposed to be and the way it would be going forward. By separating himself from the family, he could ensure not only his safety but create a level of disconnect from their buyers and their suppliers, the Sinaloa Cartel.

With his uncle in jail and the rest of his family relying on him to take up the mantle of family monarch, he had done what he thought best. But he also decided he would not end up like his uncle or some of his cousins, behind bars. If he was going to be involved, he would do it his way, and he would use his mind and a little bit of software to make it all happen from afar.

Enter the shadowing world of the Darknet and marketplaces like Silk Road and Agora. The Darknet was not a place your kids could just stumble into if they were playing on the family iPad. In fact, it was rather hard to connect and get reliable information without a good bit of knowledge about how computers and their applications worked. This world was not unlike any other marketplace that connected buyers and sellers; and from Banks's perspective, the family business could be brought into the twenty-first century. The possibilities seemed endless.

The hard part had been getting the family connections properly trained and up and running on how to communicate going forward; but once that hurdle had been overcome, it had become easier for them to hide in the shadows. Gone were the days of talking on cell phones, and for the most part face-to-face meetings were gone as well. The drop-offs were set at random by Banks and communicated with their partners. Luckily, so far there had been no attempts to steal product without payment; and that had more to do with the belief that the drugs belonged to the Sinaloa Cartel than fear of the Johnson organization. The cartel had a very nasty reputation, and none of the buyers knew that the drugs were paid for in advance by the Johnsons. What they didn't know helped create a layer of security for the Johnson family.

Banks's uncle and father had been selling weed for years in and around the Atlanta area. He had lived with his mother, Rachelle, in South Carolina while he was growing up. At the age of fifteen, when he was getting ready to enter high school, his mother had remarried and moved to Virginia. He was not very welcome by his new stepfather, so Banks had moved to Atlanta to live with his father, Raymond. Raymond had been killed during a dispute over money in South Florida back in the late 1990s, so Banks had primarily been raised by his uncle Kingston and his grandmother Maris. At an early age, he took to computers and computers took to him. At the age of seventeen, he had written some code in a contest for high school kids; and the next thing he knew, he was offered a full ride to MIT. He had taken the opportunity, left Atlanta behind, and said hello to Massachusetts.

"Ghost, you out there?" pinged the server that was dedicated to running Tor, with his chat running on Alphabay. Username Chilly had messaged him.

"Of course."

"Can you fill 50 units K?" Chilly wanted fifty kilograms of cocaine.

"Sure, no problem. Half in BTC and half on delivery," replied Ghost. Bitcoin, or BTC, was the standard monetary unit used on the Darknet. Bitcoin required a transfer of currency online that was then held by the third-party intermediary until the seller made the delivery. The system devised by Banks required buyers to put down half the money in electronic currency and the other half as cash upon delivery. "PPU 30."

"No problem; done," replied Chilly.

"Details to follow for delivery via cloud message," Ghost replied before signing out.

The current market price for a kilo of blow from their Mexican cartel connection was $18,000; and upon delivery to Chilly in New York, those same keys would sell to them for $30,000. That was a $600,000 profit upon delivery of the product to New York. The order created the next sequence of events, all of which Ghost accomplished with a few keystrokes. Once he received payment in Bitcoin, he would convert it over and forward the money offshore to the cartel so the entire transaction would have taken place without ever touching US soil or banking regulations. The cartel was moving away from the bulk of needing cash by consolidating mid-level deals and using the Internet. It made things much simpler and, quite frankly, less violent because they had their money in hand prior to ever delivering a single key. Consignment was becoming a thing of the past in the drug trade.

First Banks sent the request to the connection via Instagram with a simple photo. A predetermined sequence of photos corresponded to product types, with a second Instagram photo posted including a code for the number of units. And just like that, a meaningless needle in a haystack started a logistics request for cocaine halfway around the world from Banks's location. If anyone were to see these requests, the pictures of a black raven and a photo of "SN" or the fiftieth element on the periodic table would appear meaningless.

The Sinaloa Cartel was one of the most ruthless groups in the world; but if nothing else, they were practical with regards to some aspects of business like the need for secret communication. The Internet had always been a home to Banks; combining it with the business end of his family— moving large quantities of coke with the Web—was the genius of what he was able to bring to the table in his uncle's absence. The cartel would not accept any delays in their supply chain, so when the Black Mafia Family was all but wiped out, they had made his uncle an offer he hadn't been able to refuse. King could have refused, but he most likely would have ended up in a barrel of acid or with his head cut off in a YouTube video; but in that respect, his uncle was practical. At the time, King was facing charges, which in the cartel's book was not a deal-breaker since he had no ties to the BMF but did have some of the same connections for moving his primary product: marijuana.

King had made the move into the more lucrative business of cocaine distribution mainly because he'd had little choice. But given that marijuana legalization was around the corner in states like Colorado, it turned out that it had been a practical and profitable move to make since the street prices on his cash crop plummeted following legalization. A vast majority of clients could now legally buy their drug of choice, meaning that prices went down; and frankly, the street dealers with which he had connections changed with the times, moving into coke, heroin, or meth, where prices remained solid.

Banks's contribution came at a time when the marketplace for such drugs remained sky-high, and the anonymity of the Web allowed him to further expand upon delivery methods for the product. One might ask the obvious question: how does one become an Internet druglord?

Tor was a free software that allowed its users to have anonymity on the Web through a network of servers that hid the location of the source of websites and their users by bouncing signals off thousands of routers so a user's signal picked a random path to reach its destination. The easiest path from point A to point B is a straight line. Well, anyone trying to figure out where a user's signal was coming from would apply this same theory to return to the source of a message transmission or a website. With, Tor there were a number of layers, as in several thousand random pathways a message can take while ending up at the same point B. Your point A could be in San Juan, Puerto Rico, and you want to send a message to San Diego, California. With Tor, your message may take a path via servers in Europe to Asia down to Australia while still ending up in San Diego. This software allowed Banks to bounce his messages to the connections in Mexico, where almost all of the drugs entered the US, to arrange the beginning of the supply that would meet the demand in New York City.

And the really scary part was: he did it all from a computer in a country with no real agreement for extradition to the US—at least not for him, in a chat room that nobody but his connections knew about while he played two different video games and had conversations that nobody but the players in that room could hear.

A separate monitor pinged, signaling a new trade confirmation. Banks looked at the numbers listed on the page and smiled. One step closer to the end result. The numbers read out the confirmation of a stock purchase at their desired price.

ROSCOE JOHNSON

"**M**an, frozen lil Snickers is the shit, boys," said Roscoe as he grabbed one from the freezer in the back of the Miller Street Grocery.

The Miller Street Grocery was located in East Point, Georgia, and was a family-owned operation in a building that occupied half a city block. The front of the store was like any other midsize inner-city grocery store; but the majority of the family work went on in the back part of the building, which was equipped with loading bays and warehouse facilities. The grocery's location also serviced several other smaller grocers in the area. Located on the other half of the block was Advanced Moving Company, which specialized in long-haul relocations for families. The two businesses shared a parking lot for the trucks and a work bay in the warehouse. The warehouse facility also had a ramp that allowed a full-size moving truck to be pulled inside for any maintenance or, in this case, to be hidden from sight while Roscoe's crew did their work. All the trucks were only double axles, not massive big rigs that would require inspections as they crossed state lines. A small, thousand-square-foot office was buried in the back of the warehouse, which was divided up with pallets of food products that formed a wall and blocked all but a small walkway that went directly in front of the office. In short, none of the employees from the grocery could get past the office without being spotted by Roscoe, who held almost constant guard in the small office.

After Roscoe retrieved his Snickers bar, he noticed that the group of young men playing cards in the grocery paid him little attention. Roscoe looked over the game with interest and called out to his youngest son, "Devon, you got the truck ready for New York?"

"We almost done, and then we'll finish it up," replied the skinny kid sitting with his back to his father, concentrating on his next play. The group had picked up playing spades the last few weeks instead of the more familiar games Devon knew like crunk, poker, or gin. Really, he was watching Trey, who was playing with Demarcus to make sure they weren't passing signals.

Trey and Demarcus had grown up with Devon and Marlow Johnson and had been around the family for years. Trey was the same age as Marlow, and they had played basketball together in high school. Devon was a few years younger and nowhere near the athlete Marlow had been growing up. He had spent more time listening to music and hip-hop than playing sports. Neither of Roscoe Johnson's sons were academic giants, but both knew their way around the streets. Marlow especially understood the need to hustle and excelled at making money, even from a young age, when in grade school he would take big bags of candy and split them up, selling them as single units for a profit. Marlow was a natural salesperson.

"You fuckers haven't finished the truck setup yet!" cried Roscoe as he bit into his Snickers and looked at his son from behind a folded-up newspaper in which he was looking up his lotto numbers.

"You know Julius will be here in the next few hours, and that bullshit don't fly!"

"Man, fuck Julius. He don't need to know shit!" replied Devon.

The gazes of the other three players all fell back on Roscoe, as if they were watching a tennis match, waiting for the ball to be either hit back softly or possibly. The man moved quick as a tiger striking its prey;

the speed with which the three-hundred-pound man moved hinted at his former stature as an all-conference football player. Roscoe swept Devon backward, flipping the chair and Devon with it flat onto the concrete floor, in the process knocking the table and all the cards with it straight up in the air as Devon's foot hooked the table on his way down with a dull thud. He'd hit hard, letting out a gasp as the air released from his lungs. Before anyone could or would say anything, a large mitt of a hand grasped at the collar on Devon's loose-fitting shirt.

"Boy, I think it's about time you finished up this fuckin' game and got back to work!" said the oversize man while holding a death stare on his son.

Silently, without any further discussion, the other three players began backing away from Devon and his father. Each one moved as quietly as possible so as not to stir the confrontation taking place. Even the 220-pound Darius Pittman, also known as "Pitt," wanted no part of the man who was cradling Devon in his firm grip. Each one walked back to the loading dock bay, with Treyvon putting on his welding gloves as both he and Demarcus Jennings got back in position to finish the weld on the bottom of the rented U-Haul truck that was being prepared for its trip up north.

Devon began to catch his breath and let out a feeble "yeesss."

"Yes what!" said Roscoe, his dark-brown eyes never releasing their penetrating glare from his son, who was lying prone before him.

"Yes, sir!" said Devon "Yes, sir, and sorry—"

"You're goddamn right you're sorry . . . the whole bunch of you," snarled Roscoe. "Julius be the least of your worries."

And with that, the crew went back to their task of cutting a slot in the gas tank of the twenty-six-foot-long orange-and-gray Ford moving truck, as they had numerous times before. They would cut space for the delivery of the goods from Atlanta to one of the five boroughs of New York. Nobody in the crew knew exactly where, only that it was going north and it would be doing so in the next few days.

The group consisted of the four cardplayers: Devon Johnson, Treyvon Singletary, Darius "Pitt" Pittman, and Demarcus Jennings. A fifth member of the work crew, R. J. "Cass" Cassell, was in route to a meeting out West with the Johnson Family connection. Cass would be the one to drive the load from southern Texas through Louisiana and into Mississippi. From there, a flip of a coin would determine his path through Alabama, with nobody knowing which route or when he would arrive at a warehouse in East Point, Georgia. Cass was the primary driver to get the product to Atlanta, where it would be repacked in the cut-out fuel tank of the U-Haul and prepared for its journey up to the Bronx or maybe Queens.

Part of the changes implemented by Banks since King's incarceration had been the compartmentalization of their delivery methods. The level of risk had gone up fourfold with the decision to deal primarily in cocaine. Everyone in the room knew the story of the BMF, and nobody had any desire to spend the next thirty-plus years in jail. There were some advantages to dealing with cocaine instead of weed, namely the space needed to successfully stash and hide the cocaine was far smaller than the monetary equivalent of weed. Marijuana was also much harder to hide from drug dogs, as the scent was far stronger; and the quantities needed to make serious money required much more of it to be packaged, or multiple trips.

Each leg of the trip was handled differently, with the connection with the cartel providing the initial vehicle to be driven from the Southwest, usually starting in El Paso via Ciudad Juárez, Mexico, or Tucson via Nogales, Mexico. The only member of the crew with direct access to the meeting point was Marlow, who stayed out West, living primarily in Phoenix or San Antonio. Once the drugs made it into the US, and they always made it in, Marlow would set up the meeting with Cass and the trek would begin.

Roscoe looked at the boys working on the truck and went back to the fridge to get another Snickers. Order had been restored, and he felt like he deserved a little prize. Those little frozen peanuts covered in caramel, nougat, and chocolate were calling his name. What the fuck was nougat anyways?

R. J. "CASS"
CASSELL ROSCOE JOHNSON

ights flashed ahead of the Chevy Malibu, and the snake of red taillights was the first indication of the traffic stop ahead. Cass slowed the car, took a deep breath, and adeptly hit the speed dial on his phone, connecting him to a number that would only be used once. The international bleep was picked up on the third ring.

"Ghost, you there?" Cass calmly spoke into his Bluetooth Jawbone.

"Right here watching over you. What's the situation?"

"Traffic stop; there was a detour off Interstate 10, about 25 miles or so outside of Beaumont on Highway 124. Looks like state troopers."

On the other end of the line, Banks quickly and efficiently keyed in on a GPS locator attached to the underside of the Malibu and pulled up the blimp on his screen. He zoomed in and at the same time pulled up the information record from the Enterprise Rent-A-Car back end and blew it up on one of the multiple screens he currently had in use.

"No problem, I have you. Cover is being sent for your upcoming appointment in Beaumont with a Mr. L. J. Shelton of Beaumont Bank and Trust. Your meeting is scheduled for 4:00 p.m. this afternoon to review their security systems and the attempted breach on their data last week.

I am also loading into your email copies of your plane ticket confirmations for your flight that landed in Houston at 10:15 a.m. from Atlanta on Delta Air Lines. You know what to do." And with that, the line went silent, leaving Cass with the traffic stop and the potential thirty-plus years in jail that accompanied it if the load of fifty kilograms of Colombia's finest was found.

Within seconds, all of the necessary information had been downloaded by R. J.'s iPhone and appeared in his inbox followed by some junk mail to add further layers to the cover story, should one become necessary. The information had been carefully data mined and had been created well in advance. The original departure location for the Malibu was updated in Enterprise's system to further add the illusion being created for one R. J. "Cass" Cassell. The illusion of a thirty-four-year-old computer security specialist and owner of Cassell Security based out of Dunwoody, Georgia.

As the few cars in front of him rolled down their windows and passed licenses and registrations over, the same action was being mentally prepared and practiced in R. J.'s head. This would not be the first time he spoke to a man of authority with kilos of cocaine secretly loaded in his car, but the rush was all the same to him.

"Good morning, officer, what can I do for you?" Cass handed him his driver's license and copy of the rental-car contract.

"Nothing much, sir. We're just doing a regular check and letting drivers know the bridge just north of Walden over Hillebrandt Bayou is having some repairs and is down to one lane," spouted the officer. "You'll want to take Brooks Road or Bayou Willow Way back on over to Interstate 10 to avoid it. They cleared the wreck on I-10, and you should be far enough past it to get back on."

"Well, thank you very much, officer. I appreciate the directions."

"No problem there, Mr. Cassell, you drive safe." The officer handed the license back to Cass, not even taking a second look at the blond-haired, blue-eyed driver and forgetting him almost the second he drove off down Highway 124.

Cass calmly rolled up the window and sent a quick text saying "All good" to the number he'd just used to contact Ghost. Then he quickly deleted both the number and the text. He dismissed the incident almost as quickly as the officer had dismissed him because not only was Cass very, very cool under pressure, he had one more trait that completed his role in the Johnson operation: he was white.

Robert Jones Cassell was originally from Arlington, Virginia, but his computer skills led him to the same dorm room as one Reginald Eugene Johnson as a freshman at MIT during the late 1990s. A few indiscretions with some recreational pot in the dorm rooms later led to him being politely asked not to come back to MIT after his sophomore year, but he kept in touch with Banks online.

When asked if he was interested in a job that involved travel, adventure, and lots of cash, he decided it was worth it not to have to get a real job with very real bosses. Cass knew Banks's back story with regards to his uncle, and it didn't bother him at all. In fact, he was kind of excited to be part of the team. He considered it sort of like being a player in one of his online games. He played a part, a role, and his part was a traveling businessman. He fully trusted that if the shit ever really did hit the fan, his cover story would be airtight; and if ever questioned, he would, for lack of a better term, play dumb. All of his paperwork would make it look like the car had just been rented and he was simply an unwitting mule driving a rental car from the closest major city to his next appointment. All of this was, of course, false; but Banks could easily hack into the rental car database and plant the VIN to back up the cover story. The fact that Cass was white added to the story; and he traveled with business cards, a computer, luggage—and he even had a PowerPoint presentation on his computer memorized for just the occasion. Cassell Security was real, playing the part of a front company for his income as a security consultant.

The concern Banks had always had was having a black man drive the assets through parts of the country that were still more likely to hang up the star and bars of the Confederacy than watch an episode of *Roots*. He believed in playing the percentages; and when the math said a black man was ten times more likely to get pulled over just for being black, especially in some parts along the route, Banks made the business decision to bring in someone white whom he could trust. Banks was funny that way: once you earned his trust, he would always be there for you. Even if he wasn't in the same time zone or country, Cass knew Banks was on the other end of a random number that was sent to him as part of every trip.

The history between Cass and Banks wasn't all that long and complicated; in fact, it boiled down to one simple fact. The weed Cass got busted smoking in the dorm at MIT belonged to Banks; and instead of telling the university where it came from, R. J. kept his mouth shut and took his punishment. A trait that was rare in those days. Cass had figured that nobody else was to blame for his decision, and he accepted the consequences on his own.

The reality was, Cass liked the money. He could make more in one month driving a car listening to the latest John Grisham novel than most computer engineers made in a year. The money was the tits for him, and the risk seemed worth the reward. He didn't carry a gun in part because it didn't fit the profile of a businessman in a rental car. The only people he knew or dealt with outside of Banks, who he hadn't seen in person in over three years, were Marlow and Julius Jr. He would call J. J. whenever he arrived in Georgia, and they would set a meeting. From there, he would hand the keys to J. J.—or, more appropriately, leave the keys in a newspaper on a table in a coffee shop as J. J. walked by and disappeared into a MARTA until the next time. They used a different set of burner phones each time; and other than the brief encounters in Atlanta chosen at random, Cass never saw J. J., and in person they never spoke to each other. Kind of cloak-and-dagger, spy-type stuff; and Cass honestly felt that was part of the job's allure. That air of mystery—that, and the money. The money was really, really good. Maybe for the upcoming break he would shoot down to Atlantis in Nassau and get out of the cold for a little while. Money did make everything a lot easier, from travel to just sitting at home playing *Call of Duty* all day.

Obviously the game they were playing now was on a much higher level than taking a simple pot bust, and Cass was under no illusion that his cover story could sink as quickly as the *Titanic* in the North Atlantic; but he also really didn't like working and had found all the jobs prior to this one extremely boring. Furthermore, his options had been someone limited after being expelled from MIT, and writing code for $65,000 a year was a grind that was crushing his soul.

The truth was far less entertaining: Basically, all he did was drive a car from point A to point B and drop off the car. He did get to rack up frequent flyer miles on his way out West, and a few times a month he stayed with Marlow in Phoenix for several days to add to the illusion of business travel; but for the most part, it was pretty much just driving and listening to books on CD. Banks had covered every detail imaginable; and the only rule was nobody but the Ghost or the eye in the sky, as Cass liked to think of him, knew the route he was taking to get back to Georgia. Not even Marlow knew how he would get there or when he would arrive, but Cass did his part. Back to his own version of spy shit; he felt untouchable after a rush like the traffic stop.

And he had just played his part to perfection. He quickly switched over to his iTunes account and selected "Iron Man" by Black Sabbath. Screw the book on tape; time to kick some real tunes while driving just slightly over the speed limit. I mean, no reason to get crazy or anything.

JOHN

"Pete, sorry about your old Pats letting you down this past weekend; I don't guess it hurt Joshua's feelings too much. I seem to remember he does well when the home team loses," John said as Peter Murphy took his seat at Farm Burger in Buckhead for their weekly lunch meeting. Pete was a retired Boston police sergeant and had been with John for years.

"Yep, they sure did beat the snot out of Brady, but we should be back strong again next year," replied Pete as he took a menu. Even though he looked at the menu every time, he always ordered the same thing.

"Josh makes out all right either way the games end, but I'm sure he did just fine this past weekend."

"Let me get a burger with cheese all the way," Pete said as the brunette waitress looked at him while dropping off their drinks.

John, in his usual manner, had arrived fifteen minutes early and ordered a burger prior to Pete's arrival. Courtesies like waiting until the other party arrived to order had long sense departed their relationship. They quickly got down to business.

"Tell me what you found out on our newbie," John said as he dumped sweetener in his tea and began whipping it into a minor frenzy.

"Well, it appears that Mr. Isaac has some priors that may be problematic. Looks like he had a nasty habit of getting himself into trouble with his past girlfriends. I found at least two prior restraining orders and one investigation for domestic in Michigan that could come up. It was kind of old, but I'd be willing to bet that even your local Atlanta PD will be able to find that one." Pete pulled out a notebook and flipped to a page. "Looks like the ex was named Janet Hendrix; and she withdrew her cooperation in roughly 2003, leaving the Auburn Hills locals with no viable witness."

"What does that tell you?" asked John as he sipped his tea.

"I did a little more digging and found a car registration for a BMW at around the same time, May of 2003, in the name of one Shana Worsham, who happens to be the disabled mother of Janet Hendrix. Brand-new with all the bells and whistles for that model in that year."

"Ahhh, now that's a little more interesting, but does that make a jump all the way to possible aggravated assault with intent to kill for our guy?" asked John.

"I think it shows that your client doesn't mind tilting the wheels of justice in his favor if given the opportunity. The question is more would he do it again given his . . . uh, how do we say . . . current situation?'

"Well, his current situation is that he's locked up in Fulton and will do just about anything needed to get out of his shitty situation," John replied as his burger with fries arrived. A banana pudding milkshake would follow shortly.

John shifted in his seat. "Have you located Isaac's soon-to-be exgirlfriend?"

Pete flipped a few pages in his black notebook, past the original notes. "Seems she has taken up residence over near Dunwoody with a friend of hers named Alicia Towns."

John seemed to slow for a second while he savored the burger covered in pickled jalapeños, Duke's mayo, and a wonderful smoked Gouda. He inhaled the smell of the cooked beef before taking a bite. The look on his face changed slightly, as he had obviously bitten into one of the jalapeños.

Pete looked over at him and asked the question that was on both their minds: "Would you like me to reach out and see if a compromise can be arranged?"

John smiled a sheepish grin. "Why, I think that would be in the best interest of our client; and seeing as he has the means, perhaps that's a move he would like made on his behalf. Yes, why don't we reach out to Miss Burke and see if some time has changed her mind about the claim that poor Bradly tried to run her over with her car." John took a fry off the plate and stared off into space momentarily. "I'm sure Mr. Isaac can make it worth her while and perhaps throw in a trip for her to clear her mind."

"I'll see what her thoughts are on the matter and how that may help her see things differently." Pete made a mental note and closed his notebook, signaling an end to normal nine-to-five business talk. Everything else would be strictly off-book and committed to memory.

"Julius made contact for the next delivery," Pete said. "Return package should be here by early next week. Says it's the normal fifty runs for the Yankees."

John immediately knew the distribution point and calculated the expected return amount of cash. The code system was simple: a baseball team for each distribution point and group. A run meant a kilo of cocaine, and they made it a practice only to deal with one group per city. No need to create rivalry for product; there was plenty to go around.

"I'm heading down to the beach tonight after work; be back on Sunday night," said John without batting an eye. He felt nothing abnormal about these conversations anymore; most of the time he felt nothing at all —the booze made sure of that, and there was always plenty of booze everywhere he went.

"Sounds like there will be a second delivery to the Phillies by the end of the week as well," Pete said casually.

"How was old Julius?"

"Still black as night and looking like he wants to stab me; but other than that, he was just fucking peachy," Pete said while shifting forward in his chair. "I mean, that guy has got 'I hate your Irish ass' stamped on his forehead every time I see him."

"Don't take it personal, Pete; he pretty much hates everyone not named Della or Julius Jr.," John said with a smirk on his face. "You're just the lucky mick bastard that gets to deal with his special kind of crazy. He's still mad he has to deal with any of us since King went inside. Keep that in mind when you deal with him; you aren't considered family in his book. Never will be, either."

"Not saying I want a Christmas card, but the guy could quit being such a dick," Pete replied as his burger was adeptly delivered by the waitress. "I mean, a little professionalism goes a long way."

"I don't think professionalism is a word in Julius Johnson's vocabulary, bud," John said as he placed his folded napkin on his plate and eyed his milkshake. "As long as everything stays on track, we deal with him whether he's happy, sad, mad, or glad. No other options—it's the way King and Banks want it done, so that's the way it will be."

"No bother. I can deal with him, just speaking my mind," Pete muttered as he started in on his burger.

"I know you are—no worries. It's running as smoothly as it can. We do our part and they do their part, and the whole operation keeps marching forward." John pulled out two twenties and set them on the table. "Got to run. On my way to USP to see the King."

"Good luck with that, my friend," Pete said as John hopped up and turned for the door.

The gray sky and wind picked up as he opened the door and headed down the street. several magazines in the briefcase he hauls with him as he braced himself for the chilly winter air.

ALEX

"Cooper, you about ready to head downtown? We have reservations at Halls at six thirty. John should be at his condo by now."

"Yep, I'm ready! When you are, we can head that way," Cooper replied. "What we got coming up on the agenda for this evening?"

I looked away from the screen for a minute and up at the ceiling fan. "We need to go over the drop for early next week—the package coming down from up north. You have a flight to New York on Monday morning with a rental car pickup and meet around 1:00 p.m. at a point to be determined. Normal follow and watch. Pete has arranged a cover group there and back. We need to use the Atlanta runners this time."

I glanced out the window of my office, which was located in an ancient brick building near the historic slave market off East Bay Street. Charleston was a true gem of a city, adorned with a hint of history at every turn on every street downtown. Whether it was the black steeples, which had been painted that way during the Revolutionary War to make the British cannons less accurate, or the fort in the harbor, where the first shots of the Civil War had been fired, the history and feel of Charleston were undeniable. Luckily, Charleston had been occupied and spared the wrath of General Sherman's fires during the Civil War, unlike much of the rest of the South.

The landscape had been changed by another event that we had all lived through during our childhoods. Hurricane Hugo was a category-four storm that decimated the Charleston area September 22, 1989. In spite of all the damage done by Hugo, the restoration and recreation that followed was a renaissance for Charleston. Our city had become one of the top tourist destinations in the country because of the culture, the beaches, the food, and its touch of history. My office and, thus, our operation lay in the heart of this history, hiding in plain sight.

"Cooper, let Pete know they need to go north, up near Smyrna this time," I said as I turned in my chair behind my cherry wooden desk. Cooper was sitting at a side table inside my office.

I liked to rotate the money being run in different areas including Atlanta, parts of South Carolina, and the outskirts of Charlotte. Following a strategy similar to the one the Johnsons used with the actual narcotics, we chose not to have the illegal activity take place directly in our backyard. None of the runners actually knew who they worked for; all they knew was we had some tie to the Mexican cartel. That was enough to keep people in line, as most people valued not having their heads separated from their bodies or ending up in a barrel in the desert. Of course, we didn't tell them we weren't the cartel; but the less the runners knew, the better. Our runner system was a network of people that made deposits throughout a network of banks in random amounts to get the money into the system.

My role in our team was very simple yet very complex and required advanced planning, a proficiency with numbers, and a cat burglar's skills. Okay, maybe there wasn't really burglary involved. I was the guy who got our money clean. I handled the laundering of the proceeds from the drugs trafficked by the Johnson family. The key problem with drugs and the money they created was the logistics associated with them. On the street, $1 million of cocaine weighed roughly 44 pounds; and if you took payment in dollar bills, the cash would weigh 256 pounds—roughly the same weight as an NFL linebacker. The plan was to eliminate as much of the cash from the process as possible; and transacting most of the money offshore solved a large part of the problem, namely keeping the cartel happy, as they were paid up front and the product movement wasn't their concern. They just had to get it into the US; then the Johnson group took over and made delivery. The next level that received the product did have monetary concerns since for the most part, they were paid in cash. They had some methods for converting the cash, but we had to handle and clean at least 50 to 75 percent of the money.

The beauty of the system set up and planned for Banks and his family was that we had taken steps to eliminate some of the nasty side effects of drug trafficking—like the murders, the shoot-outs, and most importantly, the cops.

The cartel was like most businesses, after all: practical. The system we used was practical for them as well. The money was all transacted in advance for the purchase of their product. This made the *Miami Vice*-style idea of meetings in shady hotel rooms with armed guys wearing neon shirts unnecessary. As a whole, the cartel had their own problems and they used ruthless methods in their turf wars and blood feuds south of the border; but they were incredibly efficient at getting drugs, namely cocaine, into the US. All the efforts of the DEA, border guards, and immigration officials were futile given the demand and need the American general public had for the cartel's drugs.

From the supply side, the Johnson organization was pretty clever; they dealt with the same people in the same locations, and they only dealt with about a dozen different groups in eight major US cities. They ran the drugs up the Eastern Seaboard with locations including New York, Philadelphia, Baltimore, and DC. They also ran drugs south to Miami, Orlando, and Jacksonville. Drugs would also be delivered to smaller groups in Charlotte, Raleigh, to the east of Atlanta, up to Cleveland, Nashville, and to a group in Lexington, Kentucky, of all places. Some of the groups were people who had done business with King during his days delivering weed up from Mexico. One of the group's smart moves was that they actually did no distribution in Atlanta or in my state of South Carolina. This was by design and strategic planning; more simply put, we followed the doctrine of "don't shit where you eat and live." The simplicity of not attracting any attention to your primary businesses in your hometown made it far easier to clean the money and operate under the radar.

"Under the radar" was the best way to describe the Johnson organization at this point. Other than the family members in Atlanta, we never met; there was no drug trafficker's convention in Hilton Head; and we damn sure didn't advertise.

My role involved a great degree of risk and risk assessment. I developed a network of cash-based businesses in areas around the states of South Carolina, Georgia, and Virginia. We used businesses like check cashing, grocery stores, bars, and restaurants.

Money laundering in general was the introduction of illicit funds into the economy by layering it in with ordinary cash flow. The layering of the money involved making cash deposits into ordinary bank accounts to mix them with legal funds. Through a network of runners, I could direct deposits, make payments on secured credit cards for future use, and in general get cash into various types of business accounts that we could then use for operations in the States. One key way we were able to mask a lot of the movement was we had established businesses in and around Atlanta that were owned by various LLCs controlled by other LLCs that all ended up back in the Johnsons' hands.

We didn't do wire transfers out of the country. The system Banks used outside the States involved using Bitcoin for transfers; and frankly, just banking at some of the same banks in Panama, the Cayman Islands, Hong Kong, and the Bahamas as the cartels. The bank secrecy laws in Panama were close to rivaling the Swiss. The cartels wised up; basically, cash is cumbersome. Another planning item for the Johnson family was not to move huge amounts of cocaine at the same time. They used more of a real-time delivery system by having Marlow out West, ready to set up the initial phase of delivery. Banks would take an order via secure communication on the Dark Web from his key people, and the order would begin to move. The cartel was paid 100 percent in advance because, let's just be honest, nobody wanted those crazy motherfuckers on their ass. As far as everyone that made a purchase was concerned, they were getting the cartel's cocaine; they were none the wiser that it was already paid for up front. Banks required a 50 percent deposit via Bitcoin or offshore wire transfer, and then the delivery was on its way. We did have the issue of roughly $2–5 million in cash per week, but such was the life of an ongoing criminal enterprise. There was also the possibility of going to jail for thirty years to life, but that was where compartmentalization came into play.

I had never met nor ever would meet the operations side of the family. I knew their names but wouldn't have known them from Adam if we ran into each other on the street. The only people I knew who also knew me were Banks, John, and Cooper. From my perspective, that was all I needed to know and all I wanted to know. I knew of Cass, but once again couldn't pick him out from photo lineup—by design.

After King had been arrested several years ago, the game plan had changed. Banks decided if he had to keep the family business going, he was going to make some changes. Gone were the days of shady hand offs and gunplay, which I assumed played a part in his dad getting killed in Tampa around 1990. He separated operations and kept it so deliver times, routes, and dates were set at random. He began using moving vans and cover families to make deliveries for end users, and one key driver for the long haul from the Southwest to Atlanta. Marlow accepted delivery in the Southwest and set up the cars with GPS trackers for the first leg so Banks could keep his eyes on the prize during the initial delivery run. The drop-offs were randomly decided upon in Atlanta, with keys handed off to one person who delivered the goods to a setup team to get them on the road. A third team would then take them to their destination at random and drop off the truck while another truck was prepared for the return voyage with the cash. Now I wasn't kidding myself—there were a million ways it could go wrong; but in my role, that wasn't really something I saw or dealt with on a regular basis.

The key for the Johnson family was they were family and for the most part appeared to have trust with the groups they dealt with—and nobody was getting greedy. There was a lot of money to go around, and it was released back to all of them as clean currency. Hell, everyone involved got a W-2 and paid taxes. They also pretty much all kept everything they made since all other expenses were paid for by a network of companies and credit cards.

Not to sound proud, but what I had set up for them was pretty damn impressive considering nobody knew anything about it. Anonymity was necessary; and as high-tech as Banks could be with a computer, all other communication was via scheduled meetings face-to-face with no communication at all via cell phone. There were person-to-person meetings at different points; but for the most part each cell (for lack of a better term) was independent of the others, and there was virtually no way someone could connect the dots from one cell to another.

John's investigator, Pete Murphy, was the only one who met face-to-face with a point of contact regarding the logistics on behalf of the Johnson family. John met only with Kingston in prison or Julius. Banks only communicated with me, Julius, or John; and that was only through certain channels on specific days.

We had several ways we laundered the cash as it came in bulk. From the employment side of things, all of the Johnson family owned a holding company that in turn owned a construction company and a number of subs in both Atlanta and Charleston. I had come up with the idea because using construction loans from banks made it fairly easy to launder the money, and the larger loan amounts made it easier to move the cash.

The way it worked was fairly simple: First, the construction company would low-bid a job. The profitability of the job wasn't the primary concern of the LLC; instead, they were creating a vehicle. The main builder that worked for the LLC in Charleston was a guy named Michael Potter. Michael was a down-and-out builder who had been pulled off the scrap heap and offered a nice salary; in turn, he handled business a certain way. Namely, with the majority of the accounts he used and vendors he paid, he used cash. He was also given an influx of cash to purchase distressed property so the Diagram Holdings Company, or DHC, could buy and flip property. That portion of the holding company was very profitable because at this point we also used tax advantages to allow the LLC to flip the property tax-free, with the money being used to actually do the work and pay the vendors in mostly cash.

What we did was open trade lines in Potter Construction's name at big-box vendors like Home Depot, Lowe's, and a number of other retailers in both cities. Then Potter deposited cash on the credit lines, creating a surplus balance. So at, say, Lowe's, he might have 3 different accounts each paid to the positive by $25–50,000, each giving him the ability to pay for materials, etc.

The retail giants didn't follow the same rules as banks. For example, if you tried to deposit $10,000 in cash into an account that had an average balance of $1,500, it would most likely get flagged with a Suspicious Activity Report or SAR. As a general rule, anything over $6,000 would get flagged automatically; but a teller or banker could issue an SAR for less than that amount if they so chose. It made it much harder to move cash because a bank's system would still throw a flag if you ran all over town putting $5,000 into accounts in each branch, which was also another method we used, but in a different strategy—mostly in Atlanta.

With the construction loans, the borrower—let's call them Mr. and Mrs. Williams—would apply for a construction loan to build a $1,500,000 house in Charleston and would get a loan for, say, $1,000,000. Well, Potter would be less expensive than everyone else and would likely get the deal because he'd have the best price. The reason he could get the best price was he was just concerned with the number of items in the bid; he wasn't worried about turning a profit, and most builders would shoot for 15 to

20 percent in profit. Potter was able to undercut everyone else and get the deal because what we really wanted was the access to the draws from the construction line. We had a third-party bookkeeper handle Potter's books; he was just told where to get jobs and how to bid on them.

While I knew of Mr. Potter, I had never met with him, nor would I. He worked for a division of DHC and had been hired via a recruiter. He got a W-2 and paystub just like all the other employees of DHC.

Deposits were made on the lines of credit via a separate courier system. The way a construction loan worked, the contract was signed between Mr. and Mrs. Williams and DHC Construction, a subcompany under DHC. Potter and his team would start construction, usually with a 10 percent down payment, which would go to DHC via the funds from the Williamses' construction loan. DHC, in turn, would use the surplus lines of credit to fund the actual home construction, but the lines of credit would be paid down via cash transactions completed at various vendors across the Southeast. Someone walking into a Lowe's in, say, Charlotte, North Carolina, with an account number and making a cash payment didn't draw nearly the amount of attention as if it were done at a bank. The line of credit would be used and paid back by the funds, turning them into profits of DHC.

Nobody would be the wiser because all Potter had done was get a bid, build a house, and get paid; and he'd be on to the next bid. Now, certainly Potter had some notion that everything was far too easy; but at the same time, we're talking about a guy who had filed at least two bankruptcies and now just got a paycheck while his entire back office was handled by the new construction firm that backed him. The guy didn't ask too many questions because, as the recruiter told him up front: "We like what you build, but you're just not that good at managing the projects. That will be done for you by the home office."

The trick to making this method work was scalability and patience, something that the organization had been able to achieve over the last few years. At any given time, DHC Construction had 20 to 40 repair rehabs going at $100–200,000 each in 2 major markets, and at least 50 large-scale multimillion-dollar homes in 5 major cities. The collapse of the mortgage market in 2008 had created a lot of down-and-out builders. Managing the money was key, and his particular vehicle gave the organization the ability to launder roughly $90 million a year in profits. The best part was that because the company showed very little in profits after expenses and all the rehabs, DHC Construction could take advantage of a tax regulation that allowed the profits to be deferred. The money was tax-free in every sense of the word.

***

"Cooper, how's Becca doing in school?" I asked as we exited the office onto the street in one of historic Charleston's main tourist areas. We walked on the stone sidewalks toward the parking garage located behind the historic office building that housed my mortgage company. A recent fire across the street had gutted a few bars and restaurants, so the sidewalk was partially blocked with a construction chute and scaffold. We crossed the street as the weekend traffic started to file into the downtown area.

"She's adjusting; they have good schools up there," Cooper replied as he pulled out the keys to his truck. "You driving or riding?"

"I'll ride with you if you don't mind dropping me off later. I'm sure John will want to go out, and that will be all you guys," I said as I reached the passenger door. Coop had parked in one of our client parking spaces per usual.

"I should get hazard pay for having to go out with John after these dinners," Cooper said.

"Take that up with your union rep," I joked. "Being sober means I don't have to entertain John; besides, you're the single one, so you can run the streets of Charleston with him."

Cooper shot me a look that gave away his underlying feeling.

"I mean, you are single, right?" I said as he cranked the ignition of his pickup and began down the snaking lanes of the three-story garage.

"Man, you know I'd like to put it back together with Lauren; but I'm not sure I'll get the chance," Coop said. As we got to the teller's stall, he rolled down the window to hand over his ticket.

"Coop, it's been two years since you got divorced. I'm not sure of the stats on people getting remarried, but I think that ship may have sailed on you, bud," I said. "It's not like you can't find a girl in Charleston; the ratio is up to like 7:1, girls to guys."

"I don't know, man. I just want my family back," Cooper said as he pulled out of the garage and took a right onto East Bay, heading north up the peninsula.

We drove past the historic slave market, one of the top tourist destinations in our city. The market was open and teeming with tourists. The market was several rectangular brick structures with open air and half walls between the brick columns; it ran for several blocks in a straight line, with dozens of vendors selling everything from handmade sweetgrass baskets to jewelry, fudge, and works of art. Horse-drawn carriages filled with tourists could be seen during the warmer months, and the smell of horse droppings and sea salt filled the air most days. Not today—it was a crisp winter day, or at least what passed for a winter day in Charleston, with a slight breeze. The city hadn't seen snow in over a decade and only occasionally had some ice, which would usually melt by midday, even in January. Charleston was a Southern jewel of a city, and it held many wonders and secrets from years of historical events. The slave market was a reminder of the city's past, which was intertwined with its future, as it was now a hub of trade with tourists visiting the town daily. African-Americans had once been sold at the very location where tourists could now buy a piece of silver or even a piece of toffee. Charleston, unlike any other city in the South, embraced this history; the character of the town was a sight to behold.

"Looks like a cruise ship is heading out tomorrow," Cooper said as we drove down East Bay. The ship was visible at the end of Market Street.

A recent local hot-button topic was the ships, which ran from Charleston to the Bahamas and back. A new terminal had been proposed and was currently being challenged by residents.

"My favorite kind of tourists: they come, they drop off money, they leave," I said. Charleston had become one of the top tourist destinations in the country, with it having been ranked multiple times as one of the top cities to visit in America. Charleston was unique because it blended a one-of-a-kind cultural history with beaches, great restaurants, and a laid-back atmosphere. You could visit a historic civil war fort in the harbor in the morning, hit a beach for lunch, and end your evening on King Street, where a thriving shopping and entertainment district had taken hold.

We turned onto Calhoun Street, heading toward King Street and to our ultimate destination: a local steakhouse of the utmost quality.

"You think there'll be a parking spot out back?" Cooper asked. He signaled as he reached the light where Calhoun intersected King. We drove past Marion Square, a park in the middle of the city and a main area for hosting events, weekly farmer's markets, and the various festivals our city had been known to hold throughout the year.

"Should be; my guess is John is already there," I replied

We pulled in and with luck got a spot and paid the attendant, who moved a cone to allow us to valet ourselves. We both got out and went to the restaurant's back entrance, past the exterior kitchen door. A warm wooden interior welcomed us as we walked across the tile floor, past the bathrooms; the hallways was lined with awards the steakhouse had received. We came to the end of the hallway; to the right was the main room and bar with a community table and wooden interior, with two large TVs hanging over the bar. It was already packed with the local crowd fresh off of work, looking to get a cocktail and some conversation.

I looked to the secondary bar on my left and saw our compatriot already bellied up to the bar on the corner, with open chairs on either side of him. An empty martini glass sat in front of him, and a second one was being delivered by Harris, the bartender.

"Hey, boys, just in time," John said. "Harris, grab one O'Doul's and a Bud heavy for my friends."

Harris nodded a hello to us, and we slid into our seats at the bar. The secondary bar led into a newer room that had been added to Halls a year or so earlier. The expanded room had been much needed and was slightly less crowded than the main room. The warm wooden bar was like a pair of welcoming arms that pulled you in and made you feel at home.

John was dressed in a sport coat with a collared white-and-blue striped shirt underneath. His hair was perfect; dinner was obviously just the beginning of his plans for the evening.

"How was your trip?" I asked John, taking a seat as Harris pushed a cold glass filled with nonalcoholic beer in front of me.

"Quick and easy," he replied as he sipped his drink. "Coop, you go surfing this morning?"

"Actually I did; it was cold out there, but we had some good waves," Cooper said as he took off his coat and sat at the end of the bar, to the right of John.

"Well, gentlemen, to another month closer to retirement," John said as he raised his glass.

"Let's hope," I said. "Are we still on track with the exit strategy?"

"One day closer," John replied without missing a beat. "By my math, we should be about to the target."

"That we are! We should be there by the end of the year," I said, sipping my nonalcoholic drink. "You really think this will end as scheduled?"

"King may be a lot of things, but he *is* a man of his word. We will have done our part; and for the most part, they will have what they need to if they want to keep going," John said. "My impression is that King is smart enough to know when he needs to get out. The law of averages eventually catches up with everyone."

"That's what worries me, John. I mean, we've been pretty lucky here for the last few years," I said in a low voice. There was nobody else at the bar, and Harris had walked to the back area. "Either way, we need to be out of this thing sooner rather than later. I can make plenty of money slinging loans and not have to worry about going to jail for thirty years."

"I agree with you, man. I want out, too. We're close," John said with a glance. "Either way, let's save it for the table.

"Cooper, you going out with me tonight? I think there are some ladies we need to meet up with at Club Trio later this evening," John said with a grin.

With a sigh, Cooper said, "I'll be your wingman as always, John; but damn, Trio doesn't even open until like 10:00 p.m. or so. You sure you want to take it that late?"

"Coop, if you want to catch the prey, you got to go where they stay," John replied with a smile. His hair was perfect, and his smile lit up the room. "I'm sure I can find a lady friend for you."

"No worries, John, you know I'm there for you," Cooper said as he took a drink of his Bud, a look of resignation on his face, as he knew his night wouldn't end until after 2:00 a.m., when the bars downtown closed. He was going to be in for the Archibald experience that evening, whether he wanted it or not.

Suddenly a half-dressed blonde appeared. "Mr. Archibald, your table is ready. If you'll follow me upstairs . . ."

John looked over at her with a devilish grin. "Why, of course I will."

JULIUS JOHNSON

A tall man strode into the back of the Miller Street Grocery. He moved with grace and fluidity. His eyes were framed by a stylish pair of Prada glasses, and his head was freshly shaven. A neat and trim goatee lined his face; it was slightly white, which was the only sign of his fifty-seven years. His was the body of a much younger man, taut with muscle on his six-foot-three-inch, two-hundred-pound frame. He was dressed in a perfectly tailored dark suit, and his shoes shone like parquet floor. A red bowtie highlighted his look.

Julius Johnson entered the back of the store and called out for his younger brother, "Roscoe, where you at?" He looked at the U-Haul in the loading bay.

His youngest son, Julius Jr., entered the grocery, circled behind his father quietly, and took a position by the door. A mirror image of his father, he was the older of the two children born to Julius and Della. His brother, Harold, was doing a stretch for felony assault and was due out early the following year. Julius Jr. was considered to be the heir apparent to his father's position, although Harold had shown to be the far more violent of the two brothers thus far.

"In the back office, Jules!" shouted Roscoe, who was seated at a table in a private, hidden room. The room was lined with shelving systems that were stocked with store supplies. A TV played a basketball game.

Julius walked down the aisle and entered the room to see Roscoe eating a sandwich from the deli in the front of the store. Roscoe was dressed in a long-sleeved gray hoodie with jeans and work boots. His sweatshirt was sprinkled with smudges; it was apparent he had been under a vehicle, most likely working on one of the storage compartments they used to stash cocaine in the belly of delivery trucks.

"Are we ready to roll?" Jules looked at the game and then focused his attention on his kin as he set the sandwich down and wiped his chin.

"Truck is ready to go; when you expecting Cass?" Roscoe replied. He took a bite of his sandwich and looked up at the game on the TV.

"Anytime now, anytime now," Julius said as he took a seat at the table with Roscoe. "You see they caught up with El Chapo down in Mexico again?"

Roscoe turned to him with a smile. "Man, old Shorty will just tunnel his ass out again!" he said with a laugh. "You reckon we should dig a tunnel for King?"

"Fuck that, he could walk out the front door if he wanted to," Julius replied. "Supposedly, the Mexicans and some task force are rounding up all the top cartel people. Major busts at the border; could affect us, is all I'm saying. Old Shorty got caught crawling out of a manhole."

"What time you want to get underway?" Roscoe asked, looking back up at the TV. "I think they're calling for some weather up in Yankeeland."

"Don't matter none; we like the post office—neither rain nor snow," Jules said with a smile on his face. "You know his highness the King don't like no damn delays."

"Just saying, might be tricky getting up there, that's all; not questioning you, my brother," Roscoe replied as he picked his sandwich back up. "Either way, truck is ready to go."

"I expected nothing less, little brother," Julius said with a sharp glance at Roscoe. The look stopped Roscoe cold mid-bite.

"Is there something bothering you, J?" Roscoe said, now looking right at his brother.

"Heard a member of your crew may be dealing local." Julius now made a dead-eyed look at Roscoe. He reached over and closed the door behind him, and a sudden tension filled the room. "You know that's against the rules, and I need you to assure me I've heard incorrectly."

"Where you hearing that bullshit!" asked Roscoe, now fully locked in looking up at his older brother.

Jules walked to the counter beside the sink and opened the refrigerator door. He reached in, retrieved a bottle of beer, and popped the top. "I have my ways, Roscoe, you know that; and you also know what happens if someone's dealing in town." Jules slowly took a sip of the beer.

"Ain't none of my crew so much as left the building in the last two days while they been working on that truck. Where the hell they supposed to be dealing?" Roscoe said, now fully attentive to Jules as he moved back to the table and set the bottle down.

"Check your boys, Roscoe, or I will," Jules said with a calmness that spoke volumes even though he said it barely above a whisper. He stood up and walked to the door.

Roscoe just sat at the table, motionless. The gravity of the situation was square on his shoulders, and with that, he lost his appetite.

Julius shut the door and walked back to his son, waiting by the truck.

"You drop it on him, Pops?" J. J. asked.

"We'll see what the big man finds out." Jules pulled a cigarette from a silver-and-gold metal case. He retrieved a silver Zippo from his jacket pocket and lit the smoke. "You sure about your source?"

J. J. looked at his father with a sharp expression. "She knows him, and she knows what she saw." The younger Johnson was still trying to prove himself to his father in every way he could think.

"Well, then we'll let it play on out and fall where it may," Julius said as he walked to the door.

J. J. followed him out into the cold winter night. As they walked down the street, a phone in Julius's pocket vibrated, signaling a call from a number that had never used before and would never be used again after this one call on this cold night. Julius answered after the third ring. He didn't speak a word, listening to the voice on the other end as he smoked his cigarette.

RENA JOHNSON

"**G**oddamn, boy, you got a lot of energy tonight!" She rolled over, covered in sweat and wrapped in a sheet as she stood and walked toward the bathroom. She began to straighten her hair, picking up her clothing from the floor on the way.

"Well, I been working hard, Miss Johnson, and I needed to let off a little steam," replied Demarcus Jennings as he lay back in the bed.

"Stop with that 'Miss Johnson' shit right now, Demarcus!" Rena said as she walked back into the room, pulling a shirt over her head. She grabbed a pack of cigarettes from her purse before dressing in front of a full-length mirror.

"I heard Jeremiah got a letter from a college for ball," Demarcus said, cutting the TV on with the remote; the seventy-inch Samsung sprang to life with the sounds of the movie *Gladiator*. "First of many for your boy, I bet."

Rena finished getting dressed as her cell phone lit up with a call from Jeremiah. She motioned for Demarcus to be quiet before answering. She smiled and walked into the adjacent room to speak with her son.

"Hello, baby, you over at Aunt Della's?" Rena said into the receiver of her Android. She put on her high heels and got ready to head for the door. "Okay, baby, I'll be over in an hour or so to pick you up. You and Ray finish your homework."

Rena clicked off the phone and touched up her makeup in the mirror. The visits to Demarcus have become too frequent, she thought. Della's probably judging my absence right now. Della was always the judge and jury in the family, and Rena also knew that Della was not to be crossed because her opinion could change everything.

"We got to quit seeing each other so much," she said, looking over at him. "The wrong someone might find out about his shit, and that would be bad for us both."

Demarcus looked away from the TV. "Shit, you the one that keeps calling me. I'm just a simple man."

"I know, D., I know; but I don't want to see you get hurt, and we both know what would happen. Let's just stop it now and take a break for a while before someone starts thinking something," Rena said. She looked at him with a slight smile.

Demarcus stood up, exposing himself to her, and walked with her to the door. "Why, no problem, Miss Johnson," he said with a smirk. He kissed her, and they began the whole dance over with less restraint and fell back into the bed.

Rena's phone blinked with an incoming call and then went silent as it clicked over to voicemail.

KINGSTON

Kingston looked up from his magazine to see inmate number 45875-023 approach his table in the common area. All inmates at USP Atlanta had eight numbers that represented them while they were in possession of the federal government.

Donald Harrington was a con artist convicted of stealing money from investors and some lovely ladies in four different states. He sat down at King's table. "Hiya, King, you interested in a card game a little later with some of the guys in B wing?"

"Yeah, why not. What's the game tonight?" King asked as he set down his copy of *National Geographic*, looking at the friend he had acquired during his time inside.

"Hold 'em; entry is a carton of smokes," my balding, middle-aged friend said. He looked ten years older than his forty-two-year calendar count: the effects of years of hard living and too much sun in the warm months. Don had lost twenty pounds in the year he'd been inside USP Atlanta. The paleness of his skin and the lines on his face made him look closer to sixty than to his real age.

Don had come to USP after King's arrival and would be gone roughly

two years before the end of King's stretch. The two had formed an unlikely bond over playing cards and a mutual appreciation of baseball.
The pair also worked together in the laundry—not a bad position in the
prison, as it kept them busy during the day and off the labor details that
went out to work with institutions in the city.

The inmates at the low-security work camp enjoyed more free time,
including recreation in the morning. The quality of food wasn't too terrible,
and there was no perimeter fence. Visitation was Friday through Sunday
and on all major holidays. USP's satellite also allowed the inmates to work
with various groups in and around the city of Atlanta.

If he had truly wanted to, King could have walked out the door and
not come back; but then he would have been a fugitive. From his current
position, he could still run his growing empire and finish his stretch. With
Banks securely placed outside the country, if King had to, he could replace both his brothers, all from 601 McDonough Boulevard Southeast.
King had roughly four years left of his sentence; he had no reason to try
to escape.

"When you getting some visitors around this place?" asked Don.

"I think Rena is supposed to be around here this coming weekend.
She'll probably bring my youngest, Ray, with her," King replied. "You
need her to bring you something?"

"Think she could grab a few preseason baseball magazines if they're
out? Be interested to see what they think of my Mets this year. I can move
some commissary credits over."

King looked up at him as if to say no need. "Don't worry about no
credit, Don. Save your money for cards later on tonight. I'll get her to
bring some magazines in for you." King stretched his lower back and gave
a slight wave of his hand to Don.

"Well, King, that's nice of you. Tell your wife I say thank you," said
Don as he got up and walked away from the table.

King went back to his *Nat Geo*, looking at the codes in the book to take
inventory of last week's shipments. They'd had a good week and a great

month, and everything with the business was running smooth as silk.

But deep down, King worried about his daughter and his second wife. Rena had taken the last name Johnson, but they weren't really married. Maris was his daughter from a different relationship; she was nearly ten years older than Jeremiah and closer in age to Rena than her younger brothers. Maris was still his firstborn; and he knew the signs, knew that she was running with a crowd he couldn't take her away from. Their relationship was both rough and tender at the same time. The last three years he'd spent in jail had seen their relationship go from rocky to nonexistent as she'd made choices that most people her age deemed to be fun. The warning signs were there: missing work, staying out late, missing family gatherings.

King stood and walked to the TV area to try to distract his mind from his fears. He hadn't seen Maris in about a year, and their last meeting had not been pleasant at all.

What can I do from in here? he thought to himself. He needed Banks or Marlow; they were the only ones who could talk to her, and neither of them were anywhere near Atlanta. Ma Maris was too sick to do anything at this point; each of her days was a struggle as it was, without adding Maris to the equation. Roscoe and Julius wouldn't be able to relate to her; and frankly, Julius was more likely to drive her away than help her if she needed it.

Kingston recognized that the signs of her going down the dark path to drugs were staring right at him. King also knew from personal experience that the only person who could truly make a change was the individual. Drugs were very powerful, and he knew firsthand the price users were forced to pay. King had been addicted to alcohol and coke for years during the late '80s and early '90s. The death of his brother Raymond at a deal gone bad in Tampa had straightened him out. Instead of being there for his brother, he'd been out getting high, leaving Raymond to go solo to that fateful meeting in Florida.

He had failed his brother, who didn't live to see the changes he made in his life. King had gone completely sober, with not a drop of anything since the day he had buried Ray beside their father, Ray Sr. That day, King had made a promise to himself and to Raymond to change for the better.

The more he thought about Maris, the more helpless he felt. He knew there was nothing he could force on Maris that would make her change; and being in prison, he was at her mercy to even speak with him. Maybe that would be a start, just getting her to step back inside these walls to listen to what he had to say. King knew she needed to know her father loved her, and that could only be shared by looking in his baby girl's eyes. That would be the first step: to get her here to visit him. Hopefully he could begin to break down the wall between them before it was too late.

PETER MURPHY

The alarm clock woke Pete at 5:00 a.m., and he rolled over to look into the eyes of his wife. The picture was of her on their wedding day in Boston nearly three decades ago. The photograph reminded him of their life together and how much he missed her. What would his life look like if she were still alive and with him today?

Pete cut on the TV, as was his morning ritual.

"An ice storm is bearing down on the metro area, and we'll see temperature drops into the twenty-degree range by late afternoon into the early evening," said the perky blonde who delivered the early morning weather report. Obviously the shit job for the newest person in the newsroom.

Pete got ready to go to the gym in his condo to run on the treadmill and lift some weights. For a man pushing sixty, he looked to be in great shape, even after all the years of hard living. He had pretty much drunk and smoked his way through the first forty years of his life. A mild heart attack and discharge from the police department nearly ten years ago had changed his perspective. Since he'd left the force, he had migrated south for warmer weather and found work as an investigator, first with the great Donovan Howle and now with his junior partner and rising star, John

Archibald. The two had been together for nearly five years, and he had assisted in the special project known as "the Johnson family" for the last three years.

His role had some perks, namely being able to help his son Joshua safely hide the money he made from his illegal bookmaking operation in South Boston. While his father, a former cop, had his opinion on the matter, for the most part he saw nothing wrong with gambling as a vice. People had their vices; of those, gambling and women had never bothered him while he worked on the force.

John and his associates had helped Joshua clean his money and keep himself out of jail, a feat made even more complicated by the fact that his older brother, Thomas, was a lieutenant in the Boston PD. Thomas had been so detached from them since the death of his mother that he had never noticed what Josh was really doing. Truth be told, it had taken some other family friends telling Pete what Josh was doing for him to find out. After arguing and threats looked to be pushing Josh further away, Pete backed off and was later able to accept what his son was doing. Thomas dove deeper into his job; after he and his wife divorced and she got primary custody of Pete's only grandson, their disconnection grew. Thomas now worked more; and they barely spoke, even when they did get on the phone with each other.

Thomas was letting his career take over his life, and it brought memories back to Pete of when the job had done the same to him. There had been a time when he'd been every bit the overly devoted cop that Thomas was becoming. Until his heart attack, he had been all the police department had ever asked for in a cop. When the department determined he was too big a risk to keep on the force, it had destroyed him inside. To be made an outcast after all he had done for the force soured him on the whole idea of being a cop. Being told he was no longer fit to be a police officer had been more than he could take; and when he thought about all the stress and pain the job had caused him over the years, he truly felt betrayed. After the way they had discarded him, he hadn't been able to look at being a cop in the same way.

The reality was that after losing his wife, Marlene, and after the disconnection from Thomas—who was always working—grew, he couldn't have withstood another loss. For all intents and purposes, Josh was all that Pete had left at this point. Pete figured if he couldn't stop his son, he would at least try to protect him; and that was when the discussion had turned to John Archibald. At roughly the same time Pete was asking questions about how to help Josh, he was approached by John with not only a solution but a job offer. It felt great to be wanted again and back doing something meaningful, even if it meant going over to the other side of the aisle. Cops who went to work for defense lawyers lost respect from their former brothers-in-arms, but he relocated to Atlanta anyway to work for criminal defense legend Donovan Howle. The job had given him a second chance to do something meaningful. As lead investigator for the firm, he used the skills he had learned over a lifetime of being a cop. He worked directly for Howle for the first few years; and as Howle transitioned to retirement, Pete began to work directly for John Archibald. Archibald was the rising star in the firm and heir apparent to Howle. As he worked with John, Pete learned about the connection with past client Kingston Johnson and the special services provided to Kingston and his businesses. Pete saw a way to connect with Josh and approached John about being of service in this particular part of the firm's business. In a weird way, he had been able to both connect with and protect one of his sons.

While he didn't approve of the drugs, he also knew that the money side of the equation would give him the opportunity to safeguard Josh. A deal was made: he would help John and in turn, John would help Josh's gambling business stay as legal as possible. One of the major ground rules Pete and John agreed on was that they would never handle the drugs or deal with death; and if either of those came up, Pete would be out of the equation for good. Pete acted as the main courier of information between John and the Johnson organization, a very limited role, but at the same time vital to keep distance between client and attorney as services were rendered. Pete also handled the runners' cash, which needed to be placed in the Atlanta area through some private contractors he had acquired over the years as connections.

"I would suggest staying inside and off the roads late in the afternoon if you can avoid all travel; we could see a few inches of ice and sleet," said the young lady on the LG hanging from Pete's condo wall. He thought to himself that it really was amazing what a little snow or ice did to people in the South. He remembered waking up to feet of snow each morning, and then he thought about why he had moved to begin with. Why Marlene and he had come to the South in the first place: to get away from the weather and start fresh. Then she had become sick and he had been left alone. Not that it would have mattered where they'd been when she got sick, but it was ironic that they had moved south after his heart attack to reduce his stress and workload. They had moved from Boston thinking their life was starting over; and in reality, her life was a few years from ending. Cancer really was a motherfucker, and Pete had no idea why it had selected her while not taking him years ago.

Pete left his condo and went to the gym to begin his daily routine. He looked at his phone to see a text from Josh from the night before stating he would be heading Pete's way midweek and wanting to know if they could grab a bite to eat at that Italian place in Midtown. Their code for Josh bringing a suitcase full of money down. Pete thought about the Patriots losing and what that usually meant for Josh and his book. Kind of ironic that his favorite team losing actually meant big bucks for his son. He texted him back that his room was ready and he would see him soon. And with that, he was back running on the treadmill.

SPECIAL AGENT STEPHEN GOODING

"Hey, Steve, you ready for the meeting today after lunch?" asked Agent Jacob Roman, looking at his partner. The two men had been partnered together for about two years. "I think I heard some rumblings about a joint task force coming from upstairs."

Stephen Gooding glanced up from his computer screen and over at Roman with a quizzical look. "That would be interesting," Steve replied. "Who would be our dance partner? Homeland?"

"Heard it might involve one of our CIs," Roman said with a little excitement in his voice. He was the junior of the two and had only been with the bureau for about three years. He was still considered fresh out of Quantico and was a transplant to the Atlanta metro area from Ohio.

Agent Gooding had been with the bureau for almost fifteen years and took the lead in the pairing. Gooding had been as an accountant prior to joining the FBI, and he specialized in financial crimes including money laundering, tax evasion, and fraud.

"Any idea who they have in mind? I don't really see any of our informants fitting in with Homeland Security," Gooding said as he went back to his computer and the report he's been reviewing, which was on some mundane check-kiting scheme.

"It seems like if it isn't terrorism these days, it really doesn't matter," Gooding said, half to himself and half to his partner. Deep down, they both knew it to be true. Ever since the Boston Marathon bombing; the shooters in California; and the Emanuel Nine in Charleston, just four hours from Atlanta, the bureau was laser-focused on preventing any homegrown terrorists from appearing in their own backyards. Their daily focus was on pressuring informants, checking online activity, and constantly looking for these types of individual radicals; it left little time for anything else.

"How many informants are we responsible for right now?" Gooding asked, already knowing the answer. He asked more to test his junior officer than anything.

"Currently we have fifty-three total CIs in our territory, with about twenty being actively worked into ongoing investigations," answered Roman with minimal effort. "I already looked it up this morning when I heard we might get tabbed for the task force."

"Any of those fit the bill for terrorism sources?" Steve questioned.

"I can only think of about a half dozen that may have some link, but I checked our older CIs and came across a few possible candidates," said the junior agent.

"Good. I already did the same this morning, and I think we should update that list I just sent you," Agent Gooding said with a smile, having already heard the news two days ago from a source upstairs.

Agent Jacob Roman smiled when he realized his mentor was once again ahead of him. "Let me guess. Agent Thompson?" he said as he opened the email attachment.

"Good old Agent Thompson; it helps to play racquetball with the SAC's admin," Gooding said while looking at the same attachment. "Pull up the files on the CIs with ties to drugs and money; those may be worthwhile to study up on in case we get tabbed. Maybe there's some financial link we can bring to the table. Let's make sure we have solid contact points on the older ones that haven't been under regular watch; we may be contacting these guys and girls real soon," he said to Roman. "Let's be prepared. We may be knocking on some old doors for intel. My guess is it's not somebody we've been on top of because nobody in regular rotation is currently in play with any homegrowns."

And with that, Roman began to pull the files listed in the attachment in preparation of a call from upstairs. "I'll cross-reference these with the nonlocal watch lists and make sure we don't have any hits." The wheels of justice were moving forward at their own pace, but moving forward nonetheless. Names once forgotten were now back in play without any realization that the eyes of the FBI were watching and waiting.

Agent Gooding looked at his email and saw a request for him and his partner to meet with their special agent in charge before they left for the day.

KINGSTON

"Call," said Kingston, looking at his portly opponent from across the table. A middle-aged white man looked back at him from behind a pair of black-rimmed glasses.

"Pair of kings," said Thomas Streeter, flipping over his cards. Streeter had black hair and tattoos on his left arm including a tribal band around his wrist. He'd been in the federal system for seven years, doing a ten-year stretch for bank robbery. His last year would be served in PSD after his transfer for good behavior. Streeter was from out West and looked every bit of his forty-five years of age.

"Three eights," replied King as he raked the pot of cigarettes toward himself.

The group was sitting on stools that were mounted into the floor, at a metallic table in the common area. The table could seat six, but currently only four players were present. The room was divided into two parts, with tables in the front of the room near the entrance and rows of chairs located in the back.

"Thought you were playing the queen on the flop, King," said Thomas as he pitched his cards into the pile and sat up, stretching his arms. "That would have been a backbreaker in Vegas with real money. Goddamn, I can't wait to be back in a real casino."

"Thomas, that's why you always lose—you forget this is like Vegas," said Don, who had folded after the initial draw. He began to shuffle the cards for the next hand.

"Good point, Don. I guess I can't get into it considering I don't even smoke. My currency just doesn't compare to a stake of chips at the Bellagio," replied Thomas. He began turning from side to side, stretching out his back.

"I can agree with that," said the final member of the group, Roger Patterson, a disgraced former congressman from Minnesota who had been busted with cocaine and eventually found guilty of campaign finance fraud.

The other group members fit the description of white-collar criminals. None had any idea about the nature of the business Kingston was currently engaged in; to them, he was just an inmate, same as them.

As Don shuffled the red Bicycle playing cards, a man approached the table.

"Hey, Don," said the slender man as he entered the room. He looked timidly at the rest of the table, giving away the obvious discomfort he faced when meeting new faces. He had a slight beard and wore a bright-orange suit—a sign that he was new to the facility. The orange stood out like a flashing warning sign against the sea of brown that the rest of the inmates wore and the rec room's pale-green walls.

Only one guard was present, and he was half-watching TV at the other end of the room with the rest of the inmates. A sign of the nature of the facility: that one guard among twenty-five inmates stood no real danger. The medium-security facility mostly housed nonviolent offenders or inmates at the end of their sentences who were close to release and could be trusted not to leave. The annex had no walls; and most inmates worked in the community during the day, returning at night. The inmates had free time until 8:00 p.m.; then they would all be counted and the facility would be locked down for the night, which just meant that the front doors would be locked.

"Hey, Calvin, glad you could join us," Don said as he slid over to the next stool, making room for the new player at the table.

Each player had variously sized stacks of single cigarettes in front of them. King and Thomas were currently leading and had been trading Camels and Marlboros back and forth for the last half hour. Neither man smoked, making the choice of currency even more ironic.

"Guys, Calvin Simmons; he just transferred in," Don said has he distributed the first of two cards to each player. "Calvin, you can get in next go-around. Have a seat."

The inmate took a seat and looked at the rest of the members of the card-playing group.

"What you in for, Calvin?" asked Thomas as he peeked at his cards, making sure not to let anyone else at the table catch a glance.

"Bank fraud. I worked at a bank in Philadelphia, and some money went missing," Calvin said as he pulled some packs of cigarettes out and set them in front of him. He looked to be in his mid-forties, with brown hair that was just beginning to gray—but it was hardly noticeable. His face was clean-shaven, and he had the look of a banker, with rather soft features. Mr. Simmons did not look like he had worked a hard day in his life.

"Ha-ha!" cackled Thomas. "That's what I did too, but I'm innocent." A smile lit on his face as he looked over at King and Roger, searching for any indication of what they may have in their hands.

Roger smiled. "Only that money went missing at the end of a gun, Thomas."

"Allegedly," quipped Thomas.

"No offense, but you're in here now, so I think the 'allegedly' part is out the door," said King as he looked at Thomas and pushed his two-cigarette ante into the pile—a signal of a call, as Thomas was the big blind, already having his two smokes in front of him. Roger also pushed in two cigarettes, calling the other two players and leaving it to Don, the small blind.

"Fold," said Don, putting his cards down. "Calvin, don't let old Thomas scare you; we're all gentle folks in this part of the cage. None of us in here are what would be considered major criminals. I'm in for fraud, King there is in for running pot, Thomas is the closest to the end of his term for bank robbery, and Roger is in for accepting bribes . . . and doing coke with a bunch of hookers on camera. Apparently they frown upon that action, since he was a sitting congressman from Minnesota."

"Apparently," said Roger with a slight laugh. "But they didn't charge me with the hookers."

"King, tell me something," said Thomas as he threw four cigarettes into the middle of the table, a sign to increase the bet. "How are you in jail for something that's now legal in half the country? I mean, I'm from Arizona; and they have a vote this year to legalize the shit for anyone, not just sick people. That shit ain't right. They'll actually be able to grow plants at home for personal use. I know I'll be growing some myself once I get out."

"I ask my attorney that same question every time I see him," King replied, not taking his focus off the other players at the table.

"I got a medical card when I was in California a few years back; all I had to do was say I got bad headaches and they gave me one," Calvin added to the conversation. He was pulling single cigarettes out of the two packs he had brought to the game.

"Federal government hard at work," said Roger. "You know, we have incarcerated over eight million people for marijuana-related arrests since the year 2000. Damn waste of money if I ever saw one. Instead of making money, the government's spending it. I remember a report saying we lose about $3 billion in taxes, which we could be making if we taxed pot." The former politician joined in the pot with King and Thomas. "Hell, Colorado is making money hand over fist, but they can't find any banks to let them deposit it."

With that, Don flipped over three cards, showing the ace of hearts, a three of clubs, and a jack of clubs. "Isn't something like 60 percent of Americans fine with legalizing it?" he asked as he returned the deck to the table.

"Pot is legal in like twenty-something states now; the drug war against it is the biggest joke. Just like back when all the bootleggers got rich off prohibition. You're talking about something that most people want," said Roger, and he looked over the flop cards.

"Old JFK's daddy made his bones running booze," said Kingston as he waited for Thomas to bet. Thomas threw in half a pack of Camels.

"I think the guy with the plan back then was George Remus; he figured out how to get medical alcohol, and then it would get 'misplaced,'" said Roger as he peeked at his hold cards.

"Hell, Capone was held next door until he died, I think," added Thomas, taking off his glasses and wiping the lenses. "You must've picked the wrong state to get caught in, King."

"Alabama. One of the worst states for pot out there," King replied as he called Thomas, who glanced at him quickly as he made the call, trying to get a read on him. King pushed a half a pack into the middle of the chrome table; the light beat down on them.

"Too much for me," Roger said as he folded. "I saw online that Massachusetts is actually voting to decriminalize it altogether. Fucking shame for you to be in here for something that'll be legal in another part of the country, King."

Don flipped a burn card, then drew a jack of hearts from the deck and placed the card beside the other three on the table.

Thomas scratched his face and looked at King, who gave no signal one way or another as to whether the card had helped or hurt him. Thomas pushed a full pack of cigarettes to the middle of the table. "King, you know I know white guys that got less time than you for the same shit," said Thomas, trying to draw King's attention away from the cards. Kingston showed no reaction and simply slid a pack to the middle of the table.

"That's fucked up," said Calvin.

"Sure is," added Don as he flipped the river card, showing a four of clubs.

Thomas let out a little whistle. "I'm all in."

Without hesitation, King looked up and said, "You know something, Thomas, ain't much about prison fair to the black man. Call."

"Gotcha, King!" exclaimed Thomas as he stood and flipped over two aces, completing a full house. "Full house, aces over jacks!"

King just looked up at Thomas. "Ain't much fair to nobody in prison, Tom," he said as he flipped over pocket jacks.

A look of confusion passed over Thomas's face as he realized his unbeatable hand had just been beat by four of a kind. "Son of a bitch!"

King quietly pulled the pile of cigarettes to his side of the table, having been underestimated once again. Thomas walked away from the table, not saying anything else.

"Calvin, you're in this hand. Thanks for playing, Tom!" Don called as he glanced at King, who was silently stacking his winnings. The group let out a collective chuckle as Thomas walked away.

"Fuck you guys!" said Thomas as he left, heading back to his bunk. "Good hand, King!"

Don shuffled the cards, and the group went back to the game at hand.

ROSCOE

"**D**evon, if one your boys is out there selling, you best tell me right now! Can't fucking believe someone dumb enough to cross that line," screamed Roscoe at his youngest son. The two were alone in a parked Ford Expedition. Roscoe had picked up Devon so they could talk over the claim Julius had made about the crew.

"Pops, I ain't seen nobody doing nothing! I'm telling ya, Julius be trippin'!" Devon replied.

"Man, all I know is if it gets back to King, we all got problems. You know that, son," Roscoe said in a slightly less distressed but serious tone. "Straight up, he will wipe the whole crew if he thinks they're dealing at all, let alone in the ATL. This is a serious problem. We got to keep it under wraps and figure it out on our own if we can," said a somber Roscoe.

Devon looked out the window at the gray clouds and saw a plane descending from above. They had driven west of College Park, out Highway 29 toward Union City so they were close to the airport. Hartsfield–Jackson International was one of the busiest airports in the world and was a major hub for Delta Air Lines.

"You know, it's probably J. J. filing his pops's head with this bullshit," Devon said. "I think we should just be straight up with the crew and say Julius heard some shit on the street and if it is goin' on, it needs to stop."

Roscoe thought for a second, then replied, "I wish it were that simple. . . . If Julius has something, it'll blow back on everyone in this crew not named Johnson. No, we better off either handling it ourselves or staying strong and saying Julius full of shit. The only problem is if it true and he's got something . . . but what I don't get is, he won't say who it is. That makes me think he's not positive. If he were, he'd just put a bullet in the fool's skull and we wouldn't see them no mo."

Roscoe and Devon sat silently for a few minutes. Then Devon suddenly came to life. "You know what we could do is use some of the GPS trackers we use for the trucks and put them on the cars and see where everyone's going after work." He looked at his father.

"That's actually not a bad idea; we can see who's running around at night," Roscoe said, half-smiling. "Let's go ahead, but you got to be careful. I'll watch it and tell Julius we're checking up on everybody so he knows we serious about it."

"No problem. I should be able to put one on everybody by end of to-morrow," Devon said, feeling a little better about the tight spot they were in. He thought if nothing else, at least they were trying to find out who was putting it out there. "Shit, while we at it, put one on Julius and J. J.," he said, hoping his dad would agree.

"Hell no, won't do you no good to know where that fucker go at night," Roscoe replied. "Still can't believe he comin' down to start this shit with no proof of nothing. It's like he wants to cause trouble." Roscoe thought that was just like Julius, to cause problems with only one solution in mind. The more he thought about it, the more he was sure someone was going to end up gone. He just hoped it wasn't Devon because then he would have to kill Julius before he had a chance to hurt his boy.

Then Devon said the exact words his father was thinking: "Damn, Dad. Times like this, I wish Marlow was here. Can't even trust your own family."

Roscoe knew it was true. He had seen what could happen when Julius went on the warpath. He thought to himself about Jonathan Wilcox and Langston Hughes, the two young men who had faced the consequences after Kingston got arrested in Alabama. He had still never forgiven himself for the way it all had gone down, with those two paying the price. How had Julius known those two had had something to do with Kingston's bust? The thought never escaped his mind, nor did the confession, which was confirmed by J. J. and Harold. After being worked on with a hammer and drill for a day and a half, I think anyone would confess to just about anything, Roscoe thought. He thought these thoughts, but he didn't dare say anything to Devon.

He would need to keep Devon close and make sure he had everything covered because if it did go down again, he knew there would be no stopping Julius. The second King was told that someone was dealing drugs on the side and jeopardizing his empire, the purge would begin—and it would be swift and brutal. Roscoe had seen it before, and he didn't want any part of it. These boys working for him now had no idea what it would be like, and none of them understood just what they had signed up for and what had come before them.

Roscoe broke out in a sweat as he thought about what Julius would do to these boys if one of them was dealing around town, and then he started the car and headed back to East Point. He wished Marlow was with them too. Could never have too much crazy on your side in a situation like the one he might be facing.

MARLOW JOHNSON

Marlow had been in Phoenix acting as the point man for the Johnsons' growth into cocaine for three years now, since about a year before Kingston went inside. He had made his own little niche with the people out West, and so far there had been no issues with the Sinaloa Cartel.

For the most part, he had managed to stay below the radar with a few exceptions, usually at the hands of the Manuel-Rios brothers. Tonight was turning into one of those exceptions. The night had started out easy enough with some dinner and drinks. First they'd started off at Most Wanted Taco Shop and headed over to Maya Day and Nightclub. The brothers, Manny and Javier, of course came fully loaded with weed and coke.

Marlow knew how to party, but he also knew he could only take it so far with these guys. They were cartel members and worked directly under Ceasar Rojas, who was the top dog in Phoenix and Scottsdale. They ran their drugs in through tunnels near Nogales or Juárez, across from El Paso. Marlow never felt safe having to deal with them around Juárez; that place was a goddamned war zone, and everything you'd heard about it was true. Headless bodies hung from the overpasses, mass graves were plentiful, and people disappeared daily.

Tonight was going bad real quick. After hitting Maya and heading to Valley Bar, Manny had decided he wanted to see some pussy, so they headed over to The Great Alaskan Bush Company to see some strippers he knew. In the VIP room, it started with cocaine and about a half-dozen strippers, and at some point Javy started freebasing some blow. From there it went downhill pretty quickly, with a 5-foot-7-inch, 160-pound Mexican feeling like he could take on Mike Tyson in his prime. For his part, Marlow had stuck to booze and weed with Manny. But once the two brothers got going, they were fucking wild men.

Outside the VIP, Javy ended up smacking some guy with a pool stick over a game of pool. Before long, Javy was in a fight with four of this guy's buddies, who all happened to be six-foot or taller, with easily fifty to seventy pounds each on Javy. Marlow was able to break it up with Manny's help, but Manny had a look in his eye that Marlow knew meant trouble. They left the club, but were setting up to wait on the guys outside in Manny's black 2015 Escalade, which had tinted windows.

"Goddamned putas, motherfuckers!" Javy screamed as blood poured out of a cut over his left eye. His lip and jaw were already swollen, and there were cuts on his neck and hands. His left hand was swollen and looked to have at least two broken bones in the lower part; the swelling took the color to more purple than blue as the blood flowed to the hand.

"I'm gonna kill that motherfucker, Manny! Take me back over there!" Javy was going for a gun stashed under the third-row seat.

"Shut the fuck up! You aren't doing shit right here, esé!" yelled Manny.

Marlow sat in the passenger seat wondering just how far this was about to go. Either way, he knew he had to be all in with these two no matter what; he got a knife from the backpack he carried with him. His gun was in his car, back at the Valley Bar.

"Yo, Javy, close it down, son. We got this—them boys ain't walking from this! Calm it on down. We gotta be smart. This ain't Juárez, brother!" Marlow said.

Manny looked at him and gave a nod, accepting Marlow as part of the solution. "Javy! Marlow's right; we ain't letting him pass, my brother. We going to fuck them up, but we got to do it right. No cops. You know we're too far in here to go wild on them in the bar. We're going to set up and follow them to a better spot." Manny had a cold look in eyes that told Marlow this was going to go down and go down hard. Javy was in the back, taking bumps from a shooter and adding more fuel to an already hot tank. Manny lit a cigarette and rolled down the window.

It was around 3:00 a.m., and the crowd would be thinning out in the next hour as the bar closed at 4:00 a.m. Alaskan Bush looked like an old Western bar from the outside and had a U-shaped parking lot in front. The strip club was off of W. Osborn Road and had a towing company with a big privacy fence across the street. Manny had taken off north up West Osborn Road and had turned around, parked in the front of the tow-truck entrance, which at this time of night only had some lights on the signage; otherwise, the all-black SUV was hidden by the edge of the fence, but still had a clear vantage point to the front of the club and its parking lot.

Javy sat back and seemed to calm down some as he took a hit of weed, although knowing Javy, he had probably laced it with some blow. Marlow and Manny took inventory of the situation, and both became noticeably quiet and focused. Neither partook in the action Javy was laying down in the backseat.

"Javy, put the gun back up. Get me the ice picks from the cargo slot. These are civilians; we aren't going to kill them, but we are going to fuck them up." All the tension and anger had left his voice. The calmness of a predator as he watched the front door, waiting.

Marlow thought to himself, Who the fuck rides around with ice picks in the back of his SUV? But then, as stupid as it sounded, he thought, Fucking Mexican cartel members do, apparently.

"Give me the gloves and the ski masks, too."

"Shit, you come prepared, don't you," Marlow said, looking at Manny, who said nothing but just watched the doors. The silence was the only thing in the car, with the exception of the occasional snort made by Javy in the backseat.

"Always helps to be prepared, amigo," Manny said after a few minutes. His stare never broke from the parking lot. His gaze held a certain amount of fierceness, waiting for their prey. Manny most certainly was not going to let the insult to his brother or their family pass.

"These fools are probably going to break out on Wickenburg when they roll, Manny," Marlow said as he lit a cigarette and rolled down his window. "You get a good look at 'em?"

"Yep, main one that got Javy is wearing a blue-and-white striped shirt with jeans. The other three are wearing dark polos, two in blue and one in green. We should be able to pick them up; look for the striped shirt," Manny answered.

"Fuck, my hand's hurting, Manny," Javy said in a calmer tone, but I could hear the pain in his voice.

"You should have thought about that, my brother, before you hit it on a guy twice your size. Your dumb ass needs to slow it down—getting all geeked up and starting a fight in there. Marlow's right: this ain't fucking Juárez. You can't do whatever the fuck you want to do this far north," Manny said with his eyes still trained on the club's front door. "If you get jacked up—" He stopped as the group of four came out of Alaskan Bush. All at once, Manny cut on the car, without hitting the headlights, and rolled up his window. "There they are . . . putas."

Marlow felt his blood go cold as the adrenaline started to kick in; he knew the next minutes of his life would be intense, and his heart rate quickened with anticipation. He readied his knife, pulled a red bandana from his pack, and tied it around his neck, low so he could pull it up. As usual, he was already wearing mostly black. He took off his chain and watch and put them in the pack; he also took out his wallet, placing it in the pack, and put $300 in cash in his right sock.

"They're getting in that white Tahoe. Looks like they're heading north," Marlow said.

Manny was already moving slowly out of the parking lot, waiting until the Tahoe was out of the club's lot and on Phoenix-Wickenburg Highway heading north. Wickenburg was a main six-lane highway that ran from central Phoenix directly to Glendale. With any luck, these guys would be stopping far before Glendale.

The Tahoe moved down the highway, and the Escalade's shadow fell in behind, with a silver Honda Accord between them. Manny could tell by their driving that the driver was fucked up; they swerved slightly getting on the highway. Even though they were outnumbered, now they had the element of surprise on their side, because the guys in the Tahoe weren't thinking about Marlow and the brothers as they headed home in their drunken state—just another night on the town for four twentysome-thing white guys in Phoenix.

"Looks like they're getting off at N. Thirty-Third Avenue," Marlow said. Manny slowed and prepared to get off as well. "There are a bunch of apartment complexes back there off W. Indian School Road; I bet they're heading to one of those."

"Javy, you good back there?" Manny asked his brother.

"Yeah, man, don't know how much I can fight; but I'm good. I can fight," replied Javy.

"Not this time, Javy. I'm going to park us, and you're going to get up here and drive," Manny said, looking back at his little brother. "We got to be in and out, and I've only got the one mask."

"Fuck, Manny, I don't need you to fight my fight!" Javy started to raise his voice.

The Tahoe took a left on W. Indian School Road and veered off onto N. Thirty-Fifth Avenue. Manny came in behind them but was far enough back that they were none the wiser with regards to their tail.

"Fuck that, Javy, I got this. We can't kill these fuckers—just mess them up some. I can't have you kill one of these putas and make this worse. Me and Marlow got this. We going to hit 'em quick and spin out. Lay off that shit for a minute so you can get us out of here."

"All right, Manny, I get it," Javy said.

Marlow watched the Tahoe turn right and continue on, past a small strip center and into Tamarak Gardens. "I know this place; the parking lot wraps all the way around. Watch them go in, and we can turn left and circle back around."

Manny watched the Tahoe go to the front of the center past the first road. He turned left and cut his lights, taking the SUV behind two rows of rectangular apartment buildings.

"Manny, we can cut through the middle right there and catch these fuckers nappin'," Marlow said as he pulled the bandana up over his face. He looked over to see Manny slide a ski mask over his head, and suddenly a hammer appeared from below his seat to accompany the ice pick he had sitting out. He handed the second pick to Marlow.

"I got the striped shirt. I'll hit one hard; you slice the other two," Manny said as matter-of-factly as if he were ordering a pizza—almost in a dull tone that was barely above a whisper. He parked the truck and killed the interior lights to match the darkness of the night at roughly three thirty in the morning. There were lights but no cameras that could be seen from this vantage point.

"Let's go all the way," Manny said as he opened his door and slid out.

Marlow said nothing but crept out, falling in right behind him. They left Javy in the vehicle and headed through the middle of two rectangular buildings. Manny stopped and held up his hand as they passed a pool on their right. It was dimly lit in the courtyard, with most of the light splashing the pool.

The sounds of men talking in excited tones could be heard. Manny spotted them in a small parking lot that was inset at the end of the parking lot. As Manny and Marlow rounded the building, the men were heading away from them, still not aware that they were prey with two predators coming up from behind. In a fluid motion, Manny ran up to the guy in the green polo shirt and nailed him with the hammer from behind. Green Shirt immediately fell face down in the grass. At the same time, Marlow arrived at the front of the Tahoe, stuck the ice pick in the leg of one the men in blue, and swept him backward on the hood of the car beside the Tahoe. He crumbled and screamed in pain as Marlow hit him like a freight train after building up speed for thirty yards.

The other two men looked back like deer frozen in headlights. Manny was still moving forward; he hit the second guy in a blue shirt directly in the face with the hammer. Striped Shirt tripped as he backpedaled and went down, probably due to a combination of fear and alcohol. Manny slowed down and pulled the ice pick from his belt. In a deep voice, he yelled, " Give me your fucking wallet!"

Striped Shirt said, "What the—?"

In an instant, Manny struck him in the lower left side of his body with the pick, which was in his left hand, and then nailed him with the hammer, held by his right. With that, all four were down. Marlow beat the first Blue Shirt down off the hood and began kicking him until he was silent except for the groans of defeat.

Manny looked over at Marlow. "Get everything they got!" And the beating became a robbery, but Marlow realized what Manny was doing: he was making this look like something besides retaliation from the bar fight. They snatched their wallets and got two nice watches, one a TAG Heuer.

The pair cut back through the building in front of them and broke left. Almost on cue, the Escalade's lights cut on and the SUV shot forward, heading right. Manny and Marlow jumped in the backseats and Javy drove them away from the four men. They pulled out onto Thirty-Fifth and headed toward Grand Canyon University. The entire incident was over with in under two minutes from start to finish.

"Javy, slow it down. Nobody saw us. Don't draw any attention, and stay off the main highway—they got cameras." Manny looked over at Marlow. "No goddamned cameras in Juárez, amigo, at least none that work," he said with a laugh.

"Hey, Marlow, I forgot to tell you earlier, Ceasar wants a meet," Manny said. "El Chapo going back inside means a reshuffle of some people. Feds are putting major heat on Juárez. Probably going to switch to Nogales for runs for a while."

"Word, no problema, amigo," Marlow said, thinking to himself, This sure is a fucked-up time to bring up a meeting with the head cartel guy in the área. Maybe bring that up before we plant an ice pick in someone's leg outside an apartment building at four on a Thursday morning. But this was the cartel he was dealing with, and it wasn't like they had email or memos to hand out.

"Just let me know when and where." Deep down, Marlow knew a meeting face-to-face with Rojas meant something was changing. Whether it was their deal or something with El Chapo going down, he would have to be ready. A meeting with Ceasar Rojas was not a meeting without the potential for peril. A meeting that would most likely be him, by himself, in a country where bodies in barrels of acid were a daily occurrence. Meeting Rojas meant going to Mexico, into the belly of the beast that was the Sinaloa Cartel, and doing so after their leader, El Chapo, had just been captured again.

AGENT GOODING

Agent Gooding pulled into the FBI garage off Parkway at 6:30 a.m., early for the joint task force meeting, which was to begin promptly at 8:00 a.m. He parked and saw Agent Roman getting out of his car, which was in an adjacent spot.

"Morning," said Agent Roman, holding his metal YETI cup full of coffee and shutting the door of his Chevy Malibu. "What should I be expecting this morning?"

Gooding shut the door of his Tahoe and slung his briefcase strap over his shoulder. "Well, the first thing they'll talk about is the history of the Davis Whiteside Strike Force. In 2005, Whiteside—an ICE agent—was killed in the line trying to apprehend a fugitive that turned out to be a gang member. The perp had escaped custody at a traffic stop by killing two officers. Whiteside was able to get a shot into him, but died himself in the process." The two walked to the elevator and Roman slid in his keycard to activate the lift. "So in March of 2007," Gooding continued, "they named the first task force of this type the Davis Whiteside Organized Crime Drug Enforcement Task Force, or OCDETF. Since then, it has become known as the Whiteside Strike Force. It works with local

Atlanta police departments through the HIDTA program, or the High Density Drug Traffickers program. They focus on high-level traffic in the Atlanta area." The elevator opened, and they both got in.

"Most likely, the meeting today will be a meet and greet, headed by whichever special assistant US attorney is leading this particular dance. They'll name a target, and we'll go to work. My guess is they're looking at a high-level MS-13 or some tie to a biker gang. Both of those have been pretty active in the North Georgia district. They've had some real high-profile busts here in the last year. If they're calling us in, that means someone is moving money, or one of the CIs assigned to us is involved somehow."

Both agents exited the elevator and walked down the hallway. The floors were still shining from the cleaning crew that had come in the night to prepare the flooring for the daily wear and tear of hundreds of feet and rubber-soled shoes walking over them. The office was still coming to life, with a few other individuals roaming the hallways.

"None of our CIs have any ties to biker gangs," said Agent Roman. "I don't really see any with ties to MS-13 either. Looks to me like we have a bunch of has-been dealers and some lower-level guys; nobody jumps out to me as potential cartel tie-in material."

"You never know how criminals intersect; there really is no guessing," replied Gooding. "The one interesting tidbit I got from Thompson upstairs was that an ICE agent out of Houston was flying in for the meeting, along with two DEA agents. The DEA agents being here would be standard, but apparently all three of them are from Texas. The two DEA agents are based out of El Paso."

"So what does that mean to us?" asked the junior agent, cutting on the light as he unlocked the door to their shared private office.

"Well, it could mean a lot of things; but if I had to guess, I'd say it means we're dealing with drugs from south of the border via El Paso. Which means MS-13," said Agent Gooding.

"Man, those guys are like weeds: You pull one group down, and another one pops right back up," said Roman as he set his jacket and briefcase in the chair next to his desk.

"Yep, but for the most part, they aren't that hard to track down . . . but they're also usually armed to the teeth. That's where the HIDTA teams come in. Local law enforcement typically does the takedowns and gets a part of whatever we take down, cash-wise. Last one I was involved in was back in the spring of 2014, before you got here. There was a group moving drugs up in compartments in passenger buses. I think we netted around $700,000 in cash, 30 kilos, a bunch of meth, and maybe 15 to 20 arrests, all with major time serviced. Think of it as a pretty good gold star on your resume."

"Sounds like it should be entertaining," said Roman as he began opening his emails and took a sip of coffee.

Just then, a group of footsteps was heard approaching from down the hall and the voice of Assistant SAC Thompson could be heard giving a layout of the office. The group paused outside Gooding's and Roman's office, and there was a knock on the door.

"Hey, guys, good to see you in so early today," Agent Thompson said as he pushed open the door.

Both men turned and stood to meet Thompson's guests.

"Meet DEA Agents Paul Dietmer and Harley Kirkpatrick; they got in late last night from El Paso, and I picked them up on the way in this morning. They wanted to get an early start as well," said Thompson as the group all shook hands.

Dietmer sported a several-week-old beard and looked as thought he hadn't been to bed in about a month. He wore a black parka and had his shield around his neck and a pair of Ray-Bans on his head. He looked to be in his mid-forties, with a very wiry frame and the first signs of gray in his hair. Fitzpatrick was about ten years younger and appeared to be the junior. She wore a blue coat with jeans and had her red hair pulled back in a ponytail.

"Good to see some more early birds," said Fitzpatrick. "Looking forward to working with you guys on this one; should be an interesting ride."

Roman had immediately taken account of Fitzpatrick and noticed no ring on her finger—no jewelry of any type, to be more specific. He seemed to stand just a little taller than normal.

"Any details you guys want to share prior to the meeting this morning?" asked Gooding. "Maybe we can get the old interagency-sharing part of the strike force in gear early."

Thompson glanced at Gooding, but before he could say anything, Agent Dietmer spoke up. "Honestly, we're in a bit of spot on this one; and sharing might not be a bad idea. I'm sure you guys are aware that the Mexicans got El Chapo."

"Hopefully in a tunnel-proof cell," said Agent Roman before sipping his coffee.

"Who knows, with the Mexicans down there. Supposedly they're rotating him every day and watching him round-the-clock with guards," said Agent Fitzpatrick. Her ponytail whipped as she turned her head while speaking to the group of men.

"It's a world war down there right now; the Feds rounded up or killed dozens of Sinaloa's top guys, so they're all fighting over the control of the plazas."

The Sinaloa Cartel had five major plazas or entrance points it used to get drugs into the US: Mexicali, San Luis Río Colorado, Sonoyta, Nogales, and Agua Prieta. The cartel also had an ongoing relationship with the Tijuana Cartel as some type of loose agreement. Basically, that meant they weren't currently at war with each other; and both focused on getting drugs into the US as quickly and efficiently as possible. The plazas acted as superhighways for the cartel to get their products into the hands of addicts and users across the border.

Dietmer shook his head. "It won't matter until they turn him over to us. He'll find someone to threaten or bribe. Either way, they have him for now; and we've been working with them on our side of the fence to try and sweep up his lieutenants. Actually making a little progress. But, you know, down there next to Juárez and Tijuana, it will only be days—if not hours—before a new round of faces appears."

"How does that tie into Atlanta?" asked Gooding, not one to mince words. He took a seat in his chair and looked up at the guests standing in his office.

"We got some intel that a group has been running kilos for them, but it's not MS-13; and apparently this group has been highly successful for about three years now. Only problem is, we don't have a name. All we know is they have a hub here in Atlanta. Two of our informants have . . . well, let's just say 'disappeared,' but in all likelihood, they're in a mass grave south of Juárez at this point. The concern is apparently that this group is large enough and sophisticated enough that they're taking down the product offshore, and the cartel doesn't have to move money back."

Gooding leaned back in his chair and thought for a second. "So we're talking way beyond some local MS-13 gangbangers," he said as he looked at Dietmer.

"Yep, it looks that way; and that means they'll be harder to catch, especially with our only leads most likely dead and buried," answered Dietmer. "By the way, where's the coffeemaker around the place?"

Gooding thought to himself that it was strange for the DEA to be this frank and honest right out of the gate, which concerned him because it most likely meant they had absolutely no idea who they were hunting. Maybe this task force would be interesting after all—more of a challenge than some local MS-13 thugs or Mexican Mafia goons.

"Well, guys, let me get you set up in the conference room and show you to that cup of coffee, Agent Dietmer," said Thompson; and with that, the impromptu meeting was over and the work could begin.

COOPER

"Oh, shit!" said Cooper as he watched the minivan skid into the back of the moving truck on I-95. A winter ice storm had left the roads with slush, and their trip back from New York had been painfully slow. Cooper was in a black Dodge Charger that was almost gray, it had so much ice and sludge on it.

He spoke into the mic, "You guys okay in there?"

"Yep, but this ain't going to be good. Who hit me?" said the return.

"You got a minivan that slid into you. You have to pull over; they have some damage," called out Coop. He picked up a burner cell phone and selected the preprogrammed number. The phone rang twice before it was picked up.

"What's the situation?" Banks asked from the other end of the phone.

"Car wreck. Van slid into the back of the package," Cooper replied as he began to pull behind the van. The truck pulled over and cut on its hazard lights. Luckily, they were well outside of Charlotte.

"Okay, call sign Mr. Green to the driver," Banks instructed Cooper.

"And if Mr. Green doesn't work?" Cooper replied.

"Then it's code red the truck," Banks said with a calm coolness.

"Roger. I'm on it." Cooper said, then picked up the radio and called into it, "Mr. Green is here, copy."

The voice in the truck said, "Copy, we got you, Mr. Green."

With that, Cooper opened his door and walked up to the minivan. Through the window he saw a female driver with two kids in the back. She was crying hysterically and rolled down her window after he tapped it.

"How you doing in there? Everyone okay?" Cooper asked. "You kids okay?"

The woman let out a sigh and wiped her tears. "Yes, I just scared the shit out of myself. We must have hit a patch of ice. Good god, that scared me."

Cooper looked at the kids and noticed they seemed oblivious to the entire incident, as both had on earphones and seemed glued to the monitor overhead, which was playing some Disney show he couldn't make out. He walked around front to assess the damage. By this time, a black man wearing a dark-blue jacket and a Braves cap had jumped out from the passenger's side of the moving truck. He zipped up his jacket as he came to the front of the minivan, then looked at the back of the truck to see no major damage done. The minivan had a crumpled hood and slightly broken windshield.

The black man approached Coop. "Mr. Green?"

"That's right," replied Cooper to his new acquaintance, a man he recognized from the past few years of these types of trips, but someone he'd never met face-to-face—until now. A man he knew to be Julius Johnson, Jr., but still a stranger to him.

"Well ain't this a bitch," J. J. said in a hushed tone.

"Yep. You stay over here, don't approach the minivan, and make sure to turn your back to us like you're inspecting the truck. I'll talk to her and see if we can resolve this with me following her to a service station," Cooper said as they both looked at the truck, facing away from the lady behind the busted-up minivan's steering wheel. Cooper looked over to make sure she hadn't picked up her cell phone.

"If the cops pull up?" J. J. asked.

"No choice but pull up the delivery paperwork and see if we can resolve it," Cooper answered. "If she wants to call them in, we have a window of about two minutes to code red this thing."

"You serious?" J. J. said as he pulled out a cigarette.

"Yep, direct from Ghost. I just talked to him. You guys will say the truck won't restart, and I'll tell her I'm running you to the next station to get help. I'll pull up, and we're gone. By the time they figure out what's going on, we'll be in South Carolina."

"Fucking expensive fender bender," said J. J.

"No shit, but no choice. We can't sit here with the package in there. We'll call a tow truck to come get it and deliver it to Charlotte. But you guys can't be found with the truck," explained Cooper.

"So here it goes." Cooper walked back over to the lady in the minivan as she was picking up her phone. He motioned to her, and she rolled the window back down. "Hey, doesn't look too bad. No damage to them at all."

She heaved a little bit. "That's good, but my husband is going to kill me. My insurance is going to go up, and I had the kids in the car. My god, we could've been killed." She was mostly babbling at this point.

"Well, I don't see any damage to them. Can you see if your minivan will crank?"

"Okay, let me check." The van's engine turned over without hesitation.

Cooper silently breathed a sigh of relief. "That's good news. Let me see if these guys are both okay," he said to her. "Maybe we can just pull off at the next exit and deal with this without calling the insurance companies—if that's fine with you?"

"Do you think they'd do that? I mean, shouldn't we call the police?" asked the soccer mom.

"The guys in that truck told me they had a delivery deadline in Charlotte, so maybe they need to get going. It doesn't look like there's any damage to them, it's just your van. I'm right behind you, and I can follow you to the next open service station and help you get checked out. I'm sure you don't want the kids sitting on the side of the interstate."

"If you think they'd do that, I would really appreciate it. I don't want to call my insurance company if I can help it," she said, kind of coming out of her shell.

By this time, one of the little boys had removed his headphones and began asking his mommy, "Why are we stopped?"

Cooper walked back over to J. J. Luckily it wasn't icing or snowing, but it was a bitter and windy day. "All right, I think she's on board. Let's go over there and sell that you guys need to be moving on," he said.

J. J. tossed his cigarette and dabbed it out with one of the light-brown Timberland boots he wore. "Word, if you say so." He turned and walked with Cooper to the van's driver's side window.

"Ma'am, I hope you folks are all right," J. J. said with a look of concern on his face. "If it's all the same to you, our truck is fine. My boss will be more upset if we're late dropping off our load. My driver's already looking at overtime for this week. I know what he'll say if we get stuck on the side of the road and then hit traffic outside of Charlotte."

"That's fine with me. Looks like this is my fault anyway," said the lady, now more composed. She had exited the driver's side, shut the door, and was looking at the front of the van. She had left her window rolled down, and the vehicle was running. She was a slightly heavyset woman in her early thirties, by Cooper's best judgment. She was wearing a heavy winter coat that didn't do her figure any favors.

"Mommy, I'm hungry!" cried kid number two from the backseat.

"I've got two little ones with me, and I'm just thankful it wasn't any worse than it is."

Cooper looked at her and said, "Yep, I have one of my own at home in Charlotte. I know the feeling. I don't mind following you to the next exit and making sure you get there. I'm not in any rush with this weather." He glanced at a map on his iPhone and said, "Looks like there's a good-sized service station about five miles down the road—two exits down, actually."

"Thank you, that'll work for me. Let me give you my number in case your boss changes his mind and thinks there's some damage."

J. J. waved his hand. "No, ma'am, that won't be necessary. He won't know nothing about this one. Thanks, though." With that, he began to walk back to the passenger side of the moving van.

Cooper took one more look at the minivan and walked its driver back to her door. "My name is Thomas, by the way."

"Thank you, Thomas. The Lord works in mysterious ways. My name is Marlene. I sure was lucky to have a good Samaritan right behind me today."

"Yes, he does work in mysterious ways, doesn't he?" Cooper remarked as he shut the door. "I'll be right behind you. The stop is five miles down the road."

He walked back to the Charger and cranked the engine, then watched as the moving van pulled back into traffic. The rubberneckers had begun to build slightly behind them.

"You guys keep going; I'll handle the minivan," Cooper said into the radio receiver on the passenger seat.

"Got it. You calling this in to the man above?" asked J. Jr. from the truck as it moved away from the two remaining parked cars.

"Yes, I'll call it in. Crisis averted. You guys get going. I'll shoot a text to your burner when I'm on the road. Toss that burner at your next stop, and be careful—you're flying solo now."

"Got it. Good work, Mr. Green," said J. J.

"You too," chirped Cooper. He set the radio receiver down and began to follow the minivan as she pulled into traffic. Cooper thought that had been as close a call as they'd had since this had started—as close as the time the van got pulled over in Virginia. He grabbed the burner phone and dialed Banks's number.

"I see we're moving again. Everything good?" asked Banks.

"We got lucky; but yes, we look good. No cops and minor damage to the minivan. I'm following her two exits down, and I'll stay there to make sure she doesn't call the cops. The package is back on the road and heading south. They'll throw burner number one after I text."

"You do the same with yours at the stop; this number is dead after I hang up. Good work there, Cooper. That was a close call," Banks replied, then hung up.

Cooper pulled the battery from the phone and pulled out the SIM card from the disposable $40 phone he had purchased in New York. He followed the minivan, thinking how close they had been to having to leave several million dollars on the side of the road. He knew deep down they didn't have many more empty chambers left in the game of Russian roulette they were playing. He just hoped they could make it to the end of the year and get out while they still could. But he knew it wouldn't be that easy.

PETE

Joshua and his crew had arrived the night before at the condo in Midtown. He had brought three of his friends from back home and roughly $312,000 in cash in 20-, 50-, and 100-dollar bills that would need to be cleaned.

John had had his group set up a few LLCs and front businesses for Joshua as a courtesy and for a fee of $100,000. The shell companies and actual businesses Joshua owned and would use to launder his bookmaking profits had to be completely separate from anything the Johnson organization would be involved in, and the amounts of money would be drastically different. Joshua would need to clean about $1,000,000 a year, with most of that coming all at once, so a schedule and plan was put in place that would be left up to the Murphys to implement on their own. The businesses and schedules had been set up, and they often rotated which banks and areas they used. The plan also called for them to close out certain bank accounts each year while maintaining other accounts and lines of credit at main banks, where they felt most comfortable. They had been operating this way for almost three years—about the same amount of time Peter had been working with John. Joshua's business had grown at the same time as he gained the ability to use the Internet to bring employees into his South Boston businesses as well as the other ventures, which were watched over by his father in Atlanta. All of these businesses provided him with income and, more importantly, paid his taxes on his behalf and that of his crew. Each business was operated independently and had employees who knew nothing about the behind-the-scenes work being done by the owners.

"Hey, Dad, you ready to go grab lunch?" asked Josh as he walked into the living room dressed in a North Face jacket and jeans. His jacket covered his tattoos and slight 175-pound frame. Joshua was the youngest of the Murphy clan and could be characterized as the most street smart. He had blond hair and was clean-shaven in preparation for his role for the next few days. All of his tattoos would be covered up by dress shirts or long sleeves, and his jeans would be turned in for slacks with smart sport coats or suits from Brooks Brothers. He would clean up nicely for the bank tellers and have a slightly flirtatious smile ready for each of them. Josh could be very charming, and it would be on display if anything came up as they made the rounds.

"Yo, Josh, we going to eat at the Irish pub on Buckhead?" asked Nelson, one of his friends from South Boston who had made the car ride down.

"Yeah, going to get you some of that shepherd's pie," replied Josh. He was checking his website on his phone as he sat on the edge of his dad's bed.

Pete was occupied with placing deposit slips on the various stacks of money laid out on the bed. The work they'd be doing later in the after-noon required a high level of planning and setup so the smurfing— the act of concealing money by making deposits under the $10,000 mark at various banks—would go off without a hitch. The riskiest part of money laundering was the placement: getting the money into a bank or financial system. During this time, they always ran the risk of a SAR or suspicious activity report being issued by a bank teller. To be safe, the crew would mix checks, cashier checks, and money orders in with their deposits. They also stayed well below the $10,000 limit and changed up the amounts to be odd numbers, never having something even. They often included coins, and Peter always took the time to write out client names and amounts on the deposit slips to further add to the illusion of these deposits coming from paying clients. With the primary function of the business being check cashing, they wouldn't draw as much attention since the employees and managers normally made deposits involving cash. Peter made sure to hire managers who had relationships with banks in other parts of the city. A slight spike in the accounts from larger-than-normal cash deposits wouldn't be noticed. Peter also made sure that the main branches of the businesses wouldn't make any deposits on the days leading up to and during the influx of cash from Josh and the Boston group.

To effectively clean the money, Josh and his crew would come down once they hit the $300,000 mark in collections. It averaged out to about three times during the fall and winter and one trip at the end of basketball season.

"Just finishing up these slips. Remind your guys to go ahead and dress the part, okay, Josh?" Peter said without looking up from his work. He was filling out deposit slips and placing them over the piles of money, then securing them in place with rubber bands and marking them in a journal, which only he and Josh would see and which would be destroyed in a few days.

"Franco, make sure you guys are putting on your suits!" Josh called out to the exterior of the room.

All of the guys he'd brought with him worked for him, and he had grown up with them, attending high school with all three of them. Mickey Franco worked for Josh at his bar in South Boston. Nelson McGregor had been the Murphys's next-door neighbor and had known both Peter and Josh for over twenty years. The final member of the crew, Jimmy Clement, had lived a few streets over and helped Josh primarily by running the websites for his bookmaking business.

"Jimmy, looks like we're getting a lot of action on the Panthers so far," said Josh as he reviewed the total on his website.

Gone were the days of bookies being in back rooms at smoke-filled bars and restaurants. Everything was electronic. Josh had his own websites called Luck of the Irish and Cover Irish. Both sites had originally been set up by Banks and had servers offshore, but Luck of the Irish was a public site, while Cover Irish held all the clients' bets. Each client would have to be vetted and given a username and password.

All accounts were given a line of credit, and collections were made whenever someone owed more than $1,000. Josh would up the limits for his bigger players, with most of them regularly betting over $10,000 almost every weekend. Like any business, it had grown over time, and Josh now had over a hundred large players in the New England area. The main weak spot was the amount of cash he had to handle in a given week. He had a safe in the bar in Southie, and he also had one that only he knew about in a safe house—or, more appropriately, a safe condo—near Chelsea. The condo was secured, and he only used it for storing money in one of the three safes it housed. None of his guys even knew about the condo; only his dad, who would stay there when he visited Boston, had access. It was also a rental in the name of another LLC. While it was more trouble to launder the money in Atlanta, it also let Josh and his crew stay way under the radar of Boston PD—and off the radar of his older brother, Thomas.

They could also leave any leftover money in the Atlanta condo's safe, and Peter could handle placing it later if necessary; but they usually stayed in town until all the money had been placed in various banks, and then they'd fly back to Boston after taking the time to drive down in a rental car. Usually the whole trip took them a few days; and it was all time they spent with Peter, who would take a few days off work whenever it was necessary. They would also usually try to fit in some type of sporting event; but this trip was in a dead spot on the calendar, with no interesting games in town.

The setup was simple: Luck of the Irish was a legitimate website selling packages of picks for its users. The site would list odds from all the top books in the country, had banner ads, and most notably sold pick packages to its users nationwide. This particular business had the nice feature of allowing Josh and his crew to use prepaid Visa debit cards and secured credit cards to make purchases online and to deposit these revenues into their bank back home. As far as the banks could tell, it was just a successful website that made electronic deposits for $50–100 consulting purchases. The part that was most exciting to Josh was they could influence their own books by accepting regional clients to the other part of their Web-based business. Their pick packages sales gave them the ability to research their users and determine who may fit the profile to be invited to their more lucrative website, Cover Irish, which is where people actually placed their bets.

"Looks like we may want to follow Bovada's line and move the Panthers up slightly," Josh called out to Jimmy, who was dressed in a sport coat and working on his laptop in the dining area.

"I'm on it. Moving the line on Cover up a half point," Jimmy replied. "Do you want the over-under moved up the same?"

"No, not yet. We aren't seeing the cash flow on that yet. Probably be next week before we see any real action there. Make sure you have all the new prop bets that Bovada just listed mocked over to Cover before the end of the day," Josh instructed.

Basically, what Josh and Jimmy did was copy most of the same bet profiles found on Bovada, a popular offshore website, for the simple reason that they themselves used Bovada to offset their books if they got too much action on certain teams. The previous weekend had been no exception. Josh always took heavy action on the Patriots since they were the favorite team of the majority of New England and his betting clients. As a general rule, Josh always bet on the Patriots; he had to because so many of his clients bet on the Patriots. He was forced to do the same to cover the losses because the Pats usually covered. Josh would wisely lay off some of the action offshore and with some other local guys he knew.

The AFC Championship Game had been different. Josh had laid off some of his bets; but he, as any bookie would tell you, also had to side with Vegas, so he actually went with Denver. It paid off big time for him to the tune of $100,000 just on that one game because the Pats had been slight favorites and had ended up losing. Josh won $75,000 from his clients, who had all bet on the Pats; and he won $25,000 off some local bookies. Another $10,000 sat offshore after he had maxed out several of their accounts. The one limit with offshore gambling was he couldn't bet more than $1,000 a game.

Bovada acted as a blueprint for Josh's website and many like his that were out there, keeping him in the loop on the offshore lines. Jimmy monitored all the Vegas house lines daily and could update their spreads with a few clicks of the computer mouse. Mainly they wanted to be at a point where bets were split evenly so they could just collect the VIC (the money bookies made when people lost). By being even, one side basically paid the other; and the middleman, Josh in this case, got paid by both sides.

"Man, Dad, sorry your boy Brady couldn't get it done last week. But I can't say I'm too sorry," Joshua said, turning his attention to the stacks of money laid out on the beds.

Peter thought it was ironic that a sports team he loved so much meant nothing to him now that he knew his son benefited whenever they lost. He had been secretly rooting for Denver because he knew Josh would have a lot on the line if the Patriots won the game.

"Looks that way. Two trips in two months—I'd say you must be up to $1.5 for the year. That's a big increase; we need to be careful," Peter said, turning to his son. "I think we need to look at moving a few of the bank accounts as long as we have the guys down here. How many days you guys got?"

"We're good until next week—no football this weekend, so we can stay until the middle of next week, before the Super Bowl, if we need to. Sorry about your Pats losing, but it sure was good for us at the book," Josh said, looking out the window at the skyline of Atlanta. "You talk to

Thomas at all the past few weeks?"

"Yep, talked to him briefly. I know he was on some big case," said Pete to his youngest son. The reality was, Josh spoke to Thomas far more than Pete ever had. Pete could see that Thomas was following in his footsteps being a cop, and he could also see the strain it was putting on Thomas. The elder Murphy had never forgotten how he'd been set aside by the department.

"They're looking for some serial rapist that got some girl in Chelsea. Turns out the girl was the daughter of some bigwig attorney or something. So the powers that be have them putting on the full press," said Josh.

"Sounds familiar, personalized service to the rich and powerful of Boston," replied Pete with a slight tone of disgust. "Just like when I was up there, we had to drop everything if the right someone's kid went missing or got popped for drugs. You had to be paid up with the right people."

"From what he told me, it sounded pretty fucking bad. She got raped and left for dead," Josh said as he turned from the window and walked back toward his father. He took off his jacket and pulled a suit from the closet—the same dark-blue suit he always wore when he made the rounds in Atlanta. He also took out a neatly pressed shirt and tie, taking off the dry cleaner's plastic wrap before taking the shirt from the hanger and putting it on.

"You want to go over the runs with the guys real quick before we go eat?" asked Josh as he slid on his jacket.

"Yep, may as well," Peter replied and walked through the bedroom door, into the condo's living area. The condo was a well-appointed rental in the Buckhead area, only a few miles from Peter's own place. The three-bedroom rental was done through an LLC and was only used when the guys made their trips down or when Josh came to visit Peter.

"Okay, guys, let's do a rundown real quick. Nelson, cut the TV off for me," Peter said as he entered the living room, drawing the group's attention. "Let's go over what each of you will be doing today." He looked at his journal. "We will each be going to five different banks this afternoon and meeting up at Club Buckhead for drinks and dinner later today."

In keeping with the profile, the group would be dressed as businessmen to draw less suspicion. They all had the condo as their address on credit cards, a membership at the Club of Buckhead, and other identifiers if anyone ever asked. All of them worked for the check-cashing business and were listed as W-2 employees with weekly paychecks. The check-cashing business had different accounts, and each type of account had its own name. Essentially, each account had its own LLC; and the LLCs did business with one another so the money could be moved in the form of loans between the various companies.

After dealing with the placement of the money, they always met back up at the Club of Buckhead, a private club, for drinks and dinner. Peter had figured out the spot in the club where he could view the parking lot and do counter surveillance in case any of the group had been followed from their drops. He had already reserved the necessary table for seven o'clock that evening. Peter frequented the club and knew most of the members, so he would notice anyone new coming in; and without being escorted by a member, the club was closed to the general public. A cop or someone following the boys would stick out like a sore thumb. Peter would arrive an hour before each of the crew members, who knew not to come until right at six thirty and to walk in on foot from their bank routes. When they used other banks in the area, they'd use Uber or the MARTA to get back to the financial district and head to the club. The building that housed the club locked down at 6:00 p.m., and you needed to either enter through the main lobby or have a security code to enter any other locations. Club members all used the main elevator to come up to the fourth floor, which housed the facility and dining room. From four floors up, Peter could see everything coming into the crescent-shaped parking lot. If he saw someone who looked out of place, he would send out a text to the crew members with a code and they would all go their separate ways, heading out of town and back to Boston. Each person had a different escape plan, and only Peter knew all of their escape routes. He would be able to go down a back exit that led directly to a MARTA entrance and slip into a train for his own departure, if it ever came to that.

One key advantage was that in an urban area like Atlanta, there were numerous methods of travel; and it would be very hard to set up on them in advance since none of them besides Peter resided in the area. Josh and his crew only spent two or three days at a time here, and all of them could disappear back to a home base hundreds of miles and several police jurisdictions away.

"Okay, Josh, you're handling the deposits for Check 'n' Go into accounts at Citizens, America Bank, State Bank of DeKalb, Sun National Bank, and McArthur Brothers Bank. All of your deposits are under $6,000, and I've mixed in the money orders and a few cashier's checks from Peachtree Check Cashing. Remember, you are the business owner and you're making deposits for your main branch. That covers about $40,000 of the cash. I'll take $10,000 and put it into the Peachtree Check Cashing to cover the cashier's checks and money orders.

"Jimmy, good to see you're already dressed," Pete said. "You're the manager for Peachtree Check Cashing today, and you'll be making deposits at Franklin Bank, State Bank of DeKalb, State Bank of Georgia, Southern Bank & Trust, and First Financial Bank. All your deposits are under $5,000 in cash, with some money orders mixed in."

"No problem," replied Jimmy, shutting the laptop down and putting on his sunglasses. "Ready to be double-O-seven for you," he said with a laugh, and the rest of the group joined him.

"Knock it off!" Peter scolded. "Remember, guys, this is the most dangerous part of getting this money into the system. The plan is only as good as the people executing it. You have to play your parts; you want the tellers to see you as charming, but you also want them to forget you the minute you leave the bank. We're well below the limits, but they still could report you if they think anything's funny about your transaction."

"No worries, Mr. Murphy, we know the game," said Jimmy.

Franco stood, walked to the fridge, and got a can of Diet Coke out.

He was the largest of the group at 6-foot-3 and 240 pounds. A former first baseman who had played minor league ball, he was by far the most reserved and quiet of the group.

"Where you got me heading today, Sergeant?" he asked, referring to Peter's former rank in the Boston PD as he popped open the silver can.

"You get to hit the MARTA today, Frankie. You're heading south to Decatur to make the Decatur Check Cashing deposits. Same amounts as Jimmy, but you'll be hitting the same banks as Josh. All your slips are filled out for you. You'll be making a total of $30,000 in deposits.

"Nelson, you're going with me to Marietta; we'll be making deposits totaling about $60,000," Pete said, looking over at Nelson, who was putting on a light-gray suit and still had wet hair from his shower.

The plan was for each of the five to get deposits in today, then take a day off; the third day, the rest of the deposits would be made, covering all the money. Some of the money would go directly into the check-cashing safes, to be distributed over the following weeks. Pete would put the money in the businesses the week after the boys left town.

"Sounds good to me," replied Nelson.

"Look, guys, everyone remembers that what we're doing isn't above-board, so keep your cool and just make your deposits. I've mixed in checks from each of the branches that were written within the last few days as well as money orders so the deposits will look right," said Peter.

"We'll do the ATM runs tomorrow and make the payments on cards in the night drops tonight—that'll take care of about $50,000," Josh said, referring to the second phase of the plan, which involved all the ATMs they owned in the area—fifteen units that could each hold $5,000 in new bills. In the morning, Josh and Peter would withdraw new bills from the accounts into which the deposits had just been made, and mix them in with the twenty-dollar bills they had separated out that looked decent. The plan called for them to mix about $3,000 of the money from up north with brand-new $20s that they had preordered from the various banks. The ATM company would then, on paper, take a loan out from the check-cashing business; online wire transfers would be made the next morning, moving money from the various check-cashing accounts into the ATM company's accounts: the act of layering the money The difference was that the ATM company wires would total far less than what was being put in the machines, but the loan paperwork would match the totals. The first real act was getting the twenty-dollar bills into circulation. The second was creating the loan paperwork to cover the wires—loans that would never be repaid by the ATM company.

"Nelson, you and Franco will make all the drops on the secured credit cards tonight and tomorrow to load them up. Each payment will be for $2,000," said Peter, referring to payments on prepaid credit cards they'd acquired in various names and dozens of different LLCs; they would use those cards to buy picks from the Luck of the Irish website. The secured cards would actually increase the balance available as more money was deposited into them. They would make $500 cash deposits on the cards in banks' night drops and up the balances available each night while they were in town. Jimmy would then space out the buys over the next few weeks, purchasing daily picks at $100 each across the 30 different cards, generating roughly $3,000 a day in sales for the Luck of the Irish website. What this did was vary the amounts of money being cleaned and the ways in which it was getting cleaned. They would also use checks and money from the check-cashing entities to make payments on the cards. Banks wouldn't report the credit and debit card transactions the same way they did cash deposits since we were in essence lending them money by making deposits on the cash-secured credit cards. They all had limits pushed up to around $5,000 at this point, so they could effectively clean $150,000 a month if they were reduced to only using the secured credit cards.

"Bottom line is you all know what you need to do. Let's go down to the pub, get some grub, and get on it. Finish getting dressed, and let's hit it in five minutes," said Josh. With that, they all got up and finished getting ready to head downstairs.

"You ready to go, Dad?" Josh asked.

"Looks that way. I think we have everything set up," Peter said, looking at his son. "I think we need to rotate back to the Alpharetta and Roswell accounts next time you guys are down."

"Sounds good to me. At the rate we're going, we may be getting down here every other month this year," replied Josh with a smile on his face. "I think the Sox play the Braves down here this year, so we can go catch some games."

Peter thought that would be good. He had never gotten around to taking his son to a Red Sox game when they'd lived in Boston. He'd always been too busy with the police department. Now that they were breaking the law, he got to spend more time with his son than ever; and they had a certain freedom that the wealth brought. Overall, it was good he was with his son and he enjoyed the time they spent together. Josh was his life now, and he would protect him and it at all costs.

"Let's go get some of that shepherd's pie," Peter said to Josh as he patted him on the back.

KINGSTON

The Johnson ladies sat in the visiting room on a Sunday afternoon, both dressed in church colors that stood in contrast to the white stone walls of the main prison. The bright red of Rena and the deep purple of Della sat at the table, waiting on King to enter the room. They looked like bright flowers against a gray landscape. Jeremiah sat waiting for his father as his little brother looked at some comic books brought to entertain him—no electronic devices could be brought into the camp. Della and Rena had left church early to visit King, like they did at least once a month.

King walked into the room wearing the drab brown donned by the inmates. Both ladies rose to meet him as he arrived at the table. His beige was offset by the bright tones now standing across from him. Their colors overwhelmed him as they embraced.

"How you doing, baby?" Rena asked, briefly hugging King.

"Good, can't complain. I hear we got our first scholarship offer," King said as he hugged his older son.

"Yes, sir," Jeremiah responded, looking at his father. Jeremiah understood more than his little brother about why his father was where he was, and the weight of the situation could be felt in his voice.

"Hey, Daddy!" exclaimed little Ray as King picked him up and held him. Ray was about five years younger than his older brother and was very much still the baby of the family.

"Julius said to say hello; he was still at the church when we left," Della said as she hugged her brother-in-law.

Everyone returned to their seats, and King put Ray on his lap. The camp rules only allowed for a brief hug at the beginning and end of the visit. Inmates and their family were supposed to be limited to thirty-minute visits, but it was rarely enforced. The restriction had been created after two guards were attacked in the main prison in October of the previous year, but the camp saw little need to enforce the rules as a general practice. The Sunday afternoon visits were generally the busiest of the week, and there was not a week that went by that someone from the Johnson clan didn't make it in to see Kingston. Della came weekly, and Rena got in nearly as often. The boys came at least once a month.

John Archibald had been able to get King moved closer to home due to his mother's declining health. Once Ma Maris had lost the use of her legs and had become confined to a wheelchair, her visits had been less frequent; she hadn't been able to make it in to see him in nearly a year. Della had taken up the mantle and made sure Kingston had as much of a family connection as he could.

"How's Ma?" Kingston asked Della, who wore a purple hat that matched her dress.

"She has her good days and her bad," she replied. "The new medicine has been working."

"That's good to know," King said as he turned a page of his youngest son's book for him. He knew that all he could do for his mother at this point was make her comfortable. MS was a disease that attacked the nervous system and was something his mother had been fighting for years.

"King we need to talk to you about Maris," said Rena. "Jeremiah, take your brother over to the play area."

"Mom, why you gotta talk bad about Maris! She ain't here to defend herself," said Jeremiah, who was dressed in a white polo, dark pants, and dress shoes. "She was—"

Before he could get the words out, Della cut him off: "Don't you back-talk your mama, boy. You know better!" She put a hand on his shoulder. "Come on, you two. Let's go over here and find Ray another book." With that, Della led the two boys over to another table and pulled out some books that they had brought with them.

"What's going on now?" King asked Rena. He turned to her and took her hand, looking into her eyes.

Rena looked back at King and squeezed his hand. "She's got a new boyfriend, and it looks like they're partying a little too hard. I think she's hitting something a little harder than just drinking. I found some pills that looked like ecstasy. King, I can't have her in the house with Jeremiah and Ray anymore if she has drugs around. I don't know what to do with her."

"Did you confront her?"

"Not yet, I wanted to talk to you first. You know she won't listen to me." She paused and broke their handhold. "She's never listened to me . . . you know that." Rena glanced away from him. "She's out of control."

King sat, still looking at Rena. Deep down, he knew she was right. Maris was his daughter from a previous relationship, and she had never connected with Rena. They'd always had a love-hate relationship, mean-ing they loved to hate each other. Rena had entered their lives when Maris was eight years old, and they had seemed to compete for King's affection ever since. When King had been arrested and put in jail, Maris had been in college and the embarrassment created wedge in their relationship.

The younger Maris had been named after her grandmother and had a special relationship with her. Maris worked for the family grocery store and hadn't seemed to find her way yet with regards to any solid career choices. Maris knew very little about the more illicit side of the family business. She was closest to Devon in age and had grown up around Marlow and Julius Jr. She was probably closest to Marlow; but he had been out West for the better part of the last three years, further creating isolation within her own family.

"Who's the new boyfriend?" asked King.

"A guy named Kendrick Toliver; and if what I hear is true, he's part of the problem," said Rena. "Has her going out all times of night down to the Compound and Sutra Lounge. She's out in the club scene until 6:00 a.m. sometimes. Look, King, we both know what that means. We both been down that path, and I just cant have her around the boys. Jeremiah is old enough to see what his sister is doing. I need to kick her out of the house."

"That will make it worse," replied King. "She already feels alone—"

"That's a bullshit excuse, King, and you know it. She is a grown-ass woman and she needs to check herself!" said Rena in a raised tone. She withdrew from King slightly. "She is the only one that can make any changes, and she don't give a shit."

"So that means we abandon her?" asked King. "Throw her out like trash?" His voice's tone echoed that heard by millions of families struggling with the same question and discussing the same fate of addicts they cared about.

"No, we don't throw out our own," said King. "I need to speak with her. Can you get her in here to see me?"

"I can try, but she hasn't been here in over a year, so what makes you think you can say anything she'll listen to now? I'm the one who has to live with her and worry about the kids. You need to think about your two boys, Kingston!" said Rena. Instinctively, she pulled a cigarette from her purse only to become frustrated as she remembered smoking wasn't allowed. She quickly placed it back in her bag.

"King, you can't be no father to her or to them from in here," Rena said. Her words cut with the intent she had of hitting a soft spot in his heart.

He knew she was right, but it hurt nonetheless. "That's fucking cold, Rena. I'm trying," he replied, giving her a look. The anger welling up inside him was more a result of his impotence than because of what she had said to him. She was right; there was nothing a father could do for a child from behind bars. Even if he were outside, there would still be the same feeling of helplessness a parent felt for a child struggling with drugs or any addiction. It was a dark feeling and one that King knew all too well, having battled his own vices in the past.

He looked back at Rena, who was not letting up or backing down. In her mind, she was protecting her own since Maris wasn't her biological daughter and acted more as a reminder of King's previous wife.

"It's the truth, Kingston. She ain't going to listen to you and what you say from this cage."

"At least I care enough to try, Rena. Can you get her here or not?" King asked, looking in her eyes with a silent desperation in his.

Rena sensed that she had made her point. "I'll see what I can do, but I ain't making no promises. I'm the one who has to deal with her shit."

"Good," said King. "Now what's going on with Jeremiah?"

"He overhead me talking to Della about Maris. He knows about the drugs. Maris went to Della's all messed up to pick him up, and Della wouldn't let her take Jeremiah home. Della had to get your brother to come get Jerry," Rena explained.

"No more innocence left, is there?" King said. "Hard world sometimes. The truth is always hard."

"You know how he feels about Maris," said Rena. "She helped raise him as much as me or Della, especially with you being gone. He heard me say she needs to go. Damn that Toliver boy."

"Don't kid yourself, Rena. She gets that bad streak from me," said King resolutely.

"People make their own choices, King. I don't buy that bullshit—ain't nobody forcing her to do shit. The Toliver boy is just bad news; and when you put those two things together, this is what you get."

"Hard to say which way it will go, but all we can do is what we can do," said King.

"What's that supposed to mean?" replied Rena with a strange look on her face.

"All we can do is love her and hope she changes her path," answered King. "Can't nobody else make that change for Maris but Maris. That much is true."

MARLOW

The meeting with Ceasar Rojas was scheduled to take place in Nogales, Mexico. The Mexican police presence in Juárez had escalated after El Chapo's capture, and a crackdown on his lieutenants had come with dozens of arrests taking place near the border. The meeting was more out of necessity than anything else because of the shifting sands of the cartel's hierarchy. The reality was that no matter where the Mexican police stuffed El Chapo, the organization would continue to move tons of coke across the boards. The names might change, but the story stayed the same; the people of America wanted their blow, and the routes through Mexico remained open and nonstop no matter who was in charge.

Marlow sat in the back of a black Yukon Denali, which was being driven by Javy and was occupied by another cartel member who neither spoke nor looked at Marlow. The large Mexican had pockmarks on his face and a black mustache, and he was obviously meant to intimidate.

Marlow could also tell that the big Mexican disliked blacks from the look he gave as Marlow got in the SUV. Aside from the business aspect of this arrangement, he often got this same feeling of distrust from most of the cartel members. The only exceptions had been the Manuel-Rios brothers and Mr. Rojas himself. The brothers both came from Nogales and spent just as much time in Nogales, Arizona, as they did across the border. As for Rojas, he was more concerned with the color green than he was the color of Marlow's skin. He knew he needed the blacks to ensure the delivery of his product, as in the inner cities the cartel had limited access to some of their primary buyers, namely other blacks and whites.

Frankly, the initial delivery system with the Mexican gang MS-13 had proven unreliable because they really hated blacks and they scared the shit out of the whites. The general hatred and distrust Mexicans had for African-Americans made it hard for the gangs to create and maintain good business relationships with one another. In short, the racism MS-13 felt toward their black business partners usually led to problems. If there was one thing the Mexican cartel wasn't a fan of, it was problems that hindered them from making their green. The hatred Mexicans had for blacks was likely the main reason the Johnson organization was thriving. They had direct access to inner-city markets.

The Johnson family had long-standing ties to the inner cities reaching back to the early '80s, when Ray Sr. and Kingston originally started bringing up dope from Texas via El Paso. As the cartel changed their primary trade, Kingston initially rebuffed them, sticking to weed. At first, that worked with the cartel's plans because they thought they could rely on the Mexican gangs and Mexican Mafia to distribute the cocaine as that became the primary focus while the Mexicans wrestled the Colombians for control over the coke trade after Pablo Escobar's death and the weakening of the Cali Cartel. As the Mexican distribution network became more and more reliable, it eventually became the primary way to get the product into the US. This made kings out of all the various Mexican cartel leaders. If the US did one thing successfully in their effort to battle the cocaine coming into the US, it was their changing the power structure, as less coke came through South Florida and the majority of it used the porous southern border with Mexico to enter the US. Cities like Juárez and Nogales became superhighways since they directly connected to US sister cities, namely El Paso, Texas and No-gales, Arizona.

"Amigo, we're almost there," said Javy from the front seat. The Denali had swung through the center of the city down Mexican Federal Highway 15 and had stopped at the entrance to a cemetery.

Marlow looked over and saw five black Mercedes already parked. Several men were walking around outside the cemetery gates with ear-pieces and distinct bulges under their sport coats. Just their appearances told Marlow that this was not a social call.

Suddenly Mustache in the passenger's seat spoke without looking at Marlow: "Mr. Rojas is down the path waiting for you by the monument of Señor Felix B. Peñaloza."

With that, the door was opened from the outside and light bled in the car along with the brisk chill of the January afternoon. The sky was gray, and it looked like it could stay that way for days. Marlow exited the vehicle without saying a word and headed into the cemetery through the white stone gates. As he walked, he realized the cemetery was empty. Not another soul was inside the entire place, which in itself was eerie, as the expansive property covered acres in the center of the city. It spoke of fear and respect all at once, which was what the cartel was all about.

Marlow saw a man in black approaching him down the rows of above ground coffins. He recognized him as Mr. Rojas's security chief.

"Hola, mi amigo," said the large Mexican, who was dressed all in black with black sunglasses. "Raise your arms." He patted Marlow down—the third such check he'd had since crossing the border and meeting up with Javy.

"Mr. Rojas is that way." He pointed to a white cross that resembled a chess set's rook; it displayed a black, tarnished plaque that was visible from where they stood. Standing before it in a cream suit was Ceasar Ro-jas, smoking a cigarette. Marlow walked the final twenty yards, and Rojas turned to him as he heard him approach.

"Good day, my friend; I trust your journey south was a smooth one," said Rojas as he dropped his cigarette and turned to shake hands with Marlow.

"No problem at all, Mr. Rojas," replied Marlow, looking at the statue of Felix B. Peñaloza, former mayor of Nogales, Sonora.

"This is one of my favorite monuments in Nogales," Rojas said, admiring the white tower. "Let me tell you the story, and I hope you'll understand the meaning it holds for us today.

"In 1918, a citizen of Mexico was returning home and refused to be searched by a US customs agent. He was coming from Nogales's sister to the north in Arizona. It was August, when temperatures run high, and a gun battle began. Both sides took up positions, and a standoff ensued between the citizens. Both the US and the people of Mexico called for reinforcements. The Mexicans were led by Mayor Felix B. Peñaloza; and the US called up your army, your Tenth Calvary." Rojas stared at the statue and pulled another cigarette from his case, offering one to Marlow. The two lit up, and Ceasar exhaled as he spoke again. "The mayor attempted to stop the standoff and waved a white flag of truce on the end of his cane." Rojas waved his lit cigarette in the air, against the gray sky, pausing for a second. He looked at Marlow with a grave look in his eyes.

"His banner of truce was gunned down by the US military." Rojas gazed at the monument. His expression was stoic as he looked back at Marlow. A slight wind picked up and blew some dust around the graveyard. Rojas took a drag off his cigarette and blew out the smoke through his nostrils.

"Do you know what happened next?" Rojas asked. "The first permanent wall was built between the two Nogales sisters. The very first wall separating the two countries, mi amigo. This is why we now know our city as the Heroica Nogales.

"The US killed our mayor that day, but they also killed the freedom the people of this area once knew and loved when they put up those walls," said Rojas. "Their walls do nothing to prevent our trade, my friend. To my people, their walls are as useless as the politicians that built them up.

"On your way in, you passed another monument of my people. A monument of former President Benito Juárez, naked and wrestling ignorance. They should paint the ignorance red, white, and blue, because it is ignorance to think that we can be stopped from making our money." He paused and turned to Marlow, stubbing out his cigarette on the ground under his black loafer.

"Is it trade we're here to discuss today?" asked Marlow.

"Yes, my friend, it is," replied Ceasar. "I am sure you've heard that El Chapo has been arrested again."

"Yes, I saw that. What's that mean for our business together?" asked Marlow. "Good or bad?"

"You cut right to the point," Ceasar said, making eye contact with Marlow for the first time. "It means opportunity my friend. Opportunity for us both."

ALEX

"**H**eard we had some excitement on the way back from NYC," I said to Cooper as he entered my office. It was nearly seven at night, and the rest of the staff at Zachery Mortgage had gone home. Cooper only came in after-hours to meet with me. He took off his coat and laid it on the back of one of two chairs in front of my desk, then headed to the sofa.

"You could say that. Glad I was there—a cover family would have been useless. I think I got to meet one Julius Johnson Jr. in the flesh," replied Cooper as he slid onto the couch, which was situated against the exposed brick wall. The couch was a soft, broken-in piece that had survived longer than Cooper's marriage to Lauren. Cooper stretched out on the couch, a clear sign of his fatigue after driving all the way from New York. He had only been back in town an hour or so and had come straight to my office.

"I assume you kept. . .to… what do you call it . . . protocol," I said as I worked on finishing a loan application that had come in a few hours earlier.

"If you mean he has no idea what my name is, yes, I made sure to keep it out of the conversation," Cooper replied. "The money made it to

Pete in Atlanta, if you're concerned about that, by the way."

"I already knew that—got that message from John. He's on his way to Panama," I said as I closed out of a folder in my operating software. The loan for Mr. and Mrs. James Harris would have to wait till tomorrow morning. My stomach reminded me that it was past an acceptable feeding time.

Cooper picked up his head and looked at me. "That can't be good. Why is he going for a face-to-face?"

"No clue. He met with Marlow in Houston and headed south, so that can only mean something has changed south of the border." I began to shut down my computer. "You want to get something to eat?"

"You know it. What you got the taste for?" replied Cooper, sitting up on the couch and placing his head in his hands, rubbing his temples. He was clearly feeling the effects of driving for hours in an ice storm, which had made the return travel time double what it normally would have been.

The fender bender had surely raised Cooper's anxiety past normal levels. I knew he was thinking the same thing I was, which was that it had been too close a call and if our group was a cat, we would have just used a few of our nine lives.

"So many choices. . . . How about some seafood?" I suggested as I closed my laptop and picked up my phone. Cooper stood and we walked out of my office and into an open floor plan with cubicles, which housed my staff of roughly ten loan officers and support personnel. Three more private offices were set off to the right of the space, belonging to my head underwriter and two senior loan officers. The old timber beams and exposed brick walls were just two of the many charms of the building, which dated back to the Civil War. It had been modernized, but still embraced its past.

"Speaking of fishy, I saw your former partner a few days ago, before I left for New York," Cooper said as we headed to the elevator that would take us to the street, across from a three-story parking garage, which matched the height of my office building. Charleston had very few buildings over the four-story mark, and almost everything on the peninsula had some type of history to it, which meant two things: It was not going to be changed, and it was expensive as shit to own or rent.

"What's that cocksucker up to?" I asked. The mere mention of my ex-partner, Craig Youst, changed my mood.

"I didn't talk to him—just saw him running around in his Range Rover downtown like he owns the place."

"Sounds like old C. Y. Fucking fraud, in more ways than one," I said as we exited onto the back alley that would lead us to East Bay. Charleston had many restaurants, and there was no shortage of food choices within a short walk of my office. "Let's go down Market Street. We can hit Hank's or Peninsula if they're too packed," I said.

As we walked, I couldn't help but think of my former business partner. In a way, his lifestyle had led to necessity in my own. Craig had taken an accidental refund from the IRS and spent it to further his lavish lifestyle. One thing I could say for certain was that no one wanted the IRS to become one of their creditors. Our business had broken apart after that, and I soon uncovered numerous other frauds he had committed—using my license, no less. Craig Youst had managed to use my mortgage license in numerous states to create illegal loans; and for the kicker, he had put all the money in his personal account. Real stand-up guy, old C. Y. I took responsibility for the taxes and also brought the issue to the FBI, who had little interest in some minor white-collar crime and left him on the streets to rape and pillage some more. I got left holding the bag, with a ton of bills left to pay on his behalf.

To make matters even better, after I had kicked Craig out of our company, I was forced to repay the money he took because, as the IRS looked at it, I was the only man left standing. Long story short, the IRS will get their money one way or another. Around this same time, I ended up helping John with a transaction. Facing a huge debt to the world's largest collection agency, I was left with few choices. I became very upset with the entire position I'd been put in by the federal government and my former partner. John had come along and offered me a way to get out of the hole, and I have regretted that decision ever since.

But we are where we are, and we are also who we are. None of us had planned to be involved in laundering millions of dollars, but we had all made the decision to take part, each for our own reasons.

John had offered some relief by helping the Johnson family; and after I had paid back my debts to the federal government with my share, I began planning my exit strategy—and have been doing so ever since. The crappy part is I had to break the law to pay back money to the federal government—money that I hadn't taken in the first place. Kind of ironic: I repay them with money from a drug organization so they can waste it fighting a useless war. Another way to look at it was that I had repaid them with money from Kingston Johnson so they could use that money to pay the guards who kept him in his minimum-security prison. Kind of a vicious circle, if you ask me. A guy like Kingston got caught with some plants that were legal in another part of the country and was imprisoned, but a real criminal like Youst was still running around conning more and more people out of money because he'd only broken a few laws that involved paper instead of a plant that most of America had tried at some point.

"You think we'll still be on track to get out of his line of work by the end of the year?" Cooper asked as we rounded the end of the former slave market, heading west on Market Street, past a local sports bar and the various tourist traps that dotted the area.

"We're on track; at the end of the year, we'll be ready to turn it over to the Johnson family. I'm out, one way or another," I said. "You aren't planning to extend your tour, are you?"

Cooper glanced at me with a quizzical look. "Hell no, I'm only in this to protect you guys. I'm done as soon as you and John are out. Banks can take care of himself."

"Well, we are all on track and the compensation for our services is secure offshore," I said as we passed a parking lot in front of the DoubleTree

Hotel. Our destination was just down the street that ran perpendicular to the hotel.

"You think they can run things without you?" asked Cooper.

"I really don't care. They'll have to figure it out. But if Banks is on track, it won't matter because they'll all be out of the business shortly," I said. "Enough about that bullshit. Let's get some oysters."

With that, I opened the door to the restaurant; and we headed to the community table, which had some open spots at the end calling our name.

JOHN

John boarded a plane heading west to Houston, then on to Denver; and his concern over the reason for his trip was showing. He thought to himself, This can't be a good thing. Deep down, he knew that Julius requesting an unscheduled meeting between him and Marlow could only mean one thing: a message from the cartel, which would be intended for Kingston and Banks. Direct contact had long been banned by both the cartel and leaders of the Johnson organization. All messages were relayed through trusted couriers; and in this case, that meant John got on a plane heading west. The fact they needed to meet immediately—and not through electronic means—would mean a message or request from high up the food chain. Given El Chapo's recent arrest, it could be a number of things; but none of them were especially wonderful for John. He hated these errand-boy trips; he was literally counting the days until his role in this operation would be over.

"What can I get for you?" asked the first-class stewardess. Her energetic smile was highlighted by red lipstick that matched the vest she wore over a white blouse.

First class did have some perks. He would easily have a few drinks down before the in-flight movie even began to crack the screen in front of his seat. If nothing else, he would have a few hours to tie one on pretty good before having to see Marlow. Not that it would matter. Marlow was by far the easiest of the family members to deal with, besides Banks. Make no mistake, John knew a lot of details about Marlow's past; but he always found him to be easy to talk to and loyal to the family. John also had to respect that Marlow had to deal with the beast itself, with direct contact with Sinaloa. He probably deserved hazard pay for having to network with guys that liked to cut off heads and burn people alive. He probably hadn't seen that in the Johnson family employee handbook when he'd signed up. Probably not. Marlow was the most street smart of the group, and that served him well. That he had to head out West to avoid potential questioning about some assaults was also a fact John knew, because he'd been the one to suggest that Marlow leave town for a few months. Those few months turned into several years, and questions were never asked by anyone.

"Vodka tonic with a splash of OJ," John told the stewardess as he scrolled through emails on his phone. He was already on his fourth drink of the day, and it was just 4:00 p.m. This trip had not been a planned expedition.

His phone rang, and he activated his earpiece as he placed it back in his ear. "Hey, Janice. . . . Yeah, new client meeting in Denver. I'll be back late tomorrow night," said John, stirring the drink that had just been delivered. "No, nothing major. . . . I know it wasn't on the calendar—you didn't miss anything. This just came up. I'll be back in the office day after tomorrow. If anyone needs me, tell them to email me. I'll be checking in."

The reality was, there was no client in Denver; but it was a necessary lie to complete the appearance that he was just having a layover in Houston when in reality that was his destination. The meeting would take place in the Houston George Bush Intercontinental Airport, away from any potential prying eyes or ears. Got to give it to that TSA—they sure did a good job of keeping people out. The short notice and nature of the trip would make it nearly impossible for anyone to follow John or Marlow:

They were set up to meet in the middle of the country for less than thirty minutes while each waited on a flight. The only bad part for Marlow was the only flight that matched up sent him north to Detroit for the night. Nothing like twenty degrees and snow.

"Sir, please shut down your device and raise your tray table," said the stewardess. "I'll bring your drink right back to you." Before she could take the glass, John polished off the cocktail and handed her the empty glass.

"You can keep those coming, thanks," said John, closing his eyes and leaning back on the headrest. If he was going to be a messenger for $425 an hour, at least he would enjoy himself.

"Excuse me, I think I'm next to you," said a strikingly beautiful woman with jet-black hair and a smart business suit. Maybe this trip won't be so bad after all, he thought as he undid his belt and stood to help her with her bags. At least he would have some nice scenery on the flight. He could make the best use of his time for the next few hours.

AGENT GOODING

"So, where do we get started, Agent Kirkpatrick?" asked Special Agent Roman. It was nine in the morning on day two of the task force. They had broken into smaller groups and had begun reviewing potential targets in the Atlanta metro area. Working groups had identified some active targets for them to reinvestigate.

"Let's start with these case files for drug trafficking and see if we can find connections to our target profile," Kirkpatrick said. She had been stationed with Gooding and Roman. Special Agent Dietmer was working with the local police resources, checking on their options. The flow of information was less obvious when working with the lower levels of the group. The FBI had also brought in an IRS agent, Roger Christian, to help with any financial aspects of the search for connections.

Gooding was sitting at his desk reviewing names when he paused to come up for a sip of his coffee. "We do have a local in the work camp who might be worth a new interview," he said. "He's in the minimum-security pen—got busted with cash and pot in Alabama. Seems we had a CI working in his group who rolled on him a few years ago."

"Pot? I thought they were pretty clear we were looking for coke here," said Kirkpatrick as she flipped through pages of information on potential human assets.

"I know, but this guy happened to have about $2 million in cash on him; and more importantly, the CI is still on the street. You never know where criminals may connect," replied Gooding as he looked at the file on one Kingston Johnson, inmate at Atlanta PSD.

"That is a lot of cash for a guy just selling pot. Maybe he has some deeper ties they didn't get into since he was rolled on," added Christian.

"That's what I was thinking," said Gooding.

"Seems thin to me. Let's focus in on guys with ties to MS-13 or more Hispanic backgrounds," said Kirkpatrick. "They're more likely to have ties back to the guys we're looking at in Juárez."

"How well do you guys know this Rojas character?" asked Agent Roman as he turned to look for a response from Kirkpatrick. The other two members of the group also paused to listen to what the junior DEA agent would say.

"Well, he is moving up in the Sinaloa world," Kirkpatrick said. "He has a nasty reputation as an enforcer for the cartel. He was rumored to be a member of a hit squad called the Blondies—real sadistic assholes who invented the whole barrel-of-acid thing down there. He's moving into the vacuum that was created with Shorty going down. His direct boss was a guy named Angel Carrera Morales; the Fedarals got him and three of his main guys right around Thanksgiving last year. Morales was in charge of the Nogales corridor for Sinaloa or, as they call it, the Nogales Plaza. He's a real vicious cocksucker who liked to use drills to punish people he thought were informants. Hopefully Mexico is putting him in a dark hole—like they're doing with Guzmán."

"Hopefully they picked a hole he can't tunnel out of this time," muttered Roman.

"Morales was in charge of Nogales, and now there's a power play. The even money is on Rojas to win out over another Sinaloa fast-mover whose father was in charge of Nogales back in 2013. His last name is

Sosa Canisales. Rojas has the muscle and, from what we hear, is the likely successor to Morales in the Nogales area, which provides a direct pipeline into Tucson and on up to Phoenix. We know they have at least three active tunnels, and *that* is what's concerning Homeland and ICE right now. They want to shut down those tunnels. Rojas is believed to have started out as a coyote with them and has apparently kept up with the human trafficking, which could conceivably put him in touch with elements of terrorism if he were to gain control of the Nogales region."

"What do we know about Rojas?" asked Gooding.

"Not that much. He was educated in the US and stays strictly on the Mexican side of the border now. He hasn't been spotted in the US in over five years," explained Kirkpatrick. "He's been down there for a long time and was involved in Sinaloa taking complete control of the Arizona border when they took care of their competition from the Milenio, Jalisco, and Sonora cartels. Essentially, they either wiped them out or made them branches, like Sonora is now. Rojas was one of the main guys involved in taking the border for Morales and his bosses in Sinaloa."

"Damn, you need a score card and a roster to keep up with all these guys," said Agent Christian.

"Let's just say turnover is high; but at the same time, these guys are keeping distribution levels high. The Sinaloa Cartel is moving more coke than Medellin ever did, even under Escobar," said Kirkpatrick; her tone had taken a slight dip. "Remember the Blondies, which I mentioned earlier? Rojas ran the hit squad directly under Alfredo Beltrán Leyva back in 2008.

"How did they miss this guy in that operation back in 2009—what was it called . . . Xcellerator?" said Agent Gooding. "If he's been around since 2006, seems like they would've gotten a shot at him back then or when they got Alfredo in 2008."

"Wishful thinking. He apparently has ties to the Juárez Cartel and was involved in their war with the Gulf and Tijuana cartels as far back as the late '90s, so he has protection from Juárez as well. During the Xcellerator sweeps, he was in Juárez. They netted over seven hundred arrests within Sinaloa in the US and Mexico, but it hardly made a dent in their operation," reported Kirkpatrick.

"I remember that one netted something like $60 million in cash," said Agent Christian as he picked up a Starbucks cup and took a sip. "That was a big one back in 2009."

"That was a little before my time, but to give you an idea, the thought higher up is that Rojas could dominate all the plazas in the Arizona corridor." With that, Agent Kirkpatrick stood and walked over to the map of the Southwest US that had been put up just the day before. "Sinaloa has the corridor from Mexicali to San Luis Río Colorado." As she says the names, she stuck red pushpins into the map. "Rojas's brother Luis is now in control in Mexicali; and if he gains influence over Nogales, he'll have strategic control over the other two Sonoyta, located between the first two and Nogales—and then you have Agua Prieta, to the east of Nogales." Kirkpatrick marked the locations on the map with three more pins.

The other three agents studied the map.

"Didn't you say he had connections to Juárez?" said Agent Gooding, looking farther to the east of the last pin in Agua Prieta, Mexico.

"Bingo!" said Special Agent Kirkpatrick. "Now you see why this guy is important—he could consolidate power over regions all the way from Mexicali to Juárez between himself and his brother. The best thing we have had going for us is that the cartel has essentially been at war with itself since 2008."

All the agents sat silently for a minute.

"There is also a larger concern—that the Tijuana Cartel has raised a white truce flag in the San Diego corridor. If Rojas is able to take control over Nogales and consolidate the cartel's power, we would be facing the most powerful drug organization seen since Pablo Escobar having complete control over areas from San Diego to El Paso. We're talking a drug express superhighway," said Kirkpatrick. "If these guys get their acts together and stop killing each other, they may prove to be unstoppable—

especially if guys like Rojas take control." Kirkpatrick strode back to her seat and sat down. "We're talking about another Pablo or El Chapo, right before our eyes."

Gooding picked up Kingston Johnson's file and looked at the brief on the inside cover. "Confidential informant, code name Zeus, told Agent Charles Downing of a trip to be made by one Kingston Johnson from Houston, Texas, to Atlanta, Georgia, with cash and marijuana, around one hundred pounds. Johnson would be traveling via Interstate 20, with a potential route change near Birmingham that could take him to Interstate 59 or to continue on Interstate 20 into North Atlanta." He put the file down and thought for a second. That had to have come from someone close to the perp—that the CI had known Kingston might change routes struck Gooding as odd. He thought to himself, Old Zeus had to have been pretty close to Johnson to know he could have taken a route change. Gooding continued to look over the notes and saw that the decision had been made to take Kingston Johnson down on the west side of Birmingham to avoid the possible route change.

All of a sudden, a knock sounded on the door and DEA Agent Paul Dietmer walked in room with the other agents.

"Looks like we got a lead on some MS-13 gangbangers in the Lawrenceville area from the Gwinnett County Sheriff's Department. They actually have some undercovers following a group of them now with some activity," Dietmer said as he set two manila folders, each about an inch thick, on the table before the other agents. "These guys could be a good lead for us to explore." He pulled up a chair at the end of the table farthest from his partner.

"How we doing in here? Anybody to look over?" asked Dietmer.

"Nothing much," Agent Kirkpatrick replied. "Looks like some cold informants and not many ties to the Hispanic angle in these older informants. Not much juice to squeeze."

Gooding took up one of the file folders Dietmer had set on the table and began to look over some jackets on a couple of brothers named

Antonio and Juan Guillen. Both were located in the Lawrenceville area of eastern Atlanta.

Historically, the Sinaloa Cartel used primarily MS-13, a Latin-American gang with ties throughout the US; their own people; or the Mexican Mafia to move drugs into the US. Sinaloa had made Chicago its main hub for the distribution of cocaine, meth, and heroin. The concept of a group of non-Hispanics moving drugs through Atlanta was not foreign and, in fact, happened every day; but the fact that nobody knew anything about this group was perplexing. It showed a level of sophistication that was above the average street gang, biker gang, or gangbanger, for that matter. It was time to get to work; and for some reason, Gooding felt like this group was going to represent a challenge.

MARLOW

Marlow watched the plane rocket off the strip and into the grayish-blue sky. He was seated on a couch in the concierge lounge at the Hobby Airport in Houston. He had been in the club lounge for the past thirty minutes and had a Crown and coke in front of him as he waited. His one carry-on bag was placed at the end of the couch. A black goose down jacket lay beside him. Marlow was wearing a long-sleeved white shirt and black jeans. He had an iPad mini on his lap, connected to Netflix and streaming an ESPN documentary about Randy Moss, and a set of earbuds in.

Suddenly he felt a tap on his shoulder from behind. Marlow turned his head and removed the earbuds.

"Well, Mr. Johnson, good to see you again," said John as he around the couch to face Marlow. "Nothing like a little day drinking. Mind if I join you?"

"'Mr. Johnson'—shit, you know better than that." Marlow stood up and shook hands with John, patting him on the back in a half hug. "How's ATL?"

"Same old shit, my friend," John said as he worked his way around the table and took a seat across from Marlow after rolling his black Samsonite luggage to the end of the second sofa. "We get any table service in this place?"

"Yep, she'll come around in a few. All free thanks to the company Amex," Marlow said as he took a sip from his drink. He sat back on the light-beige leather couch and looked out the glass wall at the planes as they danced across the runways and into the sky above.

"Sunny Detroit this go-around; I'd say I got the better end of this meeting," John said as he waved at the girl behind the bar, then took out his cell phone and set it on the table in front of him.

"No shit, it's like two feet of snow up there right now. At least it's only overnight," replied Marlow. "How's my dad doing? You talk to him at all lately?"

"Only briefly. He and J. J. have been around the office a few times for King, but nothing much is going on. I know Jeremiah got a scholarship offer to Georgia Southern."

"Wow, already getting offers at his age; that shit is dope," said Marlow. "I bet King is proud."

"So what's the need for the face-to-face?" asked John. The waitress came over and asked for John's drink order. "Vodka soda, splash of OJ, and another one of those for him. Don't skimp on the vodka, please, sweetie."

The girl walked back over to the bar, which was about thirty feet away.

Marlow leaned in and spoke softly, "A request has been made that we expand some routes."

"A request?" asked John, looking at Marlow intently.

"Chicago, Pittsburgh, Cleveland, and Cincinnati," he replied as he stirred the half-melted cubes in his cocktail. Marlow looked out the huge, full-length window at two more planes taking off.

The lounge was behind the security lines and well within a terminal. The location had been chosen to appear as a random meeting spot to anyone who could be watching them. Marlow had already walked the entire lounge; currently it only held a half dozen other people. There weren't many travelers at this particular time of day in the middle of the week. Most business travelers would be in and out on Mondays and Fridays. Their meeting time and location was anything but random; it was one of six different points where John and Marlow could "bump into each other" during a layover as both traveled on to different cities. Given the current level of security dedicated to fighting terrorism, why not take advantage of that security, which made it next to impossible for anyone to set up in advance of them showing up.

"With an emphasis on Chicago," added Marlow.

"Fuck," said John, a sudden paleness taking over his face. "We don't do business in any of those places, and you know what's going on in Chicago—that place is a shitshow."

"No shit," Marlow said without missing a beat.

The waitress brought the round of drinks and set them between the two friends. John didn't move a muscle for at least twenty seconds.

"That's not fucking good," John said as he slowly reached for his drink.

Chicago was one of the main distribution hubs the cartel used for getting cocaine out in the US, and it was primarily run by the Mexican Mafia and various gangs, including MS-13. The bloodshed in Chicago had grown to epic proportions, with murders rates rising like rocket ships into the sky. El Chapo and the cartel had poisoned the streets of Chicago, making him only the second person since Al Capone to earn the title of "Public Enemy Number One." The drugs being funneled into Chicago made it like the Wild West, with gang members killing each other on street corners each and every day. There were over 150,000 gang members in Chicago, and roughly 80 percent of the heroin and coke they dealt came from the Sinaloa Cartel.

Both John and Marlow knew the danger of dealing with these types of individuals. The connections and their family members they dealt with had been known quantities to Kingston and his family for decades. The risks of working with new dealers increased the potential for things to go wrong—horribly wrong, which meant arrest or death, neither of which fit into the overall business plan for John or the Johnson family.

"Hey, you aren't the one out there with these crazy fuckers," said Marlow as he set down his empty glass. "This was not them asking, if you know what I mean."

"What did you say?" asked John. He took a big pull off his drink.

"I told them I had to have a meeting with the powers that be. What the hell do you think I said?" Marlow took a pull off his new drink. "Now you know why I'm day drinking."

"I know what Banks will say, and I can't really say I disagree."

"Enlighten me," said Marlow. "Because I need to know what to do here. You know all the shit that's going down now, right, with Shorty?" Marlow was talking about El Chapo's bust and was referring to the Sinaloa Cartel's boss by one of his nicknames.

"Well aware, and don't mention him," John said quickly. "That means lots of players will be changing seats, but it also means we don't know who will be in charge tomorrow." He finished his drink and took off his coat, setting it on the corner of the sofa.

Both men got quiet and watched the plane traffic out the window.

"So what do we do?" Marlow finally asked. "I didn't get the impression it was up for discussion. I'm pretty sure the Roman wants an answer." Marlow was referring to Ceasar Rojas's code name. His name was not for discussion in public . . . just in case.

"Means I have to head to a meeting with the Ghost," said John. "I guess my weekend is shot."

"At least you don't have to go to sunny Detroit. I'm assuming you'll be heading somewhere warm," said Marlow. Both men chuckled. Marlow stood and picked up his luggage. He retrieved his coat and winter cap, which had been sitting on the couch beside them.

"Fucking Detroit."

"Time for me to go. You got that last round?" Marlow asked.

"Well, you do have Detroit going for you," said John. "Cheers." With that, John gulped down the rest of his drink, Marlow walked to the door, and John began thinking to himself.

The exit strategy that had been in place from day one was now clearly in jeopardy. He had to meet with Banks and get a game plan in place as soon as possible. This request was not to be taken lightly because with the chaos at the top of the food chain with the cartel, they wouldn't know who to trust—which meant they could trust no one. The fact that the cartel wanted them to go into new markets meant some of their regular distributors had been compromised. They wouldn't be dealing with their normal business connections; instead, they would be facing new buyers, which meant new problems and, mostly likely, mountains of cash that had to be put somewhere. The level of risk had just increased exponentially, and there was no way to avoid it. They would have to come up with something fast, but there was no good answer.

The main hope John held in the back of his mind was that Banks was still following the same plan as the rest of them. That plan meant getting out—not going further into the drug trade.

This request was hardly a request at all, it was a demand; and they had to figure out how to answer it—and answer it correctly or face the consequences.

John opened the Telegraph app on his phone and sent a message to Banks. Then he went online, looking for a flight south. Guess he wouldn't be heading to Denver after all. Panama sounded much more to his liking anyway, but the reason for the trip wasn't at the top of his bucket list.

As he looked for flights, the reply came from Banks: "See you tomorrow night." The message would disappear forever in the next hour. Banks and John never needed long to get the other's message. If they were talking, it meant something bad had to be dealt with; and that could only be done face-to-face.

John put a hundred-dollar bill on the table in front of him and placed his empty glass on top. He left the lounge and went looking for a store where he could buy some board shorts; he wouldn't be needing any of the cold-weather gear he had in his carry-on. His travel plans were now in flux, just like the plans of the Johnson family. Like always, he needed to become prepared for what came next, whatever that may be.

As he walked out of the lounge, he looked for flights to Panama City, Panama—his next destination. If nothing else, Banks did reside in a pretty cool place; he just wished it was a social call and not business.

JOHN

John looked out over the sea of skyscrapers and apartment buildings from the fifteenth floor of the InterContinental Hotel Miramar in Panama City, Panama. Even in February, the city saw temperatures in the low nineties. John was sitting in an open-air private lounge waiting for Banks Johnson to arrive. As he sat there, looking out over the Pacific Ocean, he drank a cool rum punch that had been delivered to him upon his arrival in the lounge.

His thoughts drifted to his earlier discussion with Marlow, and he realized the cartel's desires were in direct conflict with the group's desire to exit the drug-delivery business by the end of the year. The plan had always been to set up the laundry end of the enterprise for the Johnsons, with John, Alex, and Cooper exiting and turning over the method and knowledge to Julius and his son. John's fear was that the cartel's desires would change Banks's and, ultimately, Kingston's minds about letting them out of their deal.

Panama City had been founded in August of 1519 by Spanish conquistador Pedro Arias Dávila; and the old Spanish style of architecture could still be found throughout the city. The city, which boasted a population nearing two million souls, was best-known for its canal, which was a modern marvel to behold. It also acted as a banking center for many types of groups that, let's just say, didn't like to share the books with their home countries. Panama was the banking destination of choice for the cartels and their business associates, with the banks' secrecy and location being prime reasons for their popularity.

It was the city's banking and secrecy, which rivaled the Swiss's, that had attracted not only the cartel but also one Banks Johnson. Banks now called Panama home and lived outside of the city near the tropical rainforest in an area called Bocas del Toro. Banks also kept a penthouse condo in the city and stayed there during the majority of the week, working to keep ahead of family affairs; this allowed him to manage their money and the logistics of family operations all from the cover of his IT services company, which he also ran out of the city. The Internet security business was booming, and Banks's company was doing tremendous business with many international banking clients in Panama. Currently he had a few dozen employees stationed in Panama, their Atlanta location, and various smaller cities in the States. They primarily defended banks and insurance companies from hackers and provided systems security services for businesses both at home and abroad.

The country's connection to cocaine had a long history, including the fact that its own dictator was, in fact, a major cocaine trafficker. General Manuel Antonio Noriega had acted as the dictator of Panama from 1983 to 1989; during that time, as well as the decades that predated his reign, he was a major drug trafficker with both the knowledge and approval of the US's CIA. General Noriega had ultimately been removed from office by the US and indicted for drug trafficking, serving roughly thirty years in an American prison. Noriega and his companions were, in part, the reason for Panama's banking status, namely because Noriega was laundering his own money.

Although publically owned, the banks of Panama could take the stand that they would fight this form of corruption; the reality was they were the banks of choice for all the major cartels and their associates. It was partly due to the need to protect their money that Banks was now located in Panama City, to both keep a safe distance from the operations but also to keep an eye on the family jewels.

From day one, Banks and Kingston had had a plan that did not include moving cocaine. They had their minds set on a different path for the family, but it still hinged on them being able to eventually get away from distributing cocaine for the Sinaloa Cartel. Part of their plan had always been to simply purchase the coke and never accept consignment with the cartel. If a person ever did end up owing the cartel, it generally wouldn't end well or easily, no matter how hard that person might try. In most cases, someone ended up dead. Kingston and Banks knew the risks and had done as much as they could to never put themselves in that position.

What the cartel now proposed was a path that could very well end up with someone either behind bars or, more likely, dead.

As John looked out over the ocean and cityscape, he didn't notice Banks come out to the patio from the double glass doors.

"John, how you doing?" Banks said as he walked up to the table. He was dressed slacks and a polo with a pair of Ray-Ban sunglasses that reflected blue.

John rose and embraced his friend with a deep hug. "Tired, my man, but making it through. The trip was a little short notice."

"I hear you." Banks took a seat, joining his childhood friend in looking out over the city and ocean before them. "Really is an amazing city from up here," he said. The breeze took the edge off the humidity, but the sun was still coming down on them both.

"To think, most of these buildings were built with drug money. Really a different world down here," said John.

"Well, you know, it's all how you look at it, Johnny. The people down here just see it as jobs and progress; they tend to overlook how the money got here and more or less focus on the benefits to their community. The buildings mean jobs for them, and they really don't care how they're getting paid as long as that money puts food on the table."

"I think it's that, more or less, that we need to discuss, don't you?" asked Archibald as he took a sip of his drink. "You want a water or diet soda?" John had changed into a white polo and a pair of shorts he had purchased in the Houston Airport. He had a pair of Rainbow flip-flops on; his shoe options had been pretty limited.

"No, I'm good. How did Marlow seem when he told you what our friends in Mexico wanted to do?"

"A little concerned, but he seemed interested," said John. "I'm sure that's to be expected."

"Has he talked to Julius Sr.?" asked Banks.

"I don't think so. I think he followed instructions and got in touch with me first. Hopefully he keeps radio silence like he's supposed to," replied John.

"He's out there on the front line with these guys, so he's got to know the danger in what they're asking," said Banks. "We should probably have rotated him out of there by now; those guys in Mexico are out there."

"Knowing there's danger and understanding it are two different things," replied John as he sipped his drink. "Does this change anything for you and King?"

"Not at all, the plan is still the same," answered Banks without hesitation. He took off his sunglasses and looked at his old friend. "We still plan to shut it down at the end of the year, and we're on track with the deal in Colorado."

John took a sip of his drink before speaking. He had a serious look on his face, and his firm tone reinforced his point. "Good to know. Because Alex, Cooper and I are all out at the end of the year, as planned. We have no interest in doing this long-term, no matter what the money looks like going forward. I heard the cartel has created a new high-octane powder form of heroin that can be snorted that they're pushing on the streets. Targeting high school kids in Chicago. You know if you go into that market, they'll want you to start taking H too."

"I agree with you; and as I said, the plan is still the same. We're going legit with all the business, and we're on track with our purchases in Colorado. I've been buying up shares in the companies, and we'll have a foothold in the dispensary industry by midyear." Banks looked over at his friend. "I know how dangerous this all is, and I want out just as soon as you do. There is no way I want to go into Chicago with the cartel. At that point, we wouldn't be independent operators; we would be one of their creatures. There is no way I'm going to let that happen. Once you start owing Sinaloa money, you belong to them. We haven't crossed that line, and we never will. None of our clients belong to them. We don't deal with the Mexican gangs at all, and I'm not about to start doing that now, when the finish line is in sight." Banks stopped talking and looked his old friend in his eyes so he could tell that he was sincere.

The point was made; both friends could tell they were on the same page and still going down the same path. Trust between the two men had been strong since they were little kids, and John knew deep down he could believe everything Banks told him. Ever since they were children, Banks hadn't been able to lie to his unofficial brother, John. By looking him in the eyes, Banks had reaffirmed that brotherly bond.

Relief washed over John, and he sipped on his drink as he looked out at the Pacific from their perch high above the city. Banks gazed out at the same sea and put his Ray-Bans back on to shield his eyes from the sun, which beat down on them both. A slight breeze knocked the edge off, but it was time to go, and it was time for them to begin taking the steps to get his family and friends out of the drug-delivery business.

"Enough about business. I know I have to entertain you this evening, so what's your pleasure?"

"You know me, Banks. I'm pretty simple to please," John said with a grin. The meeting was over. It had been necessary, but it had only approached part of the problem at hand. John knew Banks and Kingston were still planning to exit the cocaine distribution business, but they now had to deal with the larger problem of the cartel and the cartel's desires.

Sinaloa was not a group that was used to hearing the words "no thank you."

"How do we deal with Mexico on a reply?" John asked as he finished off his drink with a gulp, leaving the ice cubes to melt in the sun as he set down the glass.

"Very carefully, John. Very, very carefully." Banks stood and dropped a twenty on the table. "That should cover you. Let's get out of here, and I'll show you a better part of the city." The two men left the lounge and headed to the elevator.

If nothing else, they were on the same page, chapter, and verse; but now the key became keeping the rest of the family in line—and making sure the cartel was happy with their decision.

KINGSTON

The nervous feeling in the pit of Kingston's stomach was not something he was used to. He hadn't seen his daughter in over a year, and the last time they'd met was a miserable exchange that ended with her storming out of the facility. It had taken a lot of arm-twisting by Della to make this meeting happen, and she had to drive Maris to the prison to ensure it would even take place.

King thought back to their last meeting and the argument that had fractured their relationship. Of course, Maris knew why Kingston was in jail. There was no mystery left there. She'd been in high school when he was initially arrested in Alabama and had entered college by the time he went to prison. The split had been obvious after his arrest. At first, it was just the embarrassment she'd felt because her father was a drug dealer; and then it turned into an awkward silence between the two of them as they attempted to shield the two younger children from the reason their father would be gone from their lives for nearly a decade.

King realized now that the effort he'd put forth to protect the younger children from the truth had created a larger wedge between him and his oldest child. Rena and King had asked Maris not to discuss his jail term at all in front of the kids; and now, looking back at what they'd asked of Maris, King saw it had obviously been too much for her to handle. Maris never really got to express herself or her feelings about what her father had done; and when it finally came to a head nearly a year ago, she had erupted like a volcano. The hatred she felt for her father's actions and the cover-up that followed had been unleashed on King during their last meeting and had led to over a year of silence.

King looked up at the clock in the television room and saw it was nearly 2:00 p.m. He left his table and headed to the visiting room. The butterflies in his stomach would not stop, no matter what he did. He didn't know what to say to his daughter; he just hoped she would give him some indication that she would listen. King walked down the hall and stood at the door, waiting for the guard to buzz him through.

"Go on through, inmate," said Officer Armstrong.

"Thank you," replied King. He took a seat, looked at the entry door, and waited. He sat stock-still for about five minutes, and then they appeared. First came Della, followed by his daughter. He smiled and stood as they approached.

"Hey, King," Della said as she reached the table and hugged her brother-in-law. She was wearing a light-beige dress with a floral lace piece on the shoulder.

"Hi, Dad," said Maris. She took a seat without touching him and immediately looked off to the window and back around the room. The uncomfortable feeling was tangible.

She wore a pair of jeans with wedges and a black top that was almost sheer. She looked very natural with a beauty that immediately reminded King of her mother. He was taken aback by how much she had changed in the last year. Her hair was now shoulder-length, and she looked thin— almost twenty pounds lighter than the last time he'd seen her.

"Hey, baby, how you been doing?" asked King, taking his seat and looking directly at his daughter.

She finally glanced back at him and made eye contact for the first time. Her piercing eyes spoke volumes about how unhappy she was to be here. "I know why I'm here, and you know this will be a pointless conversation before it even starts," fired off Maris.

"Oh, do you now," replied King.

"Maris, cut the shit. You need to listen to what your father has to say," said Della. She looked at Maris and let the silence hang for a second. "What you are doing is wrong."

"Wrong, Aunt Della?" she said with a look of awe on her face. "What's wrong is selling dope and getting caught with—what, Dad? A hundred pounds of weed? Why in the hell do I have to come listen to a lecture from a convicted felon?"

"That felon is still your father, and you getting messed up so bad on drugs that you can't even drive home from my house is not going to happen!" Della said to her.

Maris popped up from the table but quickly realized there was nowhere for her to go. "I am twenty-four years old. I don't need your approval for anything!" she screeched at her aunt.

An intercom buzzed: "Table four, you need to keep it down."

"Della, let me talk to her for a second by myself," King said quietly. "Let's calm it down some. Maris, sit down now."

Della stared at her niece in disbelief and just shook her head. She got up from the table and left the room. Maris was still standing and watched her aunt leave before turning back to her father, who had remained seated. She stared at Kingston.

"Maris, please sit down. I just want to hear what you have to say. That's all," Kingston said with his hands turned up, palms facing out. His eyes showed a pain but also a caring that she hadn't seen in many years.

"What do you want to know?" asked Maris as she took a seat at the table.

"Why do you do it?"

"I do what I want to do, and it's fun. Didn't you do your fair share when you were young?" she said with a tone of disinterest. The tone millions of parents have heard from teenagers and children for hundreds of years.

"You know I have," said King. "But do you know the story of how I got sober?"

Maris looked at her father and finally focused in. "Dad, I'm just having fun with my friends. I've never been arrested, and I'm not doing too much. I still don't see why this is such a big deal to *you* of all people." Maris's eyes stared at King with defiance. "I mean, Dad, you're in jail for selling weed. Do you know how embarrassing that is for me? So let me guess: you got sober when you got arrested, and that was bottom for you."

"No," replied King, looking her directly in the eyes. "I've been sober since September 17, 1990."

A glance of confusion from his daughter. "So you're saying you've been sober longer than I've been alive? I find that hard to believe."

"It's the truth, and I know the date by heart for a reason. It's the day I buried my brother Raymond, Banks's father. It was the last day I ever had a drink, a puff, or a line of anything."

Maris was now not only looking at her father but listening.

"Think back about it, baby girl. You ain't never seen me take a drink, a puff, or anything that you can remember, can you?"

"I just assumed since you sold weed you probably used your product," she snapped back.

"Nope. Look, baby, I've done a lot of bad things in my life; and I ain't going to sit here and bullshit you. I have done a lot of bad. Coming up, we didn't have shit. I messed up a bunch in school. You know, I didn't finish past junior high and was out on them streets. That's why I always wanted you to get your education. I made bad choices, and then I was left with limited options."

"What's that got to do with Uncle Raymond?" asked Maris. For the first time, it looked like she was really hearing what King had to say.

"Well, look: we all fell in with selling weed, all of us—myself, Ray, and Julius. We got good at it, and we were dealing with people we knew, and it was a good living. I never got into it because I wanted to; it just was what I could do to provide for everyone. Hell, I couldn't get a job with no education; but I always knew how to sell."

"That doesn't mean it was right, Dad!" Maris exclaimed, and he could see her slipping back into her shell.

"I never said it was right, Maris. It just was how we knew to make money. It was easy for us—I never said it was right," replied King. "And look, I'm paying for it. Your uncle Ray paid for it with his life, and it was my fault for not being there for him."

Maris's eyes cut to him with a sharpness. "What do you mean, he paid for it with his life?"

"We were taking a load down to Tampa to a newer connection we'd only dealt with a few times. We usually dealt with the same folks all the time, but we got hooked in with some new folks. We went down, and I ended up going out and getting loaded up. I got drunk and coked up, and I left Ray and Julius to do the deal. They went to a meeting at a shady hotel called the Little Tampa Inn." King paused for a second and broke eye contact with his daughter. He hadn't told this story to anyone, and the only other person alive who knew what had happened next was Julius, his older brother.

"Back then, I usually checked out all the people we did business with in advance; but at this point, I was so far gone with blow and booze that I let it slide. Raymond and Julius went to the meeting thinking I'd done my part. In reality, I hadn't scouted ahead of time; I didn't really know this group in Tampa. I was so fucked up that I didn't really care.

"They went to that meeting and were ambushed on the way out. Raymond got shot five times, and Julius got hit once. He managed to drive them out there, but Raymond was dead by the time he got to the hospital. That was September 13, 1990."

"Wait—you said you went sober on the seventeenth," said Maris.

"I know. I was so far gone, I didn't find out for two more days that my own brother was dead. I had my last drink by his grave in Atlanta, and I've been stone-cold sober since."

King reached across the table and took his daughter's hands in his. At this point, she was listening to his every word instead of fighting with him. "What I'm trying to explain to you is that drugs take from you more than they will ever give you, baby girl. They take your time with your loved ones and replace it with cheap, often disposal people. While your uncle was getting killed, I was with some worthless scumbag in a hotel across town in Tampa doing lines of coke in the middle of a three-day bender. I abandoned those who loved me, and they paid the cost. Drugs take your soul from you, and they replace it with sorrow and false promises. You always think that next line will be enough or that next pill will be enough, but all it leaves you with is a hollowness that robs you of who you really are. It's anything—whether it be alcohol, pot, coke, or ecstasy that makes you forget yourself.

"I know telling you this while I'm in this place makes it seem less impactful, but it doesn't make it any less true. You are a wonderful, caring, and genuine person. Doing drugs will take you away from your family and yourself." Kingston paused. Maris was looking at him with less defiance and less emotion. "I can't make you change any more than anyone could make me change back then. Ultimately, you have to do it for yourself. I just hope you think there's something better out there for yourself, and I hope I'm not the reason you're doing what you do."

"I don't know why I do it, Daddy. I really don't know," Maris said, and she squeezed his hand slightly.

"I didn't ether, baby girl. Regardless, you have to realize for yourself that you want to change. That's all I can say to you about it. I can't make you want to stop—all I can do is be real with you about where I've been. Every day, I wish I could go back and make changes. Changes that could've made it so your uncle was alive. I don't want you to live the same mistakes I made."

"I know, Daddy, I know you care. I just don't know right now," she said with a tear in her eye and a crack in her voice.

"Well, baby girl, that's better than nothing. I just want you to know I love you and I want the best for you, no matter what. I'll be getting out of here in less than two years, and I want you to be there for me. I want to be there for you. I need you to know that."

"I do, Daddy. I do. And I want things to be better," she said. They looked at each other for a few minutes, both with tears in their eyes.

The buzzer went off, signaling the end of visiting time. They stood up and hugged a hug that had been a year in the making—maybe more of a lifetime in the making.

For once, Kingston felt he had been heard by his daughter; and he looked forward to a better time in front of them. A time together.

JULIUS

Julius sat in his car watching the front of the condos in Atlanta's historic Ninth Ward. He was watching the south entrance of the Studioplex apartments, a live-work grouping of offices and condos in historic buildings. The buildings surrounded a central courtyard shaped like a rectangle, complete with small trees and fountains. The businesses' storefronts opened to the area. A lively restaurant was at the end of the courtyard.

Night had just fallen. It was still early in the evening, and the individual that Julius planned to meet hadn't made an appearance.

J. J. and two other members of their crew, Shea Davis and Rodney Hamilton, had accompanied Julius on this trip. It was not a social visit. Shea was a former football player and stood an imposing 6-foot-4-inches with 270 pounds of pure muscle on his frame. Rodney was smaller but intimidating nonetheless due to his reputation with a knife and a baseball bat. Tonight he had his bat with him, as the purpose of this visit was not to kill, but only to get a message across.

"You boys know what he looks like?" asked Julius.

"I do, he's a light skinned motherfucker, bout six-two," replied Shea. "He usually gets out 'bout this time each night and heads down to the place at the end of the complex for a few drinks."

"Are you sure Maris isn't here?" Julius asked as he looked at his watch, a gold Rolex. He was wearing an Armani gray-on-black pinstripe suit with a red tie. Julius always wore red ties and dark suits.

"Yes, sir," replied Rodney. "I've been on him since he got up after lunch. She left and went to work around 1:00 p.m. and hasn't been back over here since. His Denali has been parked down the street all day."

"Best spot for us to take him is when he rounds this corner," said Shea. He wore a black jacket with a hoodie, a stark contrast to his employer, who was impeccably dressed as usual.

Hamilton was wearing a dark Adidas tracksuit with matching pants. J. J. was dressed much like his father, a clear sign of the pecking order of the crew. Hamilton and Davis were the muscle behind Julius, and both were killers when necessary.

"Bring him over to the car, and keep it quiet," Julius said quietly. "Go ahead and set up on him."

With that, the two men exited the SUV and headed to the corner of the building.

J. J. sat behind the wheel of the vehicle, looking down at his phone. A message had come in via Telegraph from Marlow. Before he could open it, there was action at the side of the building. Shea and Rodney cornered a man walking out who was wearing a camel coat with high-end jeans and a gold chain around his neck. Both Juliuses looked up as their men began talking to their target: Kendrick Toliver, Maris Johnson's new boyfriend.

Shea and Rodney had been taking turns watching Toliver for the last week and a half. Julius had wanted to find out more about the young man who was apparently keeping his niece out at all times of night. Shea had followed the couple out several nights; most of them ended with Toliver and Maris at late-night party spots or random homes in the area. It was obvious to Shea that Toliver was some type of dealer—mostly ecstasy and probably coke—based on the clubs they'd been going to and their appearance afterward. It appeared that Toliver was dealing in the same clubs at least four nights a week and taking Maris along for the ride.

Shea had been a dealer before, and he recognized all the signs: the hand offs, the meetings in the bathrooms, the constant trips to his SUV. Toliver was not the most discreet dealer he'd seen, and that was part of the problem. It would just be a matter of time before he got picked up; and having Kingston's daughter along for the ride wouldn't be a good thing for anyone, especially Maris.

As the two men watched from the vehicle roughly thirty yards away, the discussion turned into confrontation. Toliver stood no chance again Shea and Rodney, who were more than prepared to take control over him. Shea slid a small aluminum bat out from his jacket sleeve and struck Toliver in the back of his knee. As Toliver crumpled, Rodney pulled a Taser from his tracksuit and popped the dealer with fifty thousand volts. Toliver fell to the ground; after a brief moment, the two men scooped him up under his arms and whisked him over to the SUV.

At the same time, J. J. engaged the Cadillac Escalade's engine. Rodney opened the door and they slid into the vehicle in one motion, placing the incapacitated Toliver between the two assailants. As the door shut, J. J. pulled away from the curb and headed away from the complex. The entire assault had taken less than thirty seconds, and the crew was on the move with their captive.

Toliver's entire body was shaking as his head bobbed and his eyes rolled back in his head. Hamilton had only stunned him with a handheld version of the Taser for about ten seconds, but it had been enough to knock him for a loop. Toliver slowly began to regain his wits after about five minutes.

Julius had on sunglasses and looked forward as he began to speak to Kendrick Toliver, who was wedged between the two men who had just grabbed him. "The experience you're feeling is a walk in the park, Mr. Toliver. Right now, you are experiencing elevated heart rate and breathing; but it will pass. My associates wanted to ensure that we have your attention. I can assume I do, indeed, have your attention.

"I've been made aware of certain activities that concern me and other members of my family."

Toliver blinked and rubbed his face with his left hand. His right arm was pinned behind the bulk of Shea Davis, who held the small bat and had it poised to strike Toliver if necessary. "I don't-don't know what—"

Before he could finish, Julius said, "You're dating my niece Maris, and I'm aware that you have influenced her into making rather poor decisions when it comes to the use of drugs, Mr. Toliver," he said in an even tone, all while looking forward, never engaging with Toliver.

"I don't—"

"SHUT UP, you fucker!" screeched Rodney as he placed the Taser's prongs against Kendrick's back. "This is the part where you listen and shut the fuck up while Mr. Johnson talks to you. Don't you say a fucking word or I'll light your ass up again."

Toliver's body grew rigid. "No, no—please don't!"

"As I was saying, it appears you're influencing my niece into making very poor decisions," Julius said in his slow and cold tone. "I expect this behavior will stop now and you will find a reason to, let's say, no longer involve yourself with Maris."

Julius took off his glasses and turned to look Kendrick in the eyes. "Do you fucking understand me!" he asked, raising his voice for the first time. His cold eyes came ablaze as he looked at the young man.

"Yes . . . yes, sir," answered Toliver.

Julius turned away from him, once again looking forward as the SUV traveled down side roads. "Good, I'm glad we have an understanding. Let me be clear, Mr. Toliver: If you are around my niece again and we have to have this discussion again, your body will be found scattered in different zip codes.

"Pull over and get this piece of shit out of my car."

With that, J. J. pulled in behind a small building a few miles from where they'd started. In a single motion, Rodney opened the door and dragged a still uneasy Toliver out of the car, followed by Shea. As they exited, Shea released Kendrick while Rodney nailed him again with the Taser. Toliver fell to the ground, and Davis proceeded to kick him in the ribs and stomp on his back. Hamilton climbed back into the SUV as Davis finished off Toliver, leaving him in the side alley. Davis slid back into the vehicle and J. J. sped off, leaving Toliver battered and broken in their wake. Kendrick was balled up, holding his ribs and barely moving; he may have been out cold.

Julius smiled for the first time as they pulled away from their victim.

"Dad, I don't think we'll be seeing him at Sunday dinner anytime soon," J. J. said.

"Nope, J. J., I think that fucker's done," Julius replied. "Shea, you see him round Maris again, you punch that motherfucker's card. You feel me? I want you and Rod to keep an eye on her until I say otherwise."

"Yes, sir, Mr. Johnson. No problem at all," said Shea with a smirk on his face. He knew he would be seeing Toliver again real soon.

J. J. looked down at his phone as he drove the crew away. "Dad, we got a message from Marlow on Telegraph." He handed the phone over to his father, who took it and began to enter a sequence of numbers and symbols to open the encrypted message from his oldest son. A secured message from Marlow would be something important.

JOHN

John exited the elevator, entering his office and walking back into the fray on Monday morning. His slight tan was noticeable, but nobody except Janice might observe that his skin was baked from a supposed trip to Denver. He pretty much did what he wanted when he wanted, so nobody would be the wiser.

As he walked back to his office, he saw his mentor and partner, Conrad Howle, walking down the hallway with his briefcase under his arm and a cup of coffee in his hand.

"Morning, Johnny Boy!" said Howle. He was wearing a gray suit and light-blue tie. Conrad was a lawyer of impeccable reputation and John's senior by nearly twenty-five years. Their partnership had grown in the last five years, with John being the heir apparent at the firm. It was rare to see Conrad heading to any appointment on a Monday morning, so John hadn't expected to see him this early in the day.

"Where you off to, Conrad? It's early to head to the golf course, even for you," said John as he shook hands with his friend.

"Got an old client being called in to meet with our friends at Century Parkway," replied the elder attorney, referring to the street where the

Atlanta FBI field office was located. "This poor bastard has been off their radar for nearly a decade, but they want to have a talk with him."

"Well, you know the wheels of justice: they grind on no matter what," said John. "Good luck over there. I'm sure it's more of the same old—our federal government hard at work."

John walked down the hall and rounded the corner to his office. Janice was already at her post and working on her computer. His assistant was wearing a light-beige top with smart and sensible slacks. John had made sure to hire a competent assistant to whom he would have zero sexual attraction, as he was well aware of the pitfalls of dipping the pen in the company ink. Janice fit the bill, as she was fifteen years his senior and had been happily married for over twenty years. Janice was one of the hardest workers he had employed; and for the most part, she kept out of his affairs and seemed not to pass judgment on him—at least, as far as he could tell. She was a far cry from the blond bombshells and busty brunettes who acted as paralegals in other parts of the firm.

"Morning, Mr. Archibald. Mr. Murphy is in your office."

"Thank you, Janice, hope you had a good weekend."

John entered his office to find Pete sitting at the small table in the corner, reading a copy of *The Atlanta Journal-Constitution*. There were two cups of coffee on the table, one in front of him and one set in place for John. The sky's gray, cloudy haze outside the window set a somber tone to the office's atmosphere.

"Morning—" Pete took a double take after looking at John's face. "You hit a tanning bed in Denver?"

"Not quite . . . had to take a trip south," replied John as he hung his overcoat on the back of the door and placed his briefcase on the corner of the couch before heading to the cup of joe waiting for him.

"Banks?" queried Pete.

"Yep," said John.

"So you going to keep me in the dark? I assume that wasn't a planned trip," Pete said, going back to his paper.

"Request from out West that had to be dealt with in person. Nothing changes on our end. Banks wants us to start the transition to Julius as soon as possible," said John with happiness in his voice. His mood was obvious as he delivered the news.

"So the exit is in sight," said Pete. A smile had taken hold of his face, which mirrored John's. Both men had looked forward to this day since the undertaking with the Johnson family had begun nearly three years prior. Both knew it was not a long-term game that could be won; eventually they would get caught if they tempted fate too long.

"End of the year at the latest," replied John. "I'm going over to meet with Kingston the end of the week. We're on track, from what Banks told me this weekend."

"Can't say it breaks my heart." Pete had set down the paper and taken up his coffee cup, which he now raised to John. "Cheers."

"What do you need me to do?"

"Transfer the money aspect of it to Julius. We'll be out of that part of it, as planned. I got the green light from Banks to make that happen. He has them on track to purchase into their dispensary in Colorado. Banks thinks they can be out of the delivery business first part of next year, on time for King getting out of PSD. They'll be out of the delivery business by the time he's free. We just need to hand over the day-to-day on the money end of things to Julius.

"The money in the States is going into the Colorado project. They'll need that cash to operate since all of the pot business is essentially done in cash out there. No federally regulated bank can accept their deposits right now."

"Should be a money-laundering dream," said Pete.

"It should be," replied John. "The plan they had is almost completed; then they'll be able to walk away from dealing with coke."

"The question in my mind has always been: will they?"

"King and Banks will have no problems moving on from it; neither of them wanted to get into blow to begin with, it was just a means to an end.

Now Julius is the one who always concerned me," said John. "But we'll be done with him too, and that's the main reason we kept our distance."

"How do we handle him?" asked Pete.

"I'll talk to him after I talk to King, but we'll have the start by having them handle all the money going forward. How they keep up with it is between Banks and Julius, but we will start to walk away from it all. What was set up for them was a process that could be handed off at some point. Julius and his crew only know the two of us; they've never met anyone else that works with either of us."

The plan set forward by Banks and Kingston had always been to make enough money to buy into the marijuana-growing business that was booming in the Western United States. The green rush, in their opinion, was much like the legalization of alcohol after prohibition had been; and they intended to be in on the ground floor. Like anything else, it would require capital; they took the risk to get the capital necessary to buy in to the companies that would supply the marijuana industry. The buy-in was managed by Banks using offshore trading accounts and via legal means. Banks was also able to purchase a majority interest in a dispensary that would allow them to legally grow and sell weed in the state of Colorado. By getting in early, they believed they would be well-suited to grow as more states legalized weed, much like as states in the 1930s allowed alcohol back into their borders.

Banks had also taken the funds, diversified their assets, and established a number of successful businesses that they would be able to maintain and run after they got out of coke distribution. They also owned the construction company and vast real estate holdings in the Atlanta and Charleston areas.

"I know that will be a weight off your shoulders—having to deal with it, Pete. It'll sure be something I can live without in my life. I thank you for your help so far. I know the money has been good, but we need to move on from it as soon as we can." John stood and looked out over the city. "I think we're at the end of the line.

"Pete, I think I see a light at the end of this tunnel." John took a sip of his coffee.

Pete laughed a little and stood up, leaving his paper on the table. "I just hope it's not a train at the end of that tunnel, John."

AGENT GOODING

Agents Gooding and Roman entered PDS in Atlanta with very little fan-fare, having set up the interview in advance. It wasn't a good practice for any of the inmates to be seen conversing with law enforcement of-ficials, so there was a separate area that allowed the agents to enter and meet with inmates, unknown to the rest of the general population. Even in a minimum-security facility like this one, they had to be careful or po-tential informants would most likely end up silenced one way or another.

"What's the story on this guy?" Agent Roman asked Gooding. Roman was wearing a dark-brown suit and had on a thick winter coat. He was clean-shaven, and his jet-black hair had recently been trimmed. Good-ing couldn't help but think he was dressing to impress the DEA agent, Kirkpatrick, who was part of the task force. He couldn't get a read on Kirkpatrick, but he knew his partner well enough to notice the effort he was making behind the scenes.

"He's doing eight years for possession with intent to distribute. He's originally from Atlanta and got busted in Alabama on his way back into the metro," replied Gooding. He was wearing a dark-blue suit and had a cup of coffee that he'd gotten from the guards' break room.

"Do we think he's active?" asked the junior agent.

"Doubtful, but he is well-connected in the area. He refused to talk back then, but maybe the last few years in the pen have softened up his tongue and his memory."

"He has a sick mother on the outside. He got compassionately placed by his attorney to be closer to her. Maybe we can dangle something in front of him to get some new information," said Gooding.

"How you want to play this with him?" asked Roman as he got a notepad out of his case and helped Gooding set up the small room in which they would be meeting with inmate Kingston Johnson.

"Obviously close to the vest. Just try to see if he has anything to say. We'll put the release on the table, let him know what we're looking for in general, and leave him a line of contact to us. Prison walls have a way of making people remember names and things we can find useful." Gooding took a seat and made a few notes at the top of his pad.

The two agents had been meeting with current and past informants for the last few weeks with few results. Nothing new on the ring of traffickers the task force was hunting. Multiple other local authorities were doing the same thing, also with few results. Nothing new—no new names connected to the Sinaloa Cartel. In short, they were striking out and working way down the chart by the time they got to Kingston Johnson.

"Does he know about the informant?" asked Roman. "Any reason to suspect who it was that rolled on him?"

"No, it seems like he's in the dark on that matter; and let's keep it that way," replied Gooding. "That's part two of what we're looking for. We'll make contact with Zeus after this meeting and see what shakes loose. As far as I can tell, he has no idea he was betrayed by anyone at all. He reached a plea deal to stay close to his mother, so he was never confronted with the wiretaps on the informant. They caught him with like a hundred pounds of weed and over a million in cash. He was cooked without the information being brought to light. The general theory was that the organization died with him going behind bars. They watched the informant for the next year and nothing turned up, so they shelved him."

Gooding shifted and looked at Roman. "I'm going to go quick with this guy. He didn't talk years ago; he'll either bite or not on the offer, so there's no reason for us to spend a ton of time on this one. He doesn't have much time left and he may not know anything we can use, so let's just put it on the table and see where he goes."

"Makes sense to me," replied Roman as he wrote "Kingston Johnson" and the date at the top of a blank page.

There was a knock on the door and then a buzz as it was opened. A guard looked in. "You guys ready to go?" asked the middle-aged black guard as he shut the door behind him. It clicked with a locking sound. "We have your guy ready in the holding cell. We're ready to bring him in."

"Yes, sir, we're ready," replied Agent Gooding.

"All right, let me go over a few things. Remember, these guys are minimum security, so he isn't cuffed. It would look odd if we hooked him up. These rooms are used for attorney meetings, and he thinks this is a meeting with his lawyer. We have video." He pointed to the camera perched in the right corner of the ten-by-fifteen room. "But no sound—we aren't allowed to record in here. There will be a guard right outside the door if anything happens. I'll buzz him in; once he's in here, the door locks you all in." With that, the guard nodded his head, the door buzzed, and he pulled it open.

The two FBI agents stood and waited for Johnson to be brought in. As King entered the room, he looked a little surprised to see the two men, neither of whom he recognized. But the look faded almost the instant it appeared.

"Now, unless I'm mistaken, neither of you looks like John Archibald to me," King said as he took a seat on the opposite side of the table, leaving the two agents closer to the door.

The guard nodded to the agents as he exited the room and pulled the door shut.

"Well, you got us, Inmate Johnson," replied Agent Roman, taking a straightforward approach. He stood to the right of the table, on King's left.

Agent Gooding pulled back a chair, removed his jacket, and put it on the back of the chair before sitting down. He looked up at Kingston. The only items on the table were the two notepads and the small Styrofoam cup, which was half-filled with coffee.

"My name is Special Agent Roman, and this is Special Agent Gooding with the FBI."

"How are your accommodations here at PSD?" Gooding asked as he pulled out a pack of cigarettes and offered them. King waved his hand without breaking eye contact with Agent Roman. The two men engaged in a slight stare-down.

"What—are you guys fucking kidding me? You some kind of prison customer service?" King said looking at the senior agent.

"What I mean is: would you like to cut your stay in this federal facility shorter than the twenty months you have left on your sentence?" asked Gooding.

"For what? Snitching? I didn't talk in the beginning, and I ain't planning on talking now," said King, glancing at the two agents. "And it's sixteen months left."

"That's still sixteen months you could spin with your mother," replied Agent Gooding, looking King in the eyes. King looked back at him with a piercing gaze that he hid as quickly as it had appeared.

"What is it you think I can help you with?" King asked.

"We're looking back over some older files and noticed that you never talked about your connections back when you got busted. You ended up with about twice the amount of time because of that. We figured maybe all these years—during which your friends on the outside have been living life and making money while you've been our guest—may have changed your mind," Agent Roman said as he took his seat at the table.

"Shit, guys, what you think I know at this point?" Kingston said almost with a laugh. He leaned in on the table. "I ain't talked to nobody in near half a decade."

"That doesn't mean you don't know people from back when you were dealing," countered Roman.

"Sorry, can't help you," said Kingston.

"Figured you might say that," Agent Gooding said as he stood up. "We're in the local field office. If any names pop into your head, have your attorney call us."

Gooding nodded his head, and the door buzzed and was opened by the guard. Gooding put his jacket back on. The two agents exited the room, and the meeting was over.

As they walked out, Gooding looked back at King. "If your mother takes a turn for the worse, maybe your memory will get better. The offer will still be on the table. You think about it."

Kingston didn't reply; he just looked straight ahead as the door shut behind the two agents. He thought to himself that the federal government knew no shame, using his sick mother as a bargaining chip. At the same time, a hollowness was in his stomach as he thought to himself about the sequence of events that had led him to being in this prison.

He thought, Why now, after all these years? Why does the FBI take up an interest in sending two "special" agents to rattle my cage *today*? Just that little word, "special," said by the younger agent made Kingston think and take notice of how he'd said it. Why did the agent say the word "special," and why would the FBI be doing the interview instead of the DEA? All of these questions gave King a moment of clarity.

The door buzzed and opened. "Let's go, Johnson," said the guard.

King rose to his feet and thought it would be a good idea for him to talk to his attorney after all. Just not about what the agents had offered him.

RENA

Kingston's next visitor a few days later brought more troubling information.

"What do you mean she moved out!" yelled King. "I just saw her and everything was cool. What the hell happened, Rena? What did you do?!"

"I didn't do nothing, King. It was your brother!" Rena said as she sat across from him. She had just told King that Maris had left home three days earlier.

"What do you mean?" King asked as he gripped Rena's hand. He didn't want to push her too far. He knew she had a strained relationship with Maris, but she wouldn't intentionally do something to hurt his relationship with his firstborn child.

"After Della and I left here last week, I think Julius and some of his boys went and beat up Kendrick," Rena said in a hushed tone.

King closed his eyes and thought for a second. "Why the hell did he do that? I didn't tell anyone to do anything." He talked in a low voice, as the room was filled with it being Saturday, the busiest visiting day of the week. The room was rather small, and talking about crimes in the open was never a good idea—let alone talking about something King had no

178

control over. The frustration was evident in his eyes. "Why do you say Julius did something?"

"When I told Della that Maris left, she told me he was upset when he found out about Kendrick. He got Della to show him a picture of the boy."

Kingston shook his head and listened to his wife as he held her hand tightly. He squeezed it to reassure her that everything was all right, to keep talking.

"Maris came in three days ago and got all her clothing out of the house while I was at the store. When I came back, her room was cleaned out. She hasn't shown up for work at the store since, and her phone is cut off. I've been calling her, and I asked Roscoe to look for her."

Rena looked down and withdrew her hand. "Finally, last night I got a text from her that said it was fucked up for us to ruin her life with violence and that she wasn't going to take our bullshit anymore. I don't know what she's talking about, Kingston. I tried to call her, and she just sent me straight to voicemail. Nobody in the family has seen her or heard from her."

She paused for a second and shook her head. "What can we do, King? What can I do?"

Kingston just sat quietly, running scenarios through his head. None of them were good, and he felt as helpless as he had when Maris had come to visit a few weeks prior. King felt like a failure as a parent and as a man. Here he was, stuck in a prison, while his family needed him.

"I need you to get John to come see me. I need John in here first. Call him on his cell when you get out of here and tell him I need to see him—that it's an 'urgent family matter.' Make sure you use those words exactly. He'll know what that means."

Frustration was the only word to describe how Kingston felt. He was angry at his brother for doing something he himself probably would have done later, but the frustration was due to the fact that he hadn't given Julius any direction. Therein lay the problem. His brother couldn't have known that King had been making progress with Maris. The dynamic they'd set up required that Julius not come see Kingston, and all their communication was through third parties like Della or John Archibald.

King could see the point of view that had made Julius take action. If Maris got in trouble for drugs, it could put everyone at risk. A parasite like Toliver had to be dealt with, but the timing had to be perfect, and timing was not something Julius was known to consider. That had always been the problem with Julius—he was more like blunt force trauma and had no tact. The only way Julius knew was force, and it had been that way his entire life—or at least since Raymond had died. Julius had gone too far this time and this was not something that King could or would let pass lightly.

"Baby, don't you worry. I'll get this fixed up," Kingston said to Rena. "We'll get her back."

Kingston smiled, but his heart wasn't in it. He'd been an addict; and he knew if Maris was pushed, it would likely make her want to use—and then nobody would know when she would come back up. If she felt like her family had betrayed her, she could go off the deep end for a long time and may never come back to them. He couldn't help but wonder what he could have done if he had been on the outside to deal with his daughter and her issues instead of leaving it to Rena, Della, and ultimately Julius. Rena was doing what she could, but she was also not Maris's mom.

Rena half-smiled at him. It was a smile that said that both of them knew he was telling a lie. Both of them knew that neither of them knew what would happen next. But they both smiled anyway.

JOHN

John came to USP the next day. Urgent family matters were the highest priority as far as visiting Kingston was concerned. It could mean any number of things, but none of them could be dealt with by waiting to come see him on a normal schedule. As King's attorney, John had more access to his client; but more importantly, they could talk privately in a holding cell similar to where King had spoken to the FBI only a few days earlier.

John had been nursing a bit of a hangover but had called the case management coordinator at the facility to get on the schedule for the following day. Normally inmates were only allowed visitors every other day based upon an odd or even number. Kingston's visiting day had been the day before, so a visit from his attorney still needed to be scheduled in advance so a room could be reserved.

The word "urgent" told John they needed to have a private conversation, but that was normal operating procedure for them at this point. All of their conversations were had in a private room with the COs watching them; but no audio was permitted, so they wouldn't hear what was being said between John and his client.

"Archibald?" called the CO, looking out into the waiting room. John approached and showed his ID, then passed it through the slot. The CO confirmed his photo on the computer and that he was in fact the attorney of one Kingston Johnson.

"I'll buzz you through," she answered through the microphone. John approached the door and entered as it rang out and clicked. He walked forward into a separate waiting area.

"Follow me," said the slightly overweight brunette guard. "You were late on the schedule. We don't get too many of you guys on Sundays." She was referring to attorneys, who usually reserved times on Friday so their work week would end with visits to their clients being held inside the camp or the main facility.

"I'm out of the office next week so had to fit him in early. Got a trial next week," said John as they walked down the lime-green hallway. It looked like it had been painted in the recent weeks. John followed her to a room, and he was left there. The CO gave him a glance that clearly said she knew he was full of shit about the trial and the last-minute schedule addition for a private visit, but frankly he didn't care. He was his client's advocate; and he would meet with him when he wanted to and in private, as provided by the law.

John had a number of topics he needed to cover and he'd already been planning on coming in the following week to meet with King, so he didn't mind coming in on a Sunday. He did mind that he had to leave a slightly interesting but smoking-hot blonde in his bed in his condo. John looked around the room and thought about how this conversation would go; in the back of his mind, he knew these meetings would be coming to an end in the next few months. The need for his role as messenger would diminish. He wondered if maybe he couldn't call it a day on the whole Kingston Johnson experience.

He sat down at the table. He knew he had to put the thoughts out of his mind and focus on the task at hand: communicating where they all stood and addressing whatever concerns King had from in here.

Just a few more of these meeting, he kept thinking. Just a few more.

After about a ten-minute wait, the door buzzed and Kingston was led into the room by a single guard. John recognized the CO and vice versa. He had done this drill before with them.

Kingston looked the same, dressed in brown. Not a sign of any concern one way or another on his face. Stoic, almost like a statue.

"You guys know what to do. You got the room for thirty minutes today. Schedule is light." With that, the guard shut them in the box and left them to their conversation.

" Good Morning, King," John said as the two shook hands.

Kingston took a seat across from his counselor. "Wish it was, John Boy, wish it was." He put his hands together, forming a triangle with his elbows on the metallic table.

"Well, I thought I was the one bringing you news, so you tell me what's going on," asked John.

"Maris done left home," Kingston said. "Apparently she has some issues with drugs, and let's just say her uncle decided to help her resolve those matters."

"Physical?"

"Not with her," replied King. "No-good boyfriend is a pusher man, but he had a discussion with her uncle."

"When you say 'uncle,' we talking skinny or fat?" John was referring to Roscoe, who was three hundred-plus pounds, and the smaller Julius. Even with the rules, the two men took no chances. Admitting that Julius had gotten physical with Maris's boyfriend would still be talked about in code, as would much of their conversation.

"Skinny," replied King. "Maris done left home."

"Sorry to hear that, King," John said, looking at his client and pausing briefly. "Exactly how do you think I can help with this matter?"

"I know you have that investigator that works for you; I want him to look for Maris. See if he can find out where she's staying. If he can find her, we'll reach out and see if she'll come talk to me." King leaned in.

"Rena will have a package with her social, credit cards, and bank account information.

"Her uncle's actions aren't something I approve of. I'm hoping you can put Rena in touch with her so we can tell her as much."

"I see. I can probably get him on that tomorrow," replied John. "Not to be insensitive, but we do have another matter we need to discuss. Is now a good time, or would you like me to come back later in the week?"

"Now's good a time as any," said King as he leaned back and took his arms off the table.

"Ghost says all the ducks are in a row for the move to greener pastures and will be ready by the time you get out," said John, sounding as if he were reading from a children's book.

"That's good to know. Is everything ready for Uncle Skinny to take over the farm?"

"Yes," replied John, watching for King's reaction.

"Given what's been going on, I think it might make sense for us to check up on Uncle Skinny for a bit before we give him the deed. Can your guy keep an eye on him?"

Not exactly the answer John had been looking for; but given what must have transpired to make Maris leave home, he could hardly argue the point. He thought for a second; given the timeline, there was some time to check up on Julius. "How long we talking?" he asked.

"Maybe a month or two," responded King. "Need to make sure his head is on right to take control of the farm. Keep your guy on him. Tell him we need to talk, and he can come see me next weekend. I need to put eyes on him."

"Understandable. Now we are talking about some cost, and he may need a little help. You cool with that?" asked John.

"No problem," replied Kingston. "We just need to know where he's at mentally."

"And if he's off the reservation? What then?"

"Then our current farmers will need to stay in place until I can get back to the farm," said King without missing a beat.

John knew the line had just been drawn in the sand. If Kingston deemed that Julius wasn't in a good place, then John and his crew would be stuck in the middle, laundering his money. If there was friction between King and Julius, which it sounded like there was, it left very few options for someone within the family to run the cleaning aspect of the drug money. Roscoe and his crew would draw attention as sure as a heart attack. Banks was in another country, which pretty much meant that Julius was the only option within the family to manage the injection of the funds via banks. Julius had built up a network of people who could be trusted, and they had run the deposits in the Atlanta area on a few select occasions over the last year.

The businesses that cleaned the money all made central deposits to a few locations, so the managers had no real knowledge of what actually got deposited. The drug money was added to the real deposits or layered into them. This created a second set of books, which was kept up with in Charleston. The plan had always been to build a system that could one day be turned over, and that day was rapidly approaching. The only issue was that without approval from both King and Banks, John and the others would be stuck in this role. Julius had always been the heir apparent to take over this part of the operation; but if there were now issues between the two brothers, that would surely mean issues for John and his friends in Charleston.

In short, John's plan for an exit could be fucked in more than one way.

"That brings us to the next item. The short Southern man requested to take a trip to the Windy City to watch a Cubs game. He wants to get season tickets." Using code, John had just told Kingston that the Sinaloa Cartel wanted regular deliveries to Chicago.

Kingston's eyes showed a little surprise, and he shifted in his chair. He thought for a second before replying to John, putting his hands behind his head and exhaling loudly with his head leaned back. The gravity of the request was not lost on him. He turned to John. "John, you know I'm a

Braves fan. Can't do no Cubs games."

"Good to know. I will relay the message," John said, relieved that Kingston agreed it was a bad idea to further entangle themselves with the cartel.

"Yeah, make sure that message gets delivered. Especially to our skinny uncle and out West."

"I guess the next question is: how do we deliver that message? Any suggestions?" John asked as he stood up and waved to the camera to signal the end of their meeting. John at least had answers—not all of them good answers, but answers nonetheless. He also had new problems to deal with and a short amount of time to deal with them. The hangover he'd had when he arrived officially went to a four-alarm headache as he stood up.

King looked up at him. "Very carefully, John Boy, very carefully. Probably best if we just say our lineup is full. Can't take in any new games if we don't have the players."

"And if they want us to make the game anyway?" John asked.

"No way we can do it; we don't have the players." King stood up and reached his hand over to John. "Thank you for helping out with Maris. Come see me as soon as you have something, and bring Rena in here with you when you do."

"Okay, King. I make no promises on how long that will take or if he can even find her, but I can promise we'll do our best," John replied like a good attorney would, taking the middle ground.

"One more thing" said King "Couple of FBI came by to see me offering early release for intel on my contacts. Probably just a fishing expedition on my contacts but thought you should know."

John stopped in his path on the way towards the door. "Well that's news." replied John. Thinking to himself wish he had led with that piece of intel. John began to process these thoughts.

"Did you catch the Agents names?" he asked.

"Roman and Gooding" answered King.

"I will see what I can find out about this." Replied John.

The door buzzed and the guard entered the room. John finished shaking King's hand and exited the room, heading down the hall to the next checkpoint. His morning had just gotten worse, and so had the rest of his day and eventually his week. Not the news he was opening for, but at least it was something he could look into without breaking the law too much more. Now hopefully he could find Maris, keep Julius in line, and get them all out of the mess he had created.

He took a deep breath and exited USP. At least he could see the light at the end of the tunnel still, but he kept thinking about what Pete had said.

"Fuck. I hope it's not a train, Pete. Hope it's not a train," he said under his breath. He got in his BMW 7 Series and dialed Pete. Better not be a train, he thought as the number rang on a crisp Sunday morning.

JULIUS

"You got the photos with you?" Julius asked his son. The two had just parked behind the family grocery store. It was a little past ten o'clock; he had told Roscoe to meet him after the store closed so there would be less people around.

"Got 'em right here," J. J. said as he pulled a folded white envelope from a pocket inside his jacket. He was dressed in a powder-blue striped suit and looking more like his father each day both in dress and manner.

"Let's go." The two men exited the SUV, headed up the concrete ramp, and entered the back entrance, which was designated for employees. A truck being fitted for a shipment sat in the first bay as the two men entered the back door and passed through shelves stacked with goods and into the private back office.

Roscoe was sitting in his usual spot with an open bottle of diet soda in front of him. He had a basketball game on the TV hanging on the wall.

"What's up, blood?" Roscoe stood and hugged his brother and gave a head nod to his nephew. He muted the sound on the TV as the three men took seats at the table.

"Is this going to be your great reveal on one of my boys?" asked Roscoe in a serious tone, looking at the two family members who had just joined him.

"Something like that." Julius was wearing a tan jacket over a black turtleneck. He had on a pair of Gucci loafers and tailor-made pants. "I told you we have a problem; and yes, we need to do something about it."

"Well, what the fuck you got? J., show me what you got."

The younger Julius pulled the envelope from his pocket and put it in front of the stout man.

Roscoe peeled open the envelope with meaty hands and pulled out the glossy photos. He flipped through them, showing no emotion. "Julius, this ain't shit. You got some photos of my man's car? So what if he outside the club? We ain't a bunch of fucking Mormons or something. A man's got the right to live."

"You need to look closer at the window, my brother. He's making a hand off. What you're missing is we followed him all night. Look at all the different stops; he's making deliveries all over town. All those photos are from one night," Julius said.

"So you say. He could have been doing a number of things; that don't mean he's dealing."

J. J. chimed in, "What the fuck else could he be doing? Tell him about the trick, Dad."

Roscoe glared at his nephew with a stare that told him he was out of turn in this conversation. J. J. looked down from his uncle's gaze.

"We also have confirmation from a hooker that he's been pushing blow and ecstasy through them. Lady that works Midtown."

"And, what? She just fucking volunteered this information to you? Answered a hotline or some shit?" asked Roscoe with a chuckle. "Man, Julius, why you want to bring this shit in here? This don't prove nothing to me."

Roscoe stood, walked to the fridge, and grabbed a sandwich. He didn't offer his brother and nephew anything. He took a seat and opened the roast beef hoagie, which was loaded with banana peppers, onions, and lettuce. Roscoe took a bite; his body language showed indifference to the evidence being presented to him.

"J., man, you think some beat-up-ass hooker's bullshit and some photos going to make me off one of my own? Come the fuck on, you need to get to stepping. None of that means shit to me, and I know King would agree with me. We can take this up with him if we need to." Roscoe took a massive bite from his sandwich, chewing it loudly. He turned his attention to the TV and was about the grab the remote in an effort to dismiss his guests.

"Well, there's also this." Julius pulled out his phone and hit some buttons, bringing up a video. The image of a man duct-taped to a chair appeared. Roscoe stopped chewing midbite as he looked down and saw the man he knew as Treyvon Singletary, who was obviously in pain and screaming. He had been beaten and had blood all over the front of his shirt, which appeared a deep purple or dark red from all the blood loss. His left eye was swollen shut, and his face was puffy, with cuts over both eyes. His arms were taped in place on the arms of the chair; his left hand appeared to be a mangled, bloody mess.

"Please stop, man, I done told you everything! Don't cut no more of my fingers off!! NO, man—no, don't burn me again!!" The sound was garbled; Roscoe could tell Trey was missing most of his teeth.

The phone zoomed in to show a bloody stump where his left index finger used to be. It looked managed and at the same time disfigured as it had been removed. The end of the finger above the first knuckle had been removed and the nub had been burned shut, cauterizing the wound. Roscoe could see that at least two of his fingers had been removed and sealed this way.

"What you got to say, motherfucker!" yelled a voice from off camera. "What the fuck you got to say!"

"I been dealin' round town, man! What the fuck? We all boys, why you doin' this to me, Shea?!"

"You ain't my boy, motherfucker. You putting us all in danger, and you got to pay."

A second figure dressed in black appeared and hit Trey four times, splattering further blood on him. Treyvon let out a howl and then a gasp as he took the assault. After that, only a low moan could be heard.

Roscoe stood up, walked to the trashcan, and threw up his sandwich. Julius put his phone back into his jacket pocket after cutting off the video. The result a forgone conclusion in Roscoe's mind.

"Amazing what you can find out with a little effort, a pair of clippers, and a blowtorch. Thing is, Roscoe, he told us everything before we removed the first finger. That fucking weak-ass fucker talked after he lost some teeth. So what do you think that bitch would talk about if he got pinched?"

Roscoe turned back to his brother and nephew. "You are fucked up, Julius."

With that, Julius came out of his chair, moving like a big cat and taking a circular route to his brother, who was hovering over the sink beside the fridge. He never took his eyes off of his brother. He approached on Roscoe's right as Roscoe stood up straight, wiping his mouth with the back of his hand; and the two men stood toe-to-toe.

Julius's piercing eyes looked into the watering eyes of his larger, older sibling. Rage and fury took control as Julius spoke. "No, your weak-ass boy is fucked up, and now he's a memory! You feel me?" He screamed at the larger man and got within inches of his face. "I am cleaning up your mess, Roscoe! I told you what was going on and you couldn't deal with it, so I dealt with it for your punk-ass. Weak-ass motherfuckers will get us all thrown in jail, Coe."

Julius stared his brother down, and Roscoe looked away first. Julius backed off and straightened his jacket, never taking his eyes off his brother.

The larger man looked down, a tear forming in his eye as he realized that a boy he'd known for years was probably dead by now, tucked away in some dumpster. Roscoe had known Trey's mother, Clarice, for decades; and now her baby boy was gone. Just like that, a boy he'd seen almost every day had vanished. Feelings of disgust and useless loss overwhelmed him. He couldn't look at Julius; he just looked away. Roscoe had done bad things, but never to one of their own. Never to someone he considered part of the family. He hated what Julius had done, but he also knew that Julius was right—he just didn't want to admit or believe that this was what they were . . . what they had become.

"I'll have a new crew member for you to finish prepping the truck for the next delivery. Trey won't be around no more." Julius nodded at his son and headed to the door. J. J. left the photos on the table and followed his father.

Julius paused at the door and, without turning, began to speak. "Don't you ever mention King to me like he going to cover your mistakes. King ain't here, and that means I'm in fucking charge. Don't you ever say his name to me again like he gonna make a difference about what goes on right now on these streets. You feel me . . . my brother?" He pushed open the door and headed back into the dark night.

MARLOW

The meeting was to take place in the Midtown Atlanta area in a suite at The Georgian Terrace, a hotel that had been established in 1911 and once housed the cast of *Gone with the Wind*. The glorious white brick and marble hotel was located on Peachtree Street, directly across from The Fox Theater, which hosted musical acts and shows.

Marlow had arrived earlier that day and checked in to a recently renovated suite upstairs looking out over the cityscape. The room was well-appointed, with brand-new oversized couches and chairs along with sleek contemporary wooden furniture pieces. There was also a small kitchen, not that he would be cooking or even spending much time in the room during his stay. The room had been booked simply for this meeting, a meeting on the future of the Johnson family enterprise. While nothing special, the room would be the setting over the next hour for a conversation that would affect the futures of many in the family.

Marlow was sitting on the couch drinking bottled water when he heard the keycard hit the door.

"Hey, Marlow," said John Archibald as he entered, surveying the room. He was wearing a light-beige sport coat and matching pants with a white shirt and tie. "Been a while since I've been here; the renovation looks good. I like what they did with the lobby and restaurant."

"Yeah, it looks pretty dope," replied Marlow. He was wearing a black bomber jacket and jeans. Atlanta was still fighting a late spring chill, and the wind kept the temperature difficult to predict. Marlow had gotten out of Phoenix earlier that morning greeted by a late spring chill that dumped snow to his north, in Colorado.

Marlow rose and hugged his friend, patting him on the back. "Uncle J. coming to this powwow?" he asked.

"Yep—big news, I guess. I met with King last week," said John as he took a seat in a white oversized chair facing the couch.

Marlow returned to his seat. "So what's the verdict?"

"No-go on expansion," replied John. "We don't have the manpower to pull it off safely."

"I figured that would be the answer. Can't say I'm disappointed." Marlow leaned back against the couch. "How am I supposed to let Rojas know we can't do it?"

"Tell him the truth: We don't have enough men we can trust to make it happen, and we aren't comfortable going into new territory with un-proven assets."

"You think that will satisfy them?"

"Well, the way to deliver it is to say that we aren't going to take their product on consignment. Our relationship with them has always been that we paid 100 percent up front." John put his elbows on his knees, put-ting his hands together. "We don't want to risk their product with people we can't trust, and our operation is at capacity now with the routes we have in place. The way to deliver the news is that we value our relation-ship with them, and we wouldn't want to overreach."

"Sounds good when you say it that way, but the reality is these guys may not like the answer, and I'm the one who has to deliver it." Marlow had a look of concern on his face.

"Business is business," replied John. "It would be a bad business decision for both sides to expand when we can't guarantee delivery."

"We do have a short-term alternative that we can offer."

"What's that?" asked Marlow.

"Our buyers in New York and Philadelphia have agreed to double their orders for the next six months, so we'll be increasing our buys for those two areas. That's roughly five hundred more keys per month for six months."

"That's nice, but I think Ceasar had something larger in mind," said Marlow, looking over at John.

There was a knock on the door and a third keycard hit the electronic lock. The last members of the meeting arrived as Julius and J. J. entered the room. Julius was wearing a pinstriped black suit with a blazing-red tie and gray overcoat. His son was dressed in a camel-colored jacket with a white knit shirt and no tie. J. J. was clean-shaven, and Julius's goatee had been trimmed.

"Gentlemen," said Julius.

The other two men stood, and all four shook hands and exchanged the standard greetings before they returned to their seats. Julius took a seat next to his nephew, and J. J. sat in a second white chair opposite John.

"I was just telling Marlow that the decision has been made not to engage in the cartel's expansion request," John said, jumping right in.

"Can't say that's a bad thing," replied Julius. "They got blood all over the streets up there in Chi-Town."

John spent the next few minutes recapping much of the same conversation he'd just had with Marlow. The group was in agreement that the expansion was not in the family's best interest at this time. The four men talked about the upcoming months and expected delivery numbers. J. J. said very little, and his father was unusually pleasant.

"Julius, that brings us to the last piece of business," said John. "It's time for us to transition the money-cleaning part of the business to Julius."

Julius's eyes lit up, and he cracked a little half smile momentarily. "So the King has deemed me worthy of handling the family jewels?"

John looked over at him. "Now you know it's never been about that."

"I'm kidding, John. I can understand my brother wanting control while he's away. Just joking about it. We're all family, you know that."

John thought to himself for a moment. "No, really it's more about keeping on the timeline. We're on schedule to be out of this line of business by the end of the year."

Marlow and J. J. both looked at John with slight surprise.

Julius didn't miss a beat. "So the grand plan is on track, I take it," he said with a hint of sarcasm.

"Yes, it is, Julius. Any problem with that?" John looked over at him. "King is also on track to be released on schedule. The plan has always been to be completely done with running drugs when he gets out."

"Oh, I remember the plan. Just guess I'm not being clear," said Julius, and he stood up and walked over to the bar to get a bottle of water. "I never thought the day would come, and I'm glad to see it get here. That's all, John."

"Well, it is almost here, Julius; and with that, we're on schedule to shut this thing down by the end of the year," said John.

"That's good to know," replied Julius. "We got anything else to cover?"

"Nope, that's it," answered John as he stood up. "Marlow, J. J., good to see you." He reached over and shook hands with both men, who were obviously still a little struck by the news they'd just heard.

John walked over to Julius and shook his hand. "I'll see you next week for the regular intel for King." He left the three Johnson men in the suite and walked toward the elevator that overlooked the atrium below. He thought it had been too easy. He had fully expected more fight from Julius.

"Marlow, your aunt Della wants you over at the house tonight for dinner," said Julius after John had left. He looked at his nephew, who was still sitting there with a dumbfounded look on his face, still processing what John Archibald had said.

"Don't you worry none, youngblood. You come to dinner tonight. We need to talk," Julius said to Marlow, who looked up and nodded. "See you at the house around seven."

With that, Julius and J. J. exited the room and took the same path John had taken to the elevator. It was just the two men in the elevator, heading down to the lobby.

Once inside, J. J. began to speak to his dad. "Dad, what the fuck is he talking about us stopping—"

"Not here, son." Julius shot him a look that meant to keep quiet.

As they walked across the marble lobby and past the two circular couches, J. J. reached in his pocket and pulled out a valet ticket. Neither of them noticed the man who silently followed them out the door and walked away from them as they got their SUV. The man continued walking away from the father and son as they pulled onto Peachtree; then an unmarked Crown Victoria pulled up to the street curb. The man got in the passenger seat and told the driver to follow the SUV that had just pulled out.

The middle-aged white male looked over at the driver, a younger man who wore Ray-Ban Aviator sunglasses and a black leather jacket and had a crew cut. "You get the GPS in place?"

"Yep, it's in place," replied the driver as they pulled away from the curb and into traffic.

The tracking device monitor was sitting between the two men and showed a dot moving away from their position on Peachtree. The older man looked down at it, then back up at the SUV heading away from them. "Good. Let's see where they take us."

With that, they followed Julius and his son from the hotel down the street to parts unknown.

JULIUS

Marlow dialed the number again, and it went straight to voicemail. Nervous didn't really register with him because everything was relative, but it wasn't like Trey not to answer him for three straight days. In the drug-trafficking business, when people mysteriously disappeared, it was generally not a good thing. Marlow had driven by his partner's house in the Midtown area several times, and he hadn't seen his car. After the meeting with his uncle and John, he had planned to meet up with Trey to check in on their side project.

For the past six months, Marlow had been working with Trey to move keys of coke on the side to some local contacts, in direct violation of his uncle's edict not to deal in the Atlanta market. He had grown up with Trey, and they were keeping it as quiet as possible. Marlow knew from day one that King and Banks planned to end their trafficking days, but that wasn't what he had in mind. Someone would have to take up the mantle, and there was a lot of money to be made. Marlow had been building a network of guys he could trust; and while setting up the regular delivery for Cass, he had been putting together his own deliveries to Atlanta.

Marlow always knew that as the point of contact with the cartel, he may have some other opportunity down the road; and he felt that day was getting closer. So while hearing John Archibald tell him the family was getting out of the drug trade soon, he had different plans. While he didn't have his uncle Kingston's connections up and down the East Coast, that was the funny thing about cocaine: It sold itself. Marlow was making his own plans, and they did not include getting out of the business anytime soon. He had his own fortune to make, and he was still young.

All of a sudden, a phone number he recognized hit him up on his burner phone. Trey's phone, finally coming to life.

"Where the fuck you been at, man?' Marlow asked. Nervous energy made his legs spring to action as he spoke. He stood up and walked around the suite where he'd just had the meeting.

"I think it's about time you and I had a talk, nephew." The cold voice of Julius, Sr. was on the other end the line.

Marlow stopped dead in his tracks in the middle of the suite. "Uncle J.? What you doing with Trey's phone?" he said, trying to play it cool. He knew this was bad, but he was hoping to play it off.

"Cut the bullshit, Marlow. Trey told me everything I needed to know. We need to have a talk . . . right now, not on this line. Come downstairs. Shea will be waiting for you in the lobby to bring you to me." With that, the line went dead.

Marlow stood still, thinking about what had just happened. Obviously his uncle knew he'd been dealing behind Kingston's back, and he knew the penalty for such an offense. But something didn't add up. Why the act in front of John just thirty minutes earlier? What had Trey told him? Would his uncle really kill his own nephew?

None of these questions could be answered waiting in the hotel room, and he damn sure knew that he wasn't in a position to blow his uncle off. He went to the back bedroom, pulled out his knife, and put it in his jacket's inner pocket; then he went into the hotel safe and pulled out a nickel-plated revolver, which he put in the small of his back. He knew six shots wouldn't be enough against Julius and his thugs, but he would at least have something if this thing went bad. Pulling out his regular phone, he thought about calling his dad or Devon; but he realized if he made that call, he'd just be pulling them into his mess. He had no doubt in his mind that if his uncle did kill him, nothing on earth would stop Roscoe from getting revenge. At the same time, he felt there was something else Julius wanted, and he needed to let this play out to discover what that was.

As he exited the room, he pulled on his jacket and then walked to the elevator in the atrium. He hit the button for the ground floor and took a deep breath. Stay cool, Marlow, stay cool, he thought to himself. These people are family. Ain't nobody going to hurt you.

As he left the lobby, he saw big Shea waiting for him.

"What up, playa," Shea said and gave him a half hug. Marlow made sure to stay leaned over to conceal the pistol in the small of his back. A black Escalade waited for them in front of the hotel, facing back out to Peachtree. Big Rod was sitting in the front seat. Shea opened the door for Marlow and slid in behind him.

"Man, where we going?" asked Marlow as he leaned back in the SUV's pilot seat.

Rodney turned to him and Marlow saw the Glock in the man's left hand, pointing at him. "Where's yo piece, Low?" the big man said without hesitation. At the same time, Shea began to pat him down and quickly grabbed the revolver from the small of his back.

"Man, what the fuck!" exclaimed Marlow. Fear crept into his mind, knowing both of these men and their reputations.

"He's good now. Roll out," Shea said to Rodney, who engaged the gearshift and pulled out onto Peachtree. Shea put Marlow's gun in the side pocket of his jacket.

The vehicle turned east onto North Avenue.

"Low, your uncle said you need to stay cool. You understand? If he wanted you dead, you'd be dead," Shea said with a cold, even tone. "We ain't here to hurt you."

Rain started to drizzle and splattered on the windshield as the truck sped down the street, away from downtown Atlanta and toward the Old Fourth Ward. The three men were silent as the truck drove into the night, the windshield wipers sporadically wiping the glass clean.

Finally, Marlow broke the silence: "What does he want?"

"That be for him to tell you and for you to listen," said Rodney from the driver's seat.

Shea looked at Marlow from the seat beside him. "I suggest you listen."

The SUV pulled off North Avenue and onto Linden Avenue; Freedom Park, one of the largest parks in the city, was on the right side of the street. The park formed a cross shape, with The Carter Center and the Jimmy Carter Library and Museum at the center. The park and its lands had begun formation in the 1960s only to be halted in the 1970s by Jimmy Carter, ironically enough. The park had been overgrown and basically of no use to anyone until the Olympic Games came to Atlanta in 1996, and then it experienced a rebirth. It was finally completed and opened to the public in 2000.

The Escalade turned onto an access road and drove to a spot where Marlow saw his uncle's vehicle waiting. The rain was still coming down when they parked, and Shea motioned for Marlow to exit to his left. The two cars were facing each other with their headlights dimmed.

Marlow could see Julius standing outside in the drizzle. He walked toward his uncle. "What the fuck is all this about, Uncle J.?" All Marlow could see was the silhouette his uncle cast with the headlights behind him.

"Opportunity," replied the shadow.

"What you talking about?" asked Marlow. He put his hands in his jacket pockets.

"Your boy Trey told me about what you been running, and your boy Trey is not round no more," said Julius in an even voice. There was no emotion in his statements. "You can cut the bullshit. I know everything."

"So what's that mean to me?" replied Marlow. He swallowed back his grief. He had known Trey for decades, but there was no time for him to worry about that right now. He needed to figure out what his uncle wanted. "I can assume since we talking, that must mean something."

"You right about that, youngblood. Let's take a walk."

With that, the two men walked away from the SUVs and farther into the park.

"Let's just say I don't agree with my brother's belief that we can no longer do business with Mexico," Julius said to his nephew as they walked. "I think King wants out, and I think it's time for him and Banks to get out. I also think it's time for new leadership."

Marlow looked at his uncle. "You mean kill Uncle King?"

"No, boy. I wouldn't do that to my brother, but I do think it's time for us to expand the business on our own. I need you for that; and as you can see after our meeting with old John tonight, you'll need me. We need each other to make this work."

Marlow pulled a cigarette from his coat pocket and offered one to his uncle, who instead pulled out two thick Cuban cigars and handed one to his nephew.

"It's time for us to lead," he said as he pulled out a mini butane torch and lit the cigars. Julius had used the same torch to cauterize the ends of Trey's fingers after Shea had amputated them with a bolt cutter.

"So what you was saying back there with John was all a cover. You want me to take these routes down from the cartel." Marlow was realizing that this could work. He had the connection with Rojas—the same Ceasar Rojas who was shooting up the Sinaloa Cartel's ranks like a rocket heading for the moon.

"What about King and Banks? Where we going to get the money?"

"You let me worry about that. I'm gonna need you to set up the buy, and we need the routes that King and Banks don't know nothing about. This is our deal. I just need you to talk to Mexico and set it up and tell me how much. I'll send Rodney out there with you so you got some backup."

Marlow took a puff off his cigar. He thought to himself, No way Rodney will be there to protect me—more like he'll be out there to watch and eventually try to take the connection from me. "It's fine if he comes out there, but them boys down south is crazy right now. All the shit with Chapo got them backward. Ain't no way we can introduce nobody new to them right now."

"True, but you need some muscle out there; and you going to need some drivers. Rodney can bring his cousins with him to handle the driving, and you use your normal crew to do the upfit on the trucks. Just like we do going to Atlanta."

Julius stopped his nephew from walking farther by touching his shoulder. "Most important, you can't let Roscoe know what's going on. Let's get some runs under our belt and some bread in the bank before we bring him in on it. You also can't bring Cass in the loop at all—he's Banks's boy from college. We got to use our people, people we can trust. The opportunity is too great; and after watching your boy Trey fuck up in town, we got to stick together on this shit. The one thing I do agree with is we got to keep the shit out of our backyard. Too much heat."

"I know what you mean; Roscoe would go right back to King." Marlow took too deep a drag off the cigar and started to cough.

"You ain't used to no Cubans, nephew. We going to have to teach you to upgrade," Julius said with a smile. The two Johnson men were in agreement. They knew they needed each other—Marlow needed Julius and the access to the buy money, and Julius needed the connection Marlow had to the Sinaloa Cartel. But both men still questioned whether or not they could trust each other. For now, it would be this way: an alliance of necessity.

The pair laughed and walked farther into the darkness of the park. Neither were aware of the sedan that had quietly pulled into another part of the park—the same sedan that had been at The Georgian Terrace. The two men inside silently watched and waited.

MARLOW

The trip back to Arizona had been less than pleasant. Marlow'd had travel companions, and he was used to being a solo operator. The reality that his uncle had killed one of his best friends from childhood—for doing something Marlow had asked him to do—was finally setting in. Even more troubling to Marlow was that he knew he could only trust his uncle so much. If Julius trusted *him*, why did he have a hulking Rodney and two new crew members he barely knew along with him?

The new crew members were Rodney's cousins, Marcus and Quincy Dillon. They had grown up around the East Point and College Park area in Georgia. Marcus had played a little ball at Georgia State, and Quincy was a high school dropout. Combined, they probably had an IQ of about 100; but they fit the part of additional muscle. Both men tipped the scales at over two hundred pounds, with Marcus having the build of a former athlete. Both men were older than Marlow, and both were following Rodney's lead.

Since their first meeting, Rodney had only grown mildly more pleasant and slightly less dangerous since they couldn't carry weapons on the plane. They flew into Phoenix with a layover in Dallas. Marlow had already figured out that the three men would be bunking up at his house for the foreseeable future.

Marlow had already made arrangements via the Manuel-Rios brothers to meet with Ceasar Rojas the following day in Mexico. He would made it clear the meeting was to be with them only. Any contact between his new companions and the cartel was to be off-limits.

Marlow's trust in his uncle Julius had been in short supply since he killed Trey. Marlow knew that the cartel's loyalty was only so deep and that ultimately green was the only color that mattered; but with all the recent arrests at the top of the cartel, they weren't exactly looking to meet and greet new people. This would be a valid excuse for not taking Rodney and the Dillon brothers with him to Mexico.

As they arrived at Marlow's house in a Phoenix suburb, Marlow started to go over some ground rules. "All right, since you guys are going to be here for a while, we need to get some shit together and understand a few things about these cats."

Rodney sat down on the couch and stretched out, putting up his feet. The other two men took seats on either side of their cousin. Marlow had a seventy-inch Sony TV set up with a video game system. Quincy saw it and got up, approaching the gaming system. "Damn, son, you got the new PlayStation and everything."

"Don't touch that!" Marlow set down his carry-on.

Quincy looked up at him with disdain.

"Like I was saying, we got to get a few ground rules down. First, you guys need to realize you don't exist out here without me; and we have two different games going on at the same time. You guys have to be invisible around here until we can get you set up."

"What you mean by invisible?" asked Marcus. "We out here to be your backup, fool!"

"Not exactly," corrected Rodney. "Listen to what he's got to say."

"We have two different sets of shipments. Our driver will be arriving from Atlanta in a few days—don't know exactly when. We won't get a call until he's about to drop the car." Marlow opened a bottle of water he had with him. It had already been after 10:00 p.m. when their flight landed, so it was getting late. "Once we get the drop car, we'll have two loads of money. One is for the shipment going back with Cass, the Atlanta driver. Now Cass is close with Banks, and he doesn't know where I live, so you guys can't be around when I pick up the car. From there, we'll split up the payment, taking out what will go to the cartel for the Atlanta shipment.

"Julius is going to have his man in Atlanta pack the car with the cash for our buy going to Chicago. I'm going to Mexico tomorrow to set up that buy. My crew here will prepare the truck and the compartments, and they don't need to know nothing about you. You guys will drive to Chicago while Rodney stays here with me. You'll unload and return to Atlanta with the cash. On this trip, we'll use the same truck for both runs. You'll be disguised as movers, with papers and everything. The product will be in a compartment in the fuel tank. I'll show you how to load and unload it. You get pulled by a regular cop, you should be okay; but anything with a drug dog, you guys better play your parts."

"Who you want to go with you?" asked Marcus. He seemed oblivious to the facts Marlow had just laid out to him. To him, the answer to his question would tell him all he needed to know about his new crew.

"Nobody can go with me," replied Marlow.

Rodney looked at him funny. The glance told Marlow everything he needed to know. Rodney tried to play it off and cover for Marcus's question at the same time. "No problem, we can hang back," he said. "You want us to follow you?"

"Hell no!" Marlow looked at him like he'd asked if he could fuck his sister. "I don't even know where the meet will be, man. It's black bags over my head and CIA shit the whole way after I cross the border. These motherfucking Mexicans are crazy. You guys try to follow me and they will fucking kill you and bury you in the desert. The shit you hear about and read about is true, man. These cartel guys are killers, and they don't give a fuck. You fuck up and you die—it's that simple. When you guys get to sleep tonight, dream about barrels of acid. That's how fucking hard these motherfuckers are, and don't forget it. You don't meet them at all for any reason!"

Quincy's face paled, turning an ashen gray. The message had been received by at least one of the new crew members.

Rodney looked at Marlow and shook his head. "I ain't ending up in no fucking barrel. We'll cool it out right here on your couch." Rodney leaned back and took the remote. "What channel is ESPN?"

"Another thing: you guys don't mess around with the PlayStation. That's one way I talk to Banks, wherever he is, and he may be able to tell when I go online. We usually talk while playing *Call of Duty* or *Warcraft*. Nobody touch it. You guys got it?"

Marlow walked back to his bedroom knowing he was stuck in the middle of a dangerous game. On one side he had the cartel and on the other side, his uncle and his men. None of whom he could trust, and all just as likely to kill him as help him when the chips hit the table. For some strange reason, Jimi Hendrix's "All Along the Watchtower" popped into his head: "'There must be some kind of way out here,' said the joker to the thief." Marlow shut the door to his room and collapsed on his bed.

Maybe he could get a little sleep before he had to get into an SUV with a black bag over his head and meet with a druglord who could potentially be the next El Chapo at some unknown location in a third-world country. Yep, I should sleep tight tonight, he thought. At least he knew Rodney and his crew wouldn't be killing him tonight.

One simple thought came into Marlow's head: How the fuck did I get in this position, and how do I get out of it?

AGENT GOODING

Agents Gooding and Roman pulled up to the address and parked across the street. The residence of the confidential informant known as Zeus appeared exactly like it had the last time he'd made contact with the FBI, which had been a number of years prior.

"How you want to play this?" Roman asked

"Not sure yet. Let's get eyeballs on him and go from there. I'm thinking we pull him over away from the property and take him to a neutral meeting site." The agents had decided against a phone call to this particular CI since he had been cold for some time. They wanted to make sure he was still around.

Before, he had provided information that had been successful in helping stop a marijuana operation that included his own brother. The case file showed that the CI had been busted with a weapon and narcotics in the Snellville area. A hit for a previous incident in Tampa alerted the FBI to his presence in Atlanta, and they were called in when he gave up information about the large-scale delivery operation his brother was running across state lines. Once he gave up the operation, he became property of the Federal Bureau of Investigation.

"This guy's record includes a weapons charge, but he cooperated after a bust. Let's pull him over and see how he reacts."

The two agents spotted their man leaving his house and getting into a dark SUV. They followed him down the road, creeping up behind him after they drove a few miles. Roman was driving the agents; Gooding put on their lights to signal the vehicle to stop. The SUV complied, pulling over on the side of the street.

Agent Gooding exited the passenger's side and walked up to the driver's side door, his FBI badge hanging from his neck. He cautiously approached, and the window rolled down. "Afternoon."

The man behind the wheel looked at him and realized this was not a normal traffic stop. "I wasn't aware the FBI gave out speeding tickets."

"Mr. Johnson, we would like to have a discussion with you. Perhaps there's a more private place for us to talk." Agent Gooding flashed his picture ID and identified himself.

"Ain't nowhere around here going to be good for that," replied the driver. "You want to go somewhere a little closer to your place?"

"Why don't you just park here and get in the car with us. We just want to have a talk," replied Agent Gooding. "There's a parking garage right up the road about a quarter mile." Gooding opened the door to the SUV.

Roman had killed the lights on the car, making it a little less obvious, and the two men approached from the SUV. Gooding opened the door for their new companion. Once both were inside, the Crown Vic pulled back out into traffic, leaving the other vehicle on the side of the road. Traffic was light, and they pulled into the parking garage in minutes, with Roman taking a ticket and driving them up several levels until there were less than a couple dozen cars on their level. The three men had ridden in silence.

"Mr. Johnson. Do you mind if we call you Julius?" Gooding asked as he pulled a file from the dashboard and opened it. The file gave a brief write-up on the CI known as Zeus and on the operation that netted his brother Kingston. The agent who had previously handled Julius had given him that code name since he was turning on his brother, who often went by King for short. Naming him Hades may have been too close to the truth.

"Not at all, Agent . . . not sure I caught your name?" replied Julius as he sat in the back of the car. His suit was a dark charcoal with pinstripes. He remained calm, like a cardplayer waiting to see what his opponent revealed to him.

"Agent Gooding, and this is Agent Roman. Let's cut to the chase: You provided the federal government with information that led to several arrests a number of years ago. For that, you received leniency on a number of issues. Well, we're currently looking for information; and we believe you may be able to assist us again."

"I'm not sure what you gentlemen think I may be able to assist you with. I'm a legitimate businessman, and my past is not my present."

"Really? Is that how you want to play this?" asked Agent Roman, speaking for the first time.

Gooding raised his hand slightly to stop Roman from going any further. "You provided information about drug trafficking, and frankly you may be in the know about certain activity that we find of use. You may have heard of large amount of cocaine being moved through the city from Mexico."

"I thought my time working for the FBI was over. I remember something about it only being a three-year deal. Where's Agent Howard, the guy I worked with before?"

"He's retired. And you belong to us as long as we need you. What we need is information on the streets, and we have a feeling you may have something valuable to offer old Uncle Sam." Agent Gooding talked in a low voice.

"I have no idea what you're talking about. Is this some kind of racial thing? Because I'm black, you think I know where drugs hit these streets?" Julius asked with slight agitation in his voice. He quickly realized that if they were having this conversation instead of him just being arrested, the agents must have very little to go on. Perhaps this presents an opportunity, he thought to himself. Julius adjusted his tie slightly. He had on a red silk tie, and his suit cost more than the two agents in the front seat earned in a month. He reminded himself that he was in control. He could handle this. He relaxed a little and decided to wait the agents out. He remained silent until Agent Gooding spoke again.

"Now, Mr. Johnson, let's cut the bullshit. You rolled over on your own brother and you've been a free man on the streets because of that. We are interested in information; and we believe with some effort on your part, you may be able to find what we're looking for. This group would have ties to the Mexican cartels. If you know something or hear something, we would appreciate your cooperation."

Gooding stopped for a second and then turned back to Julius. "Or perhaps we can discuss this with your brother Kingston? I believe he's right over at USP here in Atlanta. You know, the prison you put him in when you ratted on him about the shipment he got busted with in Alabama."

Julius just glared at Gooding, not saying anything.

Gooding peeled a card from his front pocket and handed it to Julius. "I expect we'll hear from you if you hear anything," he said. "I think, given your status, we'll officially reactivate you as a confidential informant for the FBI. I will expect to hear from you in the next week with an update. You didn't think your freedom these last few years meant we had forgotten about you, did you?"

Agent Gooding stared right into Julius's eyes, not wavering. "You can get out now." He turned his head and torso back to face the front of the car. His message was clear that Julius was now not only working for the FBI again, but that he was also being excused and left to walk back to his car.

With that, Julius exited the back of the car. The two agents pulled off, leaving him in the parking garage with his thoughts. For the first time in a long time, he was nervous. This had not been expected; and it was an unwelcomed intrusion, given the moves he was about to make. He thought they were on obviously on the track to find their group. They were missing something—otherwise, he'd be in handcuffs right now and not walking back to his truck.

The anxiety would not be leaving him any time soon; he needed to think, and he needed to get a plan in place. There were a lot of decisions to be made, and all of them could mean prosperity or destruction for him. The next moves would be some of the most important of his life.

I guess if it's information they want, I'll need to come up with some-thing to give them, he thought and immediately brought to mind a partic-ular thorn in his side. Maybe it wouldn't be a bad idea to give them some information. They obviously didn't believe he was a legitimate business-man; and the risk of them telling Kingston what he'd done, even while he was behind bars, could be potentially devastating. Banks still controlled almost all of the family money. Julius could potentially only have access to cash he'd saved up on his own. If Kingston found out now, he could also potentially kill any deal with the cartel before they had the chance to get some money under their belts with the Chicago and Pittsburgh runs.

The next few moves are going to be critical, thought Julius as he picked up the phone and sent a message to Marlow.

When he reached his Denali, he got in and pulled back into traffic. He didn't notice the sedan that had been parked a block away and that had witnessed his meeting with the two agents. The sedan and the two men inside had stayed behind, watching his SUV. Now, the passenger picked up a cell phone and made a call as they pulled into traffic a few car lengths behind Julius.

PETE

Opening day at Fenway Park was always special, and this year the Red Sox had opened on the road for their first two series. Pete had flown up to catch the first game with Josh and his friends. The Northeast was experiencing some late-winter effects, and the needle had barely moved into the upper thirties. Luckily there was no rain in the forecast and the game would take place. It would still be a crisp day, but Pete was looking forward to all the sights, sounds, and smells of the ballpark. The cooked hot dogs, the popcorn, and the draft beer. The Fenway faithful, the bunting, and the Sox. It was opening day. A day for friends and family and baseball.

"Dad, you think the Sox got a chance this year?" Joshua asked as they walked toward one of the great cathedrals of baseball. He was wearing a down North Face jacket with a Red Sox cap turned around backward.

"The Sox have a chance every year, son," replied Pete. He was wearing a heavy coat with a black scarf, a knit cap with the Sox logo on it, gloves, and a pair of jeans. Pete had grown up around the Red Sox and raised his sons the same way. Even if they couldn't talk about anything else, they could talk baseball.

"Wish Thomas could have joined us," said Josh. "I got some great seats down the third-base line."

Nelson and Jimmy Clements had joined them, leaving Franco to run the bar back in Southie. The bar would be packed today, even with it being a Monday game. Baseball was a low-traffic game for Josh's bookmaking business, but they had just finished up a successful season of college basketball, which was Josh's second-best moneymaker, behind football.

"Copperfield's for a quick shot, guys?" Jimmy asked the group as they made their way down Ipswich Street toward a row of restaurants, pubs, and bars that were directly behind the famed Green Monster in Fenway's left field. Red Sox Nation was already out, even at eleven in the morning, starting to fill up the pubs and eateries around the stadium as everyone got ready for another season.

"Man, Copperfield's is gone. It closed end of last season," said Nelson. "Damn shame. We've been going there for years." He wore a red down jacket to protect him from the cold.

The group followed the crowd, making their way toward the street, which was closed off even now, three hours before the first pitch. Boston was celebrating a form of a working holiday; opening day for the Red Sox had taken hold of the city.

"How about Lansdowne Pub, boys? That's the closest thing to Copperfield's. No corporate shitholes like Jillian's or House of Blues. I want a true Irish shithole if we can't go back to Copperfield's," said Pete with a little laugh. He bundled his scarf around his neck one more time against the wind as they took a right onto Lansdowne. The four men walked into the Lansdowne Pub, with its rich mahogany wood paneling on brick. Large mirrors advertising Guinness beer hung on the walls. There were two patios outside; the group braved the elements and took one of the gray high-tops. Jimmy and Nelson ran inside to get the group pints of beer and some shots.

"So how did you make out on the basketball?" Pete asked Josh, who was sitting beside him. The wind whipped down the alleyway and across the patio. They were slightly off the main drag, where fans were congregating, and nobody else was outside at any of the other tables. It was slightly before lunch, but the tables would be filled shortly with fans on their way to the game stopping in for a quick bite.

The Celtics had finished a decent season, but most fans were ready for baseball after the lose by their beloved Patriots a few months ago. Pete had never gotten into basketball and quit watching the Celtics altogether after Larry Bird and Kevin McHale retired. Boston, in general, still had some deep racial undertones; and the Celtics hadn't been the same since Bird and McHale hung it up. That left two seasons in Pete's mind: the Patriots and Red Sox were the main attractions.

He had tried to follow the Braves in Atlanta; but once you have your team in professional sports, you have your team. It's hard to change allegiance after decades of loving a pro franchise. Pete followed the Sox and he tolerated the Braves.

"We did well. All the upsets got us positive early on, and we never looked back." Josh was studying his phone as he talked to his dad in a hushed voice. As Shakespeare said, "Discretion is the better part of valor."

Nelson joined them at the table and sat across from the two Murphy men. "Starting to get crazy in there." He set two pints of a light IPA in front of Josh and Pete.

"We've got about $325,000 for you to take back with you," Josh said before taking a sip from his beer.

Pete had flown up on a one-way ticket and would be driving back to Atlanta in two days. He would be taking a care package with him to spread across their metro area banks over the next few weeks.

"You guys did do good this year. That's way more than last year," Pete said as he took off one of his gloves and gripped the pint glass.

About that time, Jimmy arrived with a tray carrying a second round of beer and some shots of Jameson whiskey to warm their souls. "This wind is a fuckin' pissa," he said as he deposited the drinks on the table.

Each of the men took up one of the plastic cups of alcohol. "Here's to the Sox!" Jimmy said. "Salute!"

They all took down their drinks with a slight gasp as the warmth went over their tongues and down the back of their throats with a burn.

"Whew, breakfast of champions, boys!" said Josh as he put the plastic shot glass back on the tray. "Hopefully the Sox will show for us today."

"They had a good road trip to start the season; we should be back in the thick of it this year, my boy. It should be a good year," said Pete, taking a gulp of beer to wash down the whiskey.

Pete thought to himself about the news that John and the rest of them would soon be out of the laundry business for the Johnson family. It was shaping up to be a good year already. Pete looked at his son and his friends and thought, This is a good year after all. Pete was happy and secure; now if the Red Sox would just show up, the day would be perfect.

He looked down at his cell phone and saw some messages; he decided he'd deal with them after the game. No reason to spoil the party with work today. Today was for family and the Sox.

MARLOW

It had been near eleven at night when his journey had begun. He had crossed the border into Nogales, Mexico, and waited. A convoy of black Yukons pulled up, and he got into the middle one with Javy Manuel-Rios, who was wearing all black and had cowboy boots on. Marlow had a duffle bag with him, which Javy took and placed in the back of the SUV. They had, of course, put a black hood over his head; and then they had driven around Nogales for nearly an hour.

When they stopped and removed his hood, he saw they were in a parking lot behind a white hotel. Marlow looked up as he got out of the truck. He was wearing black jeans with a dark-blue shirt. He had on a Yankees cap and a gold chain that hung midway down his torso. The hotel was more of a motel with all the rooms facing him. There were neon lime green lights spaced in between archs. All the room doors faced the parking lot. There were five floors and to his right he saw a stair case that lead up to the third floor. He saw three more black SUVs parked on a ramp heading down. There were men with guns in the parking lot and heading up the stair case to the third floor. It was a dark night, and the building's white façade was highlighted by the bright lime-green neon lights. Marlow could see dozens of men standing around, most likely attached in some way to the cartel, a half dozen of whom were displaying fully automatic rifles. Almost all of them wore cowboy boots and hats. They were the Mexican modern-day versions of cowboys from the Old West—only they didn't trade in horses or cattle. They traded in cocaine, weed, meth, or heroin.

"This way, amigo," Javy said as he grabbed the duffel bag from the SUV.

Marlow followed him up the stairs. He couldn't help but think to himself, What the fuck am I doing. I'm in a shithole motel in Mexico with twenty armed men.

As they reached the third level, Marlow saw a sign that said "Hotel Marquis de" Something. They ushered him past. He could see flowers native to Mexico in planters to his left; he looked down at the parking lot and saw the Nogales bus station across the street.

He followed Javy down the corridor, which opened to his left. Four more armed men guarded a door. All were dressed similarly to Javy, with cowboy boots and dark clothing. One man reached over and opened the door. Marlow followed Javy into the room.

Ceasar was sitting in a chair waiting for them. "Hola, amigo!" He was wearing a black sport coat over a loose white shirt. He stood in contrast to the men working for him. He rose and shook Marlow's hand. "I'm glad to see you and look forward to our next journey together."

A second chair was beside the table. Ceasar motioned for Marlow to have a seat. Javy set the duffel bag on the bed and left; only Marlow and Rojas remained. The room was very Spartan. The walls were a drab beige with some wood finishing where the wall met the ceiling. There was a single bed with a royal-blue bedspread highlighted by bright-orange pillows and a blanket of the same color folded over the foot of the bed. The only other furniture was a small wooden dresser with a mirror on top. There was no TV, and the room smelled like cleaning solvent.

"So I assume you're willing to take up our offer and expand your services to new markets?" Rojas sat down and pulled two cigars from his pocket.

"Yes, we would like to expand," said Marlow, taking the cigar handed to him by the druglord.

"I'm glad to hear that, my friend. I admire your ambition." Rojas drew in the smoke from the cigar as he lit it with a match. There was a single glass ashtray between them. Rojas offered the lit match to Marlow and lit his cigar for him.

"Did you hear they moved El Chapo to Juárez?" asked Ceasar. "They broke him in the other prison. Those motherfuckers kept waking him up every two hours for several months. Imagine, no sleep for two months. Those cocksuckers!"

"Juárez is just a few miles from Texas," replied Marlow.

"Yes. It appears it's just a matter of time before Shorty ends up in one of your American jails.

"So we move on." Rojas took a big puff of his cigar. "We are much like the sharks of the sea. The cartel and us—we all must keep moving forward. You know, a shark never stops moving. If it stops, it can't breathe. Our business is just like this . . . much like a shark. It must move forward."

"Very true," said Marlow, feeling a little more at ease with Ceasar, all things considered.

"We will miss El Chapo—he was a fine leader—but we must move forward. I can see by the bag you brought that you are prepared to move forward with us. . . . Yes?"

"Yes, but we do need to discuss the new routes. . . . I want to have that as a separate transaction with you guys."

"By separate, you mean without your uncle and your cousin. That works with us. I assume you mean to . . . how do I say . . . branch out on your own."

"Yes, Sr. Rojas, that's what I would like to do."

Rojas took a deep breath and leaned back in his chair. "I can assume you do not want Banks or Kingston to know of our new relationship?"

"Yes. My uncle Julius and I are going our own direction. King has his way of doing business, and we have come to a difference of opinion." Marlow looked at the drug kingpin. "They don't want to go into Chicago, while we see opportunity to expand on our own."

"You understand how a new route of trade works for us? I can assume you do by the bag you have with you . . . yes?" Rojas motioned to the duffel on the bed. It held $3 million that Julius had sent to Marlow with the last shipment from Atlanta.

"Javy explained it to me," replied Marlow.

"So there is no misunderstanding, I would like for you to repeat it to me." Ceasar set his cigar down in the ashtray and looked at Marlow.

"I give you the cash to back one hundred keys. There's three million in cash in the bag on the bed. For that, I get a weekly route into Chicago. I believe the rate we get in return is $5,000 per key." Marlow had already done the math: For the $3 million he gave Rojas, they would make roughly $26 million over the course of a year. They would receive $500,000 per shipment of 100 kilos of cocaine, assuming they didn't get busted. From the cartel's perspective, they were paying roughly 5 percent of what they would make for a guaranteed delivery. If Marlow lost a load, he lost the money and most likely would eventually lose his life as well as the lives of anyone tied to him.

"Yes, this is correct; and understand that you will just deal with one man in Chicago. How you get the load to Chicago is completely up to you; but also understand if you lose the load, the money you have here is our insurance. This money is nonrefundable, and any loss is yours. Your expenses are yours. We will deliver to you one hundred keys, from Nogales to Phoenix. It is your job to, each and every week, deliver one hundred keys to your contact. You understand all of this . . . yes?"

"Yes, I understand."

"Javy told me of the piece of business you helped them with several months back," Rojas said, changing the subject. Rojas was referring to the stabbing that had taken place months before with the Manuel-Rios brothers. A slight smile appeared on his face as he blew out a blue ring of smoke.

"Yes, Sr. Rojas, I assume there was no problem with my—"

Rojas waved his hand, stopping Marlow midsentence, still with the Cheshire Cat smile on his face. "No problem at all, mi amigo, this shows me you can be trusted. This is why I am willing to grow with you. When I started with Sinaloa, I was . . . how do I say it . . . a hitter. I worked in the muscle end of the family. I was a member of, as you say in English, The Blondies; and we were responsible for keeping family business protected. When my name was called, I did what was necessary.

"The fact that you stood with Javy and his brother, without hesitation, tells me something about you. In our business, one must be willing to do what is necessary to protect one's interests. I believe you are someone we can trust and someone who will do what's necessary to protect both of our interests . . . yes?"

"Yes, I am exactly that type of person."

"Bien, Marlow, bien."

JOHN

"Cheers, boys!" John said as he raised a glass to Alex and Cooper. The three men were gathered at a seafood restaurant in downtown Charleston a few blocks from Alex's office. John had flown in to surprise his friends with the news that the end of their alliance with the Johnson family was now firmly in sight.

"Let's not get too excited yet. There's still work to do," replied a more somber Alex as he clinked his nonalcoholic beer's bottle against his companions' glasses. Alex was relieved, but he also knew that just because they were getting out didn't erase the sins of the past. "Are we sure we have no remaining ties to the Johnsons besides Banks?"

Cooper thought to himself. He'd been face-to-face with J.J. during the ice storm a few months earlier. He sensed that was one of the concerns Alex was referring to tonight at the table. "I made sure I didn't use my name, if that's what you're worried about. I was driving a rental car, and there's no connection from what happened that night back to any of us. We have always followed protocols that insulated both me and you, Alex."

Cooper took a swig of his beer. "The only one who has anything to worry about is John. He's the only one they know by face and name. So as long as our attorney keeps his mouth shut, nothing will ever happen . . . right, John?"

John looked solemnly at the two men. "I guess now would be the time to tell you about the wire I'm wearing tonight. By the way, Alex, I heard your former partner finally got what was coming to him."

Alex and Cooper both stopped for a second, then shook their heads and smiled, knowing John was kidding.

Upon hearing about Alex's former partner, Cooper glanced over at his friends with a questioning look. "That's news to me!"

"Apparently the FBI finally got around to taking some action. Old Youst went and took out a second mortgage with one lender while closing a first mortgage. Burned an attorney friend of mine, and it finally caught up to him. He'll be a felon here before long," explained Alex. He had a slight smile on his face as he thought about all the other violations his former partner had committed. Justice was weird in that way—they got him for something he did as easily as breathing."

John took a sip from his glass. "Look, I got you guys into this mess and I promised we'd get out. We're at the finish line, and we'll all have some additional assets for our trouble. Let's not act like we didn't make some money over the last few years for our efforts. Money that's safely tucked away."

The bourbon and ginger was working its magic on him. He'd had a few martinis prior to dinner, and it was starting to show. The three men were sitting at a booth looking out on the open floor of the restaurant, including a community table. John had already sent drinks to some young ladies at that table. John finished off his drink and nodded at his friends. "God, I love the guy-to-girl ratio in Charleston." He made his way over to the community table and the two young blondes he was targeting. The night was young for Mr. Archibald.

The truth was, the three friends had made millions laundering money for the Johnson family. None of them were innocent, but they had all come into this together, and it appeared they would all be leaving it unscathed—and richer.

None of the men knew that the sands of change were currently moving beneath their feet. None suspected what was to come.

ROSCOE

Roscoe sat down at the table in the back of the grocery. It was dark in the rest of the warehouse, with only a half bank of fluorescent lights still on outside the office. The rest of the employees had long since gone; it was just Roscoe and one other individual left in the building. His son, Devon, was sitting at the table with his head cradled in his hands. He was wearing a black t-shirt, jeans, and a backward Braves cap. His coat was slung over the back of his chair. He'd been crying, and the resentment from what Julius had done to Trey was now creeping into his mind. He had a laptop open on the table displaying the GPS recording application he'd installed on it. It was a basic application that recorded the movements of the global positioning trackers they'd placed on their crew's cars and trucks. Devon had been watching their movements for the last few weeks, since they installed them.

"Dad, what the fuck are we doing about Trey?" he asked as he looked over at his father.

Roscoe looked back over at his boy and let out a deep sigh. "Nothing we can do, Dev, nothing we can do."

The reality was, if they even acknowledged that Trey was in fact gone, it would be an admission of knowledge about what happened to him. That was not something Roscoe or Devon could risk, given the current state of affairs. Neither of them knew what had happened to Trey's body, but both knew that Julius would have left no trace of him anywhere. Telling Trey's family anything would open doors and create questions that couldn't be answered. The situation sucked, but all they could do was confide in each other.

"So the GPS never showed him going anywhere we should have found suspicious?" Roscoe asked.

"No, looks like he was using a different car or something. I don't know. Honestly, I didn't really know what I was looking for; I was just seeing if they were going out late at night and shit like that, Dad." Devon turned the screen to his father, who viewed the device like a caveman looking at fire for the first time.

"Show me what you mean," said the elder Johnson.

"You see, each device is coded. I listed them as A, B, and C. A is—or was—for Trey, B is on Pitt's Tahoe, and C is on Demarcus's Benz. If you click on one and access the history, it shows where they go each day. The battery lasts about a month, two months tops; and it only pings once every thirty minutes. I had them set to cut on after six each night and run to the following morning, and during the weekends. I didn't have them on while they were in the shop."

Devon clicked on Trey's history and pointed to his father. "You can see that Trey was parked most nights. He would run to Buckhead, but I wouldn't figure he was dealing because the car was parked. Then he'd head back to his house late-night. He wasn't running all over the roads. I guess I fucked up, Dad. He must've been dropping off loads or something we didn't think about."

"Son, ain't nothing we can do 'bout it now. We ain't the fucking CIA or NSA. We tried, and it's done now. *He* done now," Roscoe said as he looked at the transaction history. It listed locations and times in descending order.

"Man, Julius a monster, Dad. He killed someone we known for decades!" Devon stood and walked away from the table.

"Devon. Stop that talk! Ain't nothing we can do about this now. Aint nothing bringing him back; and after we leave this room, we need to stop talking about him!" Roscoe looked up at his son. He knew Devon was right, but at the same time he was powerless to do anything about Julius with Kingston being in jail.

"Boy, listen to me. Julius ain't the man in charge. Kingston is; and when Kingston gets out, we'll see what he has to say about what Julius has done. We can't do nothing until then."

Devon glanced at his father and then looked away. "Still don't make me feel any better."

"I know, boy, but it is what it is; and we will wait." Roscoe turned his gaze back to the screen and then picked up the TV remote to cut on SportsCenter.

"Now you go run out there to the truck and get Pitt and Demarcus and bring them in here so we can give them the 4-1-1 and be done with this bullshit. We ain't got no choice—we got to fill them in."

"All right." Devon left the room to retrieve the remaining crew members from the loading dock. They were probably wondering what was going on with them missing a body to do the work that was necessary.

Roscoe returned his attention to the computer and fumbled at a few of the keys. He pulled up the marker labeled "C," put the cursor on a day a few weeks ago, and clicked. Amazed that he could make the information come right up, he clicked on a few more dates—and then he stopped. He looked a little closer. "Fuck!"

He looked at one location listed for Demarcus's tracker and scrolled down, realizing the car had been at that location overnight. Roscoe stared with disbelief and shook his head silently. He had just come to the realization that Demarcus Jennings's black Mercedes-Benz G Wagon had apparently been parked overnight at Rena Johnson's address several of the nights they'd been tracking him. That was *not* an address he should be at overnight—or any time of night, for that matter.

Roscoe knew nothing good would come of this discovery; a bead of sweat appeared on his forehead. He slammed the computer shut and waited on the crew to enter the office, the anger already showing on his face along with a look of confusion as to how to deal with this new potentially deadly issue.

First Trey, and now another member of his crew was putting himself in harm's way. What in the hell could he do to avoid another funeral? Hell, Trey hadn't even had a funeral; his mother was going out of her mind. She had no clue her boy was gone for good; instead, she just had a black hole where her son used to be. Julius had taken him out like he was yesterday's garbage. It just wasn't right by Roscoe, and he knew Kingston wouldn't want it that way either.

Roscoe needed his older brother in the worst kind of way.

JULIUS

Julius sat in his car outside the designated meeting spot. He wore a dark suit with a deep-blue tie. He had a plan, and that plan was solid. Obviously he couldn't tell them anything that would lead back to him or his crew, but he knew some names around town he could pass along. He also knew they wouldn't go away unless he gave them something.

He thought back to his original bust, when he was arrested with a weapon and enough blow to do serious time. He hadn't been prepared back then. His only option had been to tell the Feds about a shipment they had coming up from Texas. It was supposed to involve some low-level flunkies who didn't know anyone, but instead Kingston had gone on the run because someone got sick. Back then, fucking Roscoe had picked some real idiots who couldn't be counted on.

What had happened next seemed like a nightmare to Julius. His own brother and best friend got arrested based on the intel he had provided to the DEA and the FBI.

Fucking Agent Howard—that white motherfucker—had become his handler during that time period. Once they had busted Kingston, it went downhill from there. Julius gave up some of been dealing in coke from the cartel. Julius knew better than to cross the crazy-ass Mexicans they did business with now.

About a year after Kingston went in, the FBI had seemed to lose interest in Julius. He hadn't had much left to give them that wouldn't have connected back to himself at that point.

The cartel was never discussed. Julias never dealt with them and followed his brother, lead when they started moving blow.

He was more prepared for them this time. He knew what the FBI and their brothers at the DEA wanted: names and busts. The key for Julius was making sure he gave them nothing that could lead back to him or anyone in the crew. For that very reason, he had kept his ear to the ground just in case this day came. A plan. Julius always had a plan, and he could deal with this issue just like he dealt with everything else. Stay cool, stay calm, and give them the goods, Julius thought to himself. Just like dealing coke, keep everyone calm.

With that, he exited his vehicle and entered the restaurant for the planned meet. They were meeting in Midtown for a late lunch, so there would be fewer people in the restaurant. This particular Chinese place had a few private booths in the back, and that was where they would meet—out of the prying eyes of the general public.

Stay cool, stay calm, Julius reminded himself. As he approached, he noticed a new player: a redheaded female, probably DEA. Accompanying her were the two cocksuckers from earlier—Gooding and the young one.

"Mr. Johnson, take a seat," said Gooding. "This is Agent Kirkpatrick with the DEA. She'll be sitting in with us."

Agent Gooding had a notepad, and Julius could assume there was a recorder somewhere. He took his seat and looked across at the trio. Time to play the part. Time to give them the goods. Stay calm, stay cool. Julius began to talk and give them what they wanted. The names of unsuspecting criminals across the Atlanta area started coming out of his mouth. He gave them small-time dealers involved in an operation run by some Dominicans in Cobb County that ran heroin and coke up to Virginia.

Julius had kept his ear to the ground for just this occasion. None of them had any connection back to him; nonetheless, they were now fucked. Such was the way our justice system worked. No real police work was involved—just one criminal ratting on other criminals to save his own neck. Julius played his part and did what was requested of him.

An hour later, it was over . . . for the time being. Julius headed out the restaurant and back into his life. That little speed bump had been dealt with, and now it was time to move forward. There had only been three or four staff members in the restaurant, and none had seemed to take any notice to the meeting in the back booths. He exhaled as he got behind the wheel. He straightened his tie and headed out into traffic.

His followers didn't follow this time. Instead, per their instructions, they waited. They waited to see with whom Mr. Julius Johnson had been meeting. Sure enough, the federal agents followed him out of the restaurant and then got into a Crown Victoria and headed back to the office. The followers took their time and made sure not to be made, but they followed the agents all the way back to FBI headquarters in Atlanta.

The passenger picked up the phone and made a call with the report.

ROSCOE

It had been over a year since Roscoe had ventured into the prison to talk to his brother. It was difficult for him to see Kingston in there; and knowing what they were involved in, it was doubly hard to willingly enter a federal facility that could have been his home for twenty-plus years if the cards had gone the other way. Roscoe had been the one who was supposed to make the run to Alabama that fateful day, but he had ended up not going. He would never be able to forget that his brother took all of the time on his own. He never mentioned anyone else and never even though of ratting on any other members of the family.

John Archibald had called Roscoe and said that Kingston needed to see him face-to-face. It had to be important if they needed to meet inside the prison. Roscoe knew he had to be careful and watch what he said within prison walls. He got nervous just thinking about it. He had been outside the facility for the last half hour building up the courage to go inside to see his older brother.

Should he tell him about what he found out about Rena? No, probably not the best way to open a conversation with a man you hadn't seen in a year.

"All right, big man, it's time," he said out loud as he exited his SUV and headed to the check-in line. It was a Sunday, and the line to enter the facility was short. He went through the check; because of his size, he drew a little more attention than the wives and children who were in front of him, entering the staging area.

When he finally walked into the visiting room, he saw his older brother already waiting for him at a stainless steel table, which was bolted to the floor. He looked smaller than Roscoe remembered, and he was dressed in a beige jumpsuit that all the inmates wore.

"My brother!" Roscoe exclaimed as he took part in the customary brief embrace allowed under federal rules. Roscoe was wearing a blue denim shirt with jeans. He had some scruff on his face, as he hadn't shaved in the last few days. There was some slight gray showing up in his facial hair. His head was clean-shaven, just like his brother, who again took his seat. Roscoe grinned with a wave of relieve that he was seeing one of his best friends in the world. It didn't matter to him that they were in a federal institution. He was in his brother's presence, and that was fine with him.

The plan had been to limit their contact for various reasons, not by Roscoe's choice. If it were up to him, he would visit his brother every week. The thought process was that regular visits could make the Feds think something was up—that the two men were corresponding some-how—and it could draw unwanted attention.

"You look good, King. Been too long."

"I know, Coe, been too long. Way too long," King replied as he looked at his baby brother—a man who outweighed him by a hundred and fifty pounds, give or take.

"We gotta talk about J.," Kingston said, cutting to the chase. "I talked to Maris last week."

"Yeah, I heard she came by." Roscoe folded his hands together. He talked in a low voice and leaned forward.

There was only one guard in the room, and he didn't seem very inter-ested in anything going on. King could sense his brother's apprehension.

"We got the room. I took care of it. That over there is PO Barnes, and he don't hear so good," said Kingston. "As a matter of fact, I don't think he can hear nothing, if you know what I mean."

"You heard about the Toliver thing. J.'s out running his own playbook."

"Yep, that's exactly what we need to talk about. I need you to tell J. that was *not* cool. Not something he should be concerned with, if you know what I mean. Me and Maris, we getting along better now; and I can't have issues like that popping up. I got about eighteen months left in here, and I want things to be status quo with her and the rest of the family when I get out. Julius needs to back the fuck off and quit his bullshit"

"That's the thing, King. J.—he don't ask nobody nothing; he just *does*, if you know what I mean."

"I know what you mean, and that shit's got to stop." Kingston looked at his brother with a stone face. "I need you to remind him that he answers to me. You feel me?"

"I hear you, King. I hear you. What you need me to do?"

"I need you to be by here once a month to see me. Talk to John about the schedule. I need someone I can trust. I need to know what's going on with the family. Can you do that for me, Coe?"

Kingston couldn't trust that Della had been 100 percent straight with him. Julius had a record, which meant he couldn't visit King in prison. All their communication prior to this latest issue had been through Della.

"Yeah, bro, you can count on me to be there." The big man looked at his older brother.

"What we going to do about Julius?"

"I need you to take control, Roscoe. Plain and simple."

THE DILLON BROTHERS

"**M**an, you ever think about how many people going to get fucked up off what we got riding in the back of this truck?" Marcus asked his brother.

The two men were on the outskirts of Chicago and had sent a Snapchat message to Marlow mere seconds ago. They were riding in a moving truck packed with furniture and boxes and exactly one hundred kilos of pure cocaine in a hidden compartment buried deep inside the vehicle. By design, the men carried no cell phones of their own—only a burner phone. They had no guns, only a simple bag with a change of clothing. By all appearances, they were two delivery drivers; and that was their role should something go wrong. The two men were dressed in jeans and matching polo shirts that had "Advanced Moving Company" stitched across the right breast. The truck they drove would barely make it above seventy-five miles per hour, again by design, as a governor had been placed on it. Getting caught speeding was highly unlikely. These same trucks would be used over and over again as many times as possible.

"A fucking shitload, bro. We got what, like a million lines of blow in there?" replied Quincy, who was sitting shotgun. "You know, people like to get fucked up, and what we got in here will get cut up like ten times."

The truth was, the pure cocaine they held in the belly of the truck would have a street value of nearly $10 million in the hands of the cartel's group in Chicago. They were just one of many deliveries to the distribution hub.

The plan was very simple. Marlow had given them an address only a few minutes before. They would take the truck to that address, where a second truck also marked "Advanced Moving" would be waiting for them with their contact, a man named Tito. One of the brothers was to get out and ask one question: "What address you got on your delivery?" The answer would be simple; Tito was to respond "Atlanta." The Dillon brothers would hand their invoice listing and keys to Tito, who in turn would give them a new sheet of data showing details for their delivery from Chicago to Atlanta. They would then get in the other truck and drive out of town on their way back home to Georgia. Simple, safe, and uncomplicated. No guns, no shady deals in hotel rooms. The cartel and their methods were developing into a scarily efficient model of logistics.

Their delivery route was worth about $26 million a year to Marlow and Julius, but that was just the tip of the iceberg. The hundred keys they delivered were pure. That meant the cartel would be able to cut it up and mix it with other additives, creating nearly four times as much product. The street value would hit the $10 million mark if sold per gram on the streets of Chicago. The cartel would cut up the cocaine in Chicago and deliver it to all points in the US and make anywhere from $7 million to $10 million. The weekly delivery that the Dillons would be making would be worth nearly half a billion dollars per year.

The cartel now controlled the logistics from Colombia and had driven the price down to roughly $2,000 per key, so they paid the Colombians $200,000 for a load of 100 kilos to come up from Colombia to Mexico via Central America. The Mexican cartels had guaranteed their trade routes to the Colombians, taking away the risk associated with losing the loads. The cartels in Colombia sacrificed profits in exchange for guaranteed returns. The Mexican cartels were now doing the same with their delivery partners in the US. The cycle made them incredibly powerful, and the money flowed in.

An easy delivery in plain sight with no bloodshed. The way of commerce made it much easier for them to deliver their product to the market. Bullets, beheadings, and bloodshed were, in fact, bad for business.

"How close are we?" asked Marcus.

They were driving a smaller class four-axle truck like anyone could rent at a U-Haul authorized dealer. The reason was simple: that truck wasn't required to go through weigh-in stations along highways as they crossed multiple state lines. The truck was also large enough that they could stash the drugs deep in the interior, hidden under all the various furniture, mattresses, and packed boxes that should between the back gate and anyone searching the vehicle. Their only real fear was that drug dogs could possibly be involved and smell the drugs. The steel box containing the kilos of cocaine was as far from the rolling gate as possible and welded shut.

Part of the deception was that all of their paperwork matched with a delivery of home goods for a family moving from the Phoenix area to Chicago. The hope was that no law enforcement entity would feel like unpacking a truck, especially if all the paperwork matched. If the cops did decide to unload the truck on the side of the road, the steel case would only be shielded by the large shipping crate that held it inside instead of a cooling system for a household appliance. The fridge was sealed and packed in a wooden exterior to make it look like it was brand-new.

"GPS says five miles out," replied Quincy.

The location had been chosen at random by Marlow, as had the date of the delivery. This was all part of keeping secrecy when it came to the delivery details so no law enforcement agency could set up on them. The only standard was the contact information would be given with enough time for Tito to get his truck to the correct location. Tito's truck would be rigged in the same way as the Dillons' truck, except his truck would hold payment for the delivery.

The Dillon brothers arrived at their destination and saw their truck's twin waiting in a strip mall's parking lot in Tinley Park in south Chicago.

"Okay, here we go." Quincy climbed out of the passenger's side; at the same time, a Latino holding a clipboard climbed down from the passenger's side of the other truck. Both were wearing polo shirts with "Advanced Moving" on them.

"Where you delivering to, my man?" asked Quincy.

"My truck's going to Atlanta," replied the Latino. He had a mustache and slicked-back hair.

"That works for me," replied Quincy, and the two men exchanged clipboards. Quincy looked over his shoulder and nodded at his brother, who jumped out of the cab carrying their duffel bag. Without saying a word, a second man got out of the driver's seat of the other truck and walked to the driver's side of the Dillons' truck. He nodded at Marcus as he passed.

And with that, the Dillon brothers entered the gassed-up truck with paperwork for a delivery of furniture from Chicago to the suburbs of Atlanta for the Miller family. Marcus cranked the engine and pulled out of the parking lot.

"Okay, man, get me a route to Interstate 57 on the GPS, and let's head south," Marcus told his brother.

The drug transaction had taken place in less than a minute. The Dillon brothers were now drug traffickers, and they headed home with the payoff. At the same time, the second truck pulled out heading north into the waiting arms of dealers and pushermen in the Windy City so they could poison people in various cities. The commerce of cocaine had taken place as it did every day, everywhere. The beast that was the American appetite for drugs needed to be fed, and this was just a small piece of the greater puzzle that was the American drug love affair with cocaine.

JULIUS

Dressed in a sport coat with a polo shirt, Julius entered the back of the grocery on Miller Street for a meeting with his brother. Roscoe had called him and said they needed to talk in person and to meet him up at the store after closing. It was a little after ten on a Saturday.

Julius was feeling pretty good. The first shipment to Chicago had gone off without a hitch, and the truck had arrived in Atlanta early that morning. The wheels were in motion; the money would be moving into the new bank accounts he had set up a few weeks earlier. He would send the next set of buy-in money—a couple million—back out West with the next run Cass made. Eventually he would just have one of the Dillon boys drive it out West; but for now, no reason to break up a good thing. He had to admit that Cass being white made that part of the operation run more smoothly. The Dillon boys also needed to prove themselves before they could be fully trusted. Putting the money with Cass for now was the smart play, especially since he never knew how much was being purchased or how much money he was hauling on his trips.

The plan was coming together nicely. Sure, the interference by the FBI was a problem, but nothing he couldn't deal with. He'd fed them some good intel that should keep them satisfied for now. He had even gone as far as to rat on Kendrick Toliver's connection, some fucking Haitian with a questionable immigration status. That had been a no-brainer and would also probably end with Toliver needing to be tied up.

Julius entered the back of the office and found Roscoe sitting at the table with the NBA playoffs on the TV. "What's up, my brother?" asked Julius as the two men half hugged. There was something slightly off about Roscoe.

"Man, ain't no easy way to say this, Julius. I went and saw King last week in prison," Roscoe said firmly.

"Really. What, did you do go run to him about our little disagreement?" Julius took a seat and leaned back, showing no concern about what his brother was saying. "How was the King?"

"Honestly, he was pissed off about the Toliver shit. He said he wants me to handle the business going forward. Said you need to take some time off," Roscoe replied as matter-of-factly as someone ordering food at a restaurant.

"Ha-ha! Didn't know you were a fucking comedian, Coe. That's some funny shit." Julius was watching TV more than he was listening to the words coming out of his brother's mouth.

"And what exactly does 'take a fucking break' mean, Coe?" Julius now stared at Roscoe, his tone changed.

"I guess it means you need to stay the fuck out of here and stay away from the shipments. I guess it also means that Banks is on his way into town. That's what the fuck it means," Roscoe said as he looked right back at his brother, doing his best to match his gaze.

"Oh, really. So Prince Banks and the King want me to step aside after all these years! And who the fuck is going to—"

Roscoe slammed his fist into the side of his brother's jaw and put all three hundred pounds in motion, taking Julius to the ground before he could finish his last insult. Roscoe pounded his hands—the size of small hams—into Julius's face a half-dozen times. The blood poured from his nose, which had been broken by one of the savage blows from Roscoe's attack. Julius wasn't able to put up a fight because the beating had caught him by surprise. Even if he had been able to, the anger built up in Roscoe would have overwhelmed anything Julius would have had to offer.

Julius was half-conscious and spitting up blood. Roscoe had knocked out several of his teeth, and blood soaked his shirt and dripped onto the floor. Roscoe stood over him, waiting to see if he would attempt to counter.

"King said to make sure you got the fucking message, J. You out. The beating is for Toliver and for what you did to Trey. You come at me or any of my crew again, and King said you dead—brother or no brother. You feel me?" He backed away from Julius and picked up a baseball bat.

Julius had rolled over and was crawling for the door. "Wha the fuck, Coe, I'm yo brotha," he spat out through a bloody mouth that was missing teeth. His eye, where Roscoe had nailed him with one of the first blows, was beginning to swell shut. It hadn't been a fight; it had been a beating. Julius crawled to the door.

"Julius, I swear if you come back at me or my crew, ain't going to be no mercy from Kingston. He told me to tell you that, and he meant it." Roscoe patted down his brother, trying to make sure he didn't have any weapons. "Now we still brothers, but you got to be held accountable for what you done. You crossed the line, and this is the punishment. This is all there will be—unless you want to start more trouble. I suggest you get outta here and don't come up here no mo'." Roscoe held the bat over Julius. He couldn't be sure what would happen next. He stood a few feet away from Julius as he came to his feet.

"So it be . . . it be like tha . . . Coe," Julius sputtered out of his mangled face. Roscoe tossed him a towel to stop some of the blood.

"Yeah, Jules, it's like that. And don't think I wouldn't have killed your ass if Kingston told me to. You my brother, but we done with each other. You ain't right, and you out. Now go on."

With that, Julius left the Miller Street Grocery. He climbed into his black SUV and wheeled out of the parking lot. More than anything, he was in shock that Roscoe'd had the balls to attack him like that. He knew now that it eventually may come down to blows or bullets. He pulled out his phone as he drove to his house, which was a few miles away from the store. He texted Shea to meet him in a half hour. He would need to get cleaned up and plan the next steps.

Out of the business. Who the fuck did King think he was messing with? It was time. Julius had known it would come to this eventually. He'd always known, and he had planned just in case. This trespass by Roscoe would not be let to go lightly, but first he had to get his pieces in place. The money he'd put into the laundry today—that was the key. He had the connection through Marlow—well, at least as long as he needed Marlow . . . eventually he would have to take care of him as well. Thank god he had opened up his own accounts for the Chicago money because if Banks was involved, he was most likely locked out of all the operational money. He had his own money saved up—easily a million in cash—around town in safety deposit boxes. Not the high finance that Banks and his white boys out of town had set up, but he had his cut for the last few years.

Fuck King, and fuck Roscoe. He didn't need either of them. He had Marlow and the connection. Everything would be fine. Goddamn, his head hurt. He looked in the rearview and saw the damage. His left eye was swollen shut, and blood was coming out of the corner from a cut over the eyelid. His nose was broken, and his front four teeth had been knocked out. Blood was all down the front of his shirt.

But he was a survivor, and he would make sure his revenge would be swift and fucking violent. His own fucking brothers.

As Julias pulled in front of his house, Shea's text hit him back saying he would be at the house shortly. He sat there for a second, typing a text for him to bring some supplies. Time to arm up, just in case. He sent the text and opened his door, then paused for a second. What the fuck was he going to tell Della? Fucking Kingston had put Roscoe on him. What the fuck would he do about what had just happened?

He had to show strength. That was always the answer, in his book.

Violence meant violence. What would his response be to Roscoe and, by extension, Kingston? The message had to be clear that Julius was not to be fucked with. Kingston would need to realize that he was not in control of these streets.

As he exited the truck, he saw a shadow off to the back of the SUV move to his left, into his blurred view. Maybe if his eye were open, he would have seen the figure coming from around the vehicle.

"What the fuck! . . . You!"

A silencer-assisted muffled shot rang out, striking Julius in the forehead and blowing his brains out the back of his head and onto the opened door and hood of his Escalade. He fell to his right knee and backed up against the open car door. Two more shots struck him in his heart, and then there was a metallic click as the weapon was dropped on the concrete driveway. The blood started to paint the ground. The sounds of the city were all that could be heard in the distance. The figure walked off into the darkness.

Julius Johnson was dead.

JOHN

It was early in the morning, and John was still drunk from the night before. He recognized the number calling his phone as Della Johnson. He looked past the blonde in his bed to the clock, which showed it was near 3:00 a.m. He looked at his cell; she had already called seven times, since about two that morning. He thought, Oh fuck, this can't be good news. This usually means someone is in jail or worse.

"Hello. . . . Della. Slow down. What . . . ?" Della told him that Julius had been killed in front of their house. John listened between the wails and crying, and he got out of bed. He went into the kitchen and began making coffee. Fuck, this is going to be a bad day, he thought to himself. No way I'm going back to bed now.

"I'm on the way; and Della, don't say anything to anyone until I get there."

John set his phone down and put both hands on the marble countertop that made up the island in his penthouse condo's modern kitchen. He was trying to process everything he had just heard and think of the next step.

He quickly fired off a message via Telegram to Banks.

What had just happened?

He picked up his phone and went to his home office. He pulled out a notebook and looked up the emergency number for Banks. The number began the drone of the international ping to a burner phone, just one in a series of numbers that would only be used once. There was no immediate answer.

He wondered if he should warn Alex and Cooper. Was this something larger? Were they all in danger now? Was this the cartel? No, that made no sense; the last load had been delivered to Philly several days ago with no issues.

Wait, he thought. I can call Marlow. It's only midnight out West. He dialed Marlow's number; at this point, a call from his attorney telling him about his uncle's death would not be of concern, so he broke protocol and called directly from his cell. Marlow answered after a half-dozen rings.

"Marlow, it's John. I have . . . I have bad news. Your uncle Julius is dead," he said in a lawyerly kind of way, just in case someone was listening.

"I don't know what happened yet. I'm heading over there now. I know he was shot to death."

John headed to his bathroom and started the shower.

Right then, the line beeped. "Marlow, it's your cousin from out of town. I called him too. Let me talk to him. Probably a good idea for you to start heading home."

He clicked off, and the line went live with Banks on the other end. "Banks. What the fuck, man. Julius is dead. Tell me everything's okay!" John listened to Banks, and the nightmare of that Sunday morning began for Mr. Archibald and the Johnson family.

"I'll go see King for you," John said minutes later as he ended his call with Banks.

He walked back to the coffeepot and poured a cup. After a moment's hesitation, he grabbed a bottle of bourbon and glass, poured a shot, and took it down. John looked at his phone, wanting to call someone—anyone—but there was nobody else he could call at this point. So he just looked out his window at the cityscape of Atlanta with all of its lights blinking back at him. The silence was deafening. This meant something was happening that John could not control, and he was scared. As scared as he'd ever been. He knew this was going to be a problem for him, and he could already feel the pull back into the abyss.

KINGSTON

He sat in his cell, alone. Alone with his thoughts. A second brother dead. Was this his fault as well? Kingston hadn't left his cell since John had come and delivered the news earlier that day. Had he gotten his brother killed by his decisions? Was Julius's blood on his hands, like Raymond's had been nearly a decade before?

He held one of the few photos he'd brought in with him. It showed the four brothers as young men all dressed in their Sunday best. He thought it was from Easter, but he couldn't be sure. Raymond was wearing a jacket as blue as the sky. Julius was wearing one of Ray's hand-me-downs in a similar color of blue. Roscoe had on just a white shirt with a thin black bowtie. He'd looked like a round mound even back then. King was wearing a red suit that was probably two sizes too big for him. They hadn't had much, but they'd had each other.

He couldn't help but feel he had failed Julius just like he had failed Ray so many years ago. Kingston had made the decision to start dealing cocaine, and he felt that decision had ultimately led to what happened to Julius. Julius was no saint, but he was King's brother, and now he was dead.

A tear dropped from his eye as he lay back on his bunk. He quickly wiped it away and thought to himself that the toll that had been paid by his family for his decisions was too much. Two of his brothers were dead. His sons were growing up without a father. His mother was dying of a disease without him to help or comforter her. Rena and Maris were out there making their way without him. He was completely isolated.

The real pain was in the fact that he could walk out the front door of this prison at almost any time and just disappear. He had the means to do it, but then he would be a fugitive for the rest of his life. Was he selfish not to walk out and take them with him?

"Just got to get it done," he said out loud, speaking for the first time since John had visited. "Five hundred and seventy." The number of days until his release. He said it again: "Five hundred and seventy." The number both renewed him with resolve and silently scared him with the large number of days he had left inside.

He thought, I can do it, no problem. And no matter what, I am never coming back to a prison. Ever. They got me once, but never again. We're going to end this bullshit and make things right for the family. Make things right for all I've done.

Just got to finish it up.

"Goodbye, J. See you on the other side," Kingston said. He figured they would both be going to hell for their sins, but King wasn't there yet. He still had time to make some things right. As soon as he got out of this prison, he could make things right. He had time. It wasn't too late.

THE FUNERAL

It was a crisp spring day, with the sun shining down on the funeral of Julius Alton Johnson Sr. in Westview Cemetery, the largest cemetery in the Southeast. Westview opened in 1884 and had over 100,000 souls committed to its grounds. Julius's family and well-wishers had gathered at the Abbey Chapel in Westview for the service, with a graveside burial to commence after the pastor's words. The Abbey was a stone structure with truly gothic designs. Its main hall had vaulted ceilings with an arch and a ribbed ceiling. On the exterior were three large portals stacked one on top of the other for a total of six. In the middle entrance of the Abbey was a picture of Christ with open arms, welcoming the mourners and the recently departed.

The funeral itself was taking place several weeks after Julius's death, as the incident was officially being investigated as a homicide and required an autopsy; but it didn't take a rocket scientist to figure out the cause of death was the hollow-point that had removed the back of his skull and placed his brains on the interior of his vehicle.

Shea had been the first to arrive and find Julius. Della had been over at a friend's house that evening playing bridge when the murder took place. The police had arrived shortly after Shea had found Julius's body, and the circus had begun.

The grieving had been immediate, but the resolution was as far away as possible at this point. The police had no leads; but interestingly enough, the FBI had become involved in the investigation behind the scenes. The College Park Police Department was investigating the murder with Agents Roman and Gooding keeping constant tabs on their progress. Needless to say, when a confidential informant got murdered days after passing information to his handlers, it drew attention. All of the information Julius had passed along was now being checked and double-checked for any potential leads by the task force with a renewed level of interest that had not previously existed. An informant who had been of little interest to the group was now a high priority due to his murder. The College Park police detectives had been dispatched to watch the funeral and the comings and goings to be held at Westview Cemetery that breezy and sunny midweek afternoon. They were there to watch and record visitors to the funeral of Julius Johnson Sr.

One of these visitors was John Archibald, but he was present for an entirely different reason than to say goodbye to the man. He had been summoned by Banks, who had arrived from Panama the day before. John would soon discover that Banks was not alone in his travels. John's head hurt from the recent binge he had been on since Julius's death, but he was dressed neatly in a black suit and dark-blue tie, giving off the impression of total sobriety.

The uncertainty of the chain of events had made everyone uneasy. Roscoe had come to John and told him about his fight with Julius beforehand, and the lawyer in him had to spring into action. They had documented the slight bruising on Roscoe's hands and taken a statement from him for future use if and when the police came asking. John had been one of the few people allowed to view the body; he went with Della to identify Julius's corpse in the morgue. John was actually slightly relieved to discover that the gunshot wounds had done the work to cover up any damage done by Roscoe's strikes. The shot to the head had been final and devastating. The two to the heart for good measure showed the signs of a professional; that in itself sent John's head spinning.

Had something gone wrong with the cartel? Was King sending a stronger message than a beating from Roscoe? Roscoe had told him about the incident with Kendrick Toliver, and that opened up that possibility. John was in a very difficult position. While solving the crime would be the police's goal, John was very aware that they weren't the type of group that needed a lot of law enforcement around them. Truth be told, Julius had probably deserved what he got; but it couldn't have come at a worse possible time for John and his friends.

His meeting with Banks was to take place well before the funeral, which would take place at 1:00 p.m. and last for hours, as most African-American funerals do. John was waiting in a back room reserved for family and friends of the dead. He couldn't help but feel that he was on the way to his own funeral. Julius Johnson's death would be felt throughout the organization; and John had a bad feeling that his exit would now be, at a minimum, delayed. As he waited, he looked at the ornate crosses and pictures in the room and couldn't help but see the irony of the meeting about to take place doing so in the eyes of God. What they would be discussing was about as far from God as one could get.

A knock on the door. He looked up, expecting to see Banks as he entered; instead, he saw a huge Hispanic man dressed in black suit followed by a wiry-looking middle-aged white man, also dressed in black. Neither man spoke to John as they entered the room. He saw Cass standing outside, appearing to have been posted as sentry.

Finally, his old friend entered and their meeting could begin. "Thanks for coming today, John. Let me introduce you to Juan Machado and Cain Rowland." As he talked, he pointed to each man, as if the names alone would not have hinted at their owners. Machado did not move to shake John's hand and, in fact, said nothing. He was about 6-foot-2 and looked to be 220 to 230 pounds of pure muscle. He had a scar on his cheek and an obvious bulge under his jacket—presumably, a weapon. Rowland, on the other hand, moved toward John and extended his hand. "Wish our meeting were under better circumstances, Mr. Archibald," he said as they shook hands. Rowland was in his mid-forties with a clean-shaven face and slightly muscular build. He was about 6-foot and 170 pounds. He was dressed in a black suit that John recognized as high-end; it appeared he would be attending the funeral. Rowland walked over to a window and leaned against the ledge while Banks joined John, sitting in a pew that faced the picture of some nameless saint looking down on them. Banks's eyes had a dark quality, and his face was chiseled stone, with no emotion. He looked every bit like an FBI agent or government official—only dressed in a two thousand dollar suit, which showed he had moved far beyond a government salary. He looked formidable.

"I've hired Mr. Rowland to run the investigation for the family, and I would appreciate it if you would assist him by bringing him up to speed. He is a former homicide detective from Miami and now works as a private investigator," said Banks to his friend. Banks's black suit was highlighted by a red carnation, which John recognized as something Della would have added to his outfit. Red had been his late uncle's favorite color.

"Della wanted me to thank you personally for everything you've done these past few weeks." Banks handed him a red carnation similar to the one he wore. "She has asked all the family to wear one of these to remember Uncle J." John took the flower and affixed it to his suit's lapel. "She also told me about her thoughts about Kendrick Toliver."

"How is Ma Maris holding up?" asked John as he made sure the flower held in its place.

"She says it ain't right for a parent to bury a child, no matter how old the child is. . . ."

John glanced at Banks with a look that asked his next question before he could even utter the words.

"Yes, Mr. Rowland is aware of the family business. His compensation and contract ensure absolute secrecy. He's here to investigate my uncle's death and my uncle's death only," explained Banks.

"Are we sure that's a good idea at this point? No offense, Mr. Rowland, but do we want an outsider involved?" The lawyer in John had taken over; he felt a little taken aback that Banks hadn't consulted him prior to making such a move. But he also thought maybe this meant Banks was going to honor releasing John and his team as they had discussed during his visit to Panama.

"No offense taken," replied Rowland. He showed no emotion in response to the words coming from John's mouth; his face looked stoic. He took a glance out the window and then appeared to be sweeping the room with his eyes, looking for anything that was out of place. John noticed a slight bulge at the back of his jacket, where it appeared a gun was hidden in the small of his back.

"Mr. Rowland comes recommended from our banker friends in Panama, whom he has done . . . let's just say some work for in the past," Banks said. John leaned back and tilted his head up, thinking for second. "He has no connection to Shorty." This was an obvious reference to the cartel.

"So that means this issue with Julius wasn't related to our contacts south of the border?"

"I don't believe so. They reached out to me offering assistance," answered Banks. "But the reality is, I think they wanted to disavow any involvement. They were pretty clear that they see this as an attack on their extended family, and they're willing to assist if necessary. Either way, something isn't right for them to have reached out so quickly. They knew about Julius the morning afterward. We need to get in front of this thing."

John's mouth dropped for a second, and once again Banks beat him to the question he was about to ask. The realization that the cartel had known about Julius dying so quickly was slightly unsettling. Why would the cartel know that Julius was dead so soon after the murder? While the cartel knew who Julius Johnson was, why would they move so quickly to contact Banks? Were they feeling out the Johnsons, or did they believe there was some larger issue? None of the possibilities were good.

"I of course told them we didn't need their assistance and that we would be looking into resolving this matter as quickly and quietly as possible. That's where Mr. Rowland comes in. He's a former homicide cop, but he is also a very, *very* private consultant. Our friends in Mexico agree with me that we need to keep tabs on the investigation into Uncle Julius's death and make sure it doesn't interfere with the sensitive nature of our relationship."

John nodded his head in agreement. "So Mr. Rowland will be—"

"I need you as the family attorney to request that both you and Mr. Rowland be involved in any questioning of family members or associates. I will also be posting a reward offering for any information about my uncle's death on behalf of the family. This senseless murderer must be brought to justice as soon as possible. I don't think we need the local police—or anyone else—poking around the family too much for too long."

What Banks said made sense to John. The reward would bring in dozens, if not hundreds, of crank calls, all of which would bog down the local police. Any police department would tell you that a cash reward is one of the worst possible ways to actually solve a murder. John could see that clearly the cartel was more concerned about losing business than who actually killed Julius. The involvement of this Rowland character probably meant that King and Banks feared exposure more than anything else. Millions of dollars were at stake, and having a little thing like a murder investigation slow up commerce would not be accepted. And having the local College Park PD stumble upon how they made their money wouldn't be accepted either. On the bright side, it appeared on the surface that the Sinaloa Cartel had had no involvement in killing Julius. Otherwise, they probably wouldn't be having this conversation, because the cartel would have probably killed the entire Johnson family if it were that type of issue.

"So who is Mr. Machado?" asked John.

Banks looked over at the big man. "I've hired him as a private bodyguard. He is Venezuelan and has no ties to the cartel. He works for me," replied Banks. That Banks now saw reason to have a bodyguard was not lost on John. "He has been working for me down in Panama for the last few years."

Banks placed his elbows on his knees. John knew what was coming next. "This brings us to the next piece of business. I need you guys to stay on while we sort this mess out."

The news John had feared had been delivered.

"I need you to help me, John. I don't have anyone in the family right now who can do what you guys do."

"Banks, I've already told my guys we were out end of the year," John said, looking in his friend's eyes. "They really don't want any further part in moving money for you guys."

"I know that, John, but I need you guys while I figure this out. I need you until I can get set up with a new system here locally. I can't trust that someone connected to Uncle Julius is responsible for what happened to him."

John stood up and paced for a minute or two. He knew he couldn't abandon his friend in his time of need. He also knew that Banks could push the issue for more forcibly if he wanted to. But just like the time when they were kids, he knew the correct answer.

"How long we talking?" John asked, resigned to the fact that he was being pulled back in.

"Maybe six more months after the end of the year. I want to keep you guys on as close to Kingston's release as possible. Also, I don't expect you to do me this favor for nothing. I want to take you up five more points as compensation for your work."

John knew it wasn't about the money for Alex and Cooper, but he also knew they would help Banks out, given the circumstances. The money would help it along, but they would still want out. He needed an ending point. Kingston would be released in no less than seventeen months, which put them a year past the initial deadline. So another year in the business of laundering drug money for the Johnson family.

"Okay, I'll talk to them and let them know; but I'm pretty sure you know we'll help you out as long as we still have a deal to end our involvement by the time King gets out. Is that fair?"

"Deal," replied Banks. He stood, and the two men hugged—the embrace of a friendship that spanned almost three decades.

"So what's next?" asked John.

"Well, first off, I'm staying here while we figure this out. I'll be in town, and you'll see a lot more of me. It's time for me take control of this thing and figure out who killed my uncle. This is an attack on my family, and I can't let that slide. I'm going to figure out who did this, and we will make them pay for it. I'm back, and I'm going to be here until justice gets done."

With that, the two men left the room, heading into the main room where the funeral would be held. His uncle's body was waiting in a closed casket. The chamber holding the coffin was quiet, as it would be a few more hours before mourners arrived. Banks walked over to the coffin and bent a knee, saying a prayer for his slain uncle.

John couldn't help but realize they were entering into a new mission. He also couldn't help but wonder where this would take them all. Julius had been gunned down by what appeared to be a professional hit; and given the circles the family ran with, nobody could be excluded as a suspect at this point. John closed his eyes and said his own silent prayer.

He decided he would get some fresh air before everyone else arrived, so he walked outside the Abbey and stood in the rays of the midday Southern sun. The heat was already in the mid-nineties, and the summer stickiness of the South had surrounded him the second he walked outside the chapel. John looked up to the sky and took in a deep breath. He exhaled and walked down a small path under some cherry trees, realizing the journey to the answer was sure to mean more bloodshed.

He noticed the red carnation that Banks had given him, and he thought to himself: Who killed Julius Johnson, and do they understand the world of trouble that's heading their way?

ABOUT THE AUTHOR

Jason Myers is a mortgage broker who was born and raised in Charleston, South Carolina. He has published several books specific to the mortgage industry. *Criminal Enterprise* is Myers's first fiction novel, and the first of a series of crime novels.

www.ingramcontent.com/pod-product-compliance
Lightning Source LLC
Chambersburg PA
CBHW020743250626
47155CB00003B/887